FAMILY AND HONOR

JACKY LEON BOOK TWO

K.N. BANET

1

CHAPTER ONE
MARCH 9, 2019

I t was another Saturday, another night at the bar, and I found myself staring at Joey, an eyebrow raised in question. My phone was going off, but it could wait. I had to address the foolish human in front of me.

"Are we going to do this every week?" I asked, making it clear what I was talking about. He knew. He knew very well what I meant, and still, he gave me a cheeky smile, daring me to make him stop.

"*Jacky*. Heath is driving here right now, just like he does every Saturday. Now, I'm pretty sure you're a werewolf because he hangs around like you're one of his wolves, but you just refuse to admit it."

It was a game. Over the months since whatever Dallas was, this conversation had become a game.

"Not a werewolf. Never will be a werewolf. *Can't* be a werewolf." I grabbed a rag and a dirty glass and started wiping it down. I would still need to throw it in the dishwasher, but it gave me busy work to wipe them all down beforehand. Busy work was useful when uncomfortable questions and implications were being thrown my way.

I had given up months ago with Joey. Every werewolf in Jacksonville and Tyler had told him I wasn't a werewolf. Some humans were more perceptive than others, and Joey was one of them, having a small sixth sense for the supernatural. Since he'd gotten some form of confirmation of his not-so-secret belief, thanks to the mess last August, he was going to hang onto it like a dog with a bone.

But still, I played the game.

"You can't be a werewolf?" Joey snorted. "Why don't I buy that?"

"I've never lied to you. I'm not a werewolf." I grinned. That was true. I wasn't a werewolf. Werecats weren't werewolves. Couldn't be werewolves. Had a long-standing bad history with werewolves, even. The fact that two lived in my territory was unheard of, never done. Sometimes, territories would accidentally overlap, but those incidences were quickly corrected. Werecats gave everything a wide berth, preferring their own company normally. I was no exception.

But I had let two werewolves move right in with no intention of ever making them leave. It was selfish, honestly. With them came a little human girl named Carey, and she deserved the world. Even after months, I still felt the ache in my chest, demanding me to pick up my phone and call to see how she was doing, to see if she was safe. I was never truly released from my Duty, instead offering my protection for the remainder of her life as long as she lived in my territory. A stupid thing to do, but I had done it.

"Do you deny that Heath is on his way here right now?" Joey countered. "Werewolves only stick around for their pack. They're very adamant about that. They check in and make sure businesses being run by their people are doing well. He makes an obvious show of supporting your business."

I gave him a weak glare. I had a natural connection to the earth I claimed as mine, a piece of magic every werecat had. Werecats watched and felt their territory all the time, making sure no supernatural intruders were on the way or had to be dealt with. Since I let the wolves move in, my magic was constantly in overdrive, always accounting for the location of the two wolves, instinctual warning bells playing in the back of my head that they were there, and I hadn't yet forced them to leave.

So, there was no way I could deny Heath was in his car heading toward my bar for his standard Saturday night drink, forcing Landon to stay at home with Carey. Sometimes they got a babysitter, and both would show up but not tonight. Tonight, it was only Heath.

"He's on his way," I said softly, admitting some piece of defeat to Joey. "Heath coming to my bar doesn't make me a werewolf, though. I helped him out last year. What if we're just friends?"

"Sure." Joey was grinning like a fool now. "Friends."

I schooled my face. The way he was saying it made it

sound like Heath and I were secret lovers, a thought I didn't toy with for long. If it weren't for the question of my humanity, that would be exactly the sort of thing people would assume by Joey's choice of words and tone.

"Joey, leave her alone!" someone called out. "It's your turn. Come get your damn stick, and let's play!"

"Yeah, Joey. Go play with your friends. I have a business to run." Waving him away with my rag, he relented. I dropped the rag, knowing it was finally time to deal with whatever was going on with my phone. Everyone knew not to call me during business hours, so it must have been important, something I needed to know immediately or the moment I had a break. I *never* got calls like that.

I grabbed it from my cubby behind the bar and frowned at the name on the screen. Two missed calls and three texts. Fantastic.

None were Hasan, something that surprised me. Instead, both calls and all the texts were from Jabari, his oldest son and right hand. Jabari was also one of two biological children Hasan had. The rest of the brood were all turned, just like me.

Why is dear older brother calling me?

I was almost scared to unlock my phone and check. It took a moment, but I mustered up the courage. I didn't have time to listen to my voicemail, but the texts made up for whatever I was missing there.

Jabari: We've gotten reports of two dead werecats in the PNW. Hasan is having me tell everyone to keep their heads down.

Jabari: Stay safe, watch your back.

Jabari: Let me know when you've gotten this.

I started typing quickly and deleted it just as quickly. What did I say to that? Two dead werecats across the country from me didn't really pose quite the threat that a werewolf war on my doorstep did.

I continued to think, a sinking realization about what Hasan and Jabari were thinking. They were old cats from before recorded history and had survived a devastating war with the werewolves.

I started typing again, frowning. The sinking feeling didn't stop. I ignored it as best as I could, trying to carefully word my reply.

"Good evening, Jacky," someone said from the other side of the bar. I jumped back, then cursed as I saw who it was, my heart pounding. Heath lowered his eyebrows in concern. If he were a human, he would have gotten a laugh because men liked to laugh at women when they got spooked, but we both knew what had just happened was concerning. "I spooked you," he pointed out immediately in a soft voice like he was trying not to draw more attention to us.

"I was a little distracted." I waved my phone at him, hoping he would dismiss the entire thing. "Let me finish what I was doing, then I'll get you a beer."

"What could have distracted—"

"Don't worry about it." I finished my text without care and hit send before shoving the phone into my pocket. "Nothing that concerns you." The sinking feeling wouldn't leave. It dampened a little, but it wouldn't leave.

"Okay." He seemingly dropped it just like that.

I busied myself pouring him the promised beer and slid it across the bar. It was faster than I normally slid glasses across the bar, and for a moment, I worried it would go over the edge. He grabbed it before that happened, too fast for the natural human eye to see—the very behavior supernaturals tried to avoid in front of humans. He didn't make a comment about it.

"You look good tonight."

I looked down at what I was wearing then leveled him with a flat stare. I had on an old black t-shirt, jeans torn at the knees, and dirty steel-toed boots. I didn't wear makeup and was certain I had done nothing with my hair that would warrant any compliments. It was in a ponytail, with pieces falling out everywhere, especially over my face. It hadn't been the best of days before the texts from Jabari. I barely got any sleep before opening, which had started the day off on the wrong foot.

He kept an innocent expression on his face as if his statement wasn't completely out of left field.

"Don't try flattery," I finally said pointedly. "It won't get you the information you want."

"Who says I'm looking for information?" he countered, raising an eyebrow, matching the one I liked to give people.

"The look on your face." Shaking my head, I grabbed an empty glass and served myself a drink—water. I didn't drink while I worked. Leaning on the bar, I eyed him warily. "What do you need tonight, other than being in my business?"

"I came for my customary Saturday night drink," he replied, his bland innocence refusing to abate and show me what he was thinking. I took a long sip of the water as I watched him, taking in every smell, hoping I could somehow discern what he was thinking.

"Then I'm getting back to work." I stepped back, putting my drink down at the same time. While he was alone, sitting at the bar proper, there were humans by the pool tables and sitting in a couple of my new booths along the opposite wall who would be needing drinks soon. Most were regulars and those I could prepare for. I knew what they drank, what they didn't like, and their habits.

"Well, I was hoping you would do something for me," he added before I made it two steps away. "But really, I'm just here for my drink. We can talk about the other thing later tonight."

I bit back the groan. "Just tell me, Heath. No reason to make me wait all night for one of us to forget, then you'll leave and bother me tomorrow with it." I grabbed my rag again, another dirty glass, and went back to the busy work that kept me occupied, waiting on him.

"You're going to hate it. You're really going to chafe with this request."

"Heath, don't play games with me right now." I wiped down the glass with more pressure than I really should have. I worried it was going to crack soon.

"Carey wants all of us to go bowling tomorrow."

I stopped what I was doing, giving him the most

exasperated look I could muster. "Well, why didn't you say that sooner?" *It would get me out of the house on a boring Sunday. I'm always okay with that.* "Heath."

"I wanted to mess with you a little," he admitted, a smirk forming. "It's really a lot of fun."

"I hate you," I growled softly. "I really do."

"Of course, you do." He took a long swallow of his beer. Watching him, with his classic good looks in his perfect suit, totally out of place in my shithole of a bar, I wondered how I ever found myself in this position. Sure, I had gotten involved with his war in Dallas, but I didn't have to let him move into my territory. His excuse about having me help protect Carey was probably honest. He was technically a werewolf Alpha of two, him and his son, and they were the only defense his human daughter had.

My answer had been spur-of-the-moment. Looking back, I knew I should have told him no, that it drew unnecessary attention to me, or I didn't want an Alpha werewolf hanging around in my space, but I said yes because of things like this. Opportunities to have those elusive things called friends. Some form of community that didn't involve my own kind, which I was actively avoiding and had for several years.

"So, bowling. Tomorrow. What time?" I pressed for more information, trying not to sound too excited or desperate. I liked bowling, and just the idea of going with people was exciting.

"The place on 69 opens at three. Do you know it?"

With my nod, he continued. "Meet us there by three-thirty." Heath was still smirking into his glass.

"Sounds good. Gives me time to get some sleep." With that, I yawned, realizing just how tired I was. For some reason, the last week had been a long one, with only a few nights when I got a full night's sleep. "I hate long weeks."

"We've had one ourselves. Landon and I had to spend two nights in Dallas, thanks to some meetings. Our old pack wanted us to check in as well, make sure everything was going well. Nothing official, just old friends, but very important old friends. A lot of the werewolf council had flown in."

"They don't have spies?" I asked, smiling because I knew the answer.

"No, they don't. They can't seem to convince anyone to come out here and check on us. Something about everyone scared of the big...supernatural who runs Tyler and Jacksonville and the surrounding area." He grinned back at me.

Our plan was working. Heath was able to pull Carey out of the werewolf world and be her father, and I was the nuclear deterrent who got some friends out of that world. It wasn't perfect, but it was holding. Sometimes, I thought the polite man in front of me was overreacting to what happened in Dallas, but I was always quick to remind myself I didn't know all of his history. I didn't know how many enemies he had or who they could be. I only knew he thought they were a danger to his daughter.

Things I maybe should have asked about before letting him move in. Too late now.

"Must be some scary supernatural," I commented lightly.

"Truly. Shook up a lot of my old pack when it rolled through Dallas and showed them who the dominant predator was."

I wanted to laugh, but I bit it back. We had to be careful about talking openly about too many supernatural things. What surprised me was his comment about her being the dominant predator. In a one-on-one fight, we both understood I could wipe the floor with him. His son, too, but no self-respecting werewolf Alpha, retired or not, admitted to something so vulnerable. It exposed a weakness when weaknesses got wolves killed.

"You're a fool," I whispered, looking down to pour him another beer.

"For admitting it?" he inquired, obviously knowing where I was going with my comment.

"Yeah. Aren't you supposed to maintain that you're the strongest? It's how you get other wolves to fall in line. One of the ways." I gave a half shrug, silently trying to dismiss my knowledge. I knew a lot about other supernatural species, something Hasan made sure was a frequent part of my education shortly after I was Changed.

"That mattered when I ran a pack, but...that supernatural showing up and doing what it did reminded every wolf in North America that we don't run the world. Everyone is quietly eating that dose of reality right now."

My stomach sank a little more, remembering Jabari's texts and what the implications of two dead werecats could mean. "You all already knew about..." I didn't know how to finish that without giving away anything more. I glanced around the bar, glad to see every human in the room was instinctively avoiding the two dangerous predators at the bar. It always happened. Once Heath walked in, they gradually drifted to the other side of the room, hiding by the booths and pool tables. They would claim it was a sign of respect for Heath, but Heath and I knew the truth.

"We did know but seeing is believing. Seeing the truth is different from hearing it. Harder to ignore, harder to deny. Don't worry, none of them are really angry or upset. They're cautious. Actually, I know a couple of Alphas who have reached out to introduce themselves to some...cousins, hoping to start better relations." Heath sipped on his beer. I put the new one in front of him, causing him to chuckle. "Wolves are social things. Insular in our own ways but more social than the rest of our world. We adapt to a new player on the stage, even if it's really one of the oldest players, and this time, many wolves are making sure we're allies."

"That's good," I mumbled. "I'm not really involved with politics, so thanks for that news."

"It's been going on for months, and no one told you?" He narrowed his eyes playfully, but there was no missing the cunning, curious light in his eyes.

"Nope. I don't want to be involved. I don't care to be involved."

"Strange because..." He leaned in closer, his voice dropping to a barely audible whisper. No human ears would pick up what he said. "You're right in the middle of it, letting wolves live near you, in your space."

"Don't make me throw you out," I snapped, suddenly fighting a bolt of hostility. His comment sounded like trouble, and like always, I wanted no part in it. I didn't want attention. "Out of the bar, my territory, and out of the state. You drag me into anything else, and we're going to have real problems."

"I just figured we were on the topic, so I would give you the recent news. I'm not looking to draw attention to myself, promise. Or you. Word is, many supernaturals have been curious and confused by the new living arrangement here, but they don't have any reason to talk about it. They're just curious."

"Once an Alpha, always an Alpha. Natural politicians, the lot of you." I made it sound like an insult— it was and wasn't. Supernaturals like Heath stayed alive because they were so good at making the right allies and playing the field without pissing off too many people. Had he made mistakes? Yeah, that was pretty clear from what happened last year, but even I could tell he was a survivor.

Politicians still sucked, though.

"Always, even without a pack. It's not something I can turn off."

I had long figured *that* out.

"Well, forgive me, but I don't plan on telling you

anything on my end. Whenever I learn about something from..." I couldn't say 'my family,' so I trailed off, trying to find the last word. He only watched me, too curious, too insightful for my liking. He wanted to know so much more about me, and I fought to say anything for a minute under his gaze. "When I learn something, it's normally told to me in confidence. Something that can't join the world of rumors."

"Of course." He was still smiling, though. "The only time I ever hear about...your kind is when one crosses paths publicly with another group." He had phrased it very carefully, something I was grateful for as I looked over his shoulder and saw Joey watching us with suspicion.

"I can't tell you all my secrets. Sorry." I threw in the apology because I knew there was an expectation. He'd given me information I either didn't know or was purposefully ignoring, and I refused to return the favor. "And can you talk to that man?" I didn't need to say who. Heath sighed heavily in return, telling me exactly how bad he felt about who I was dealing with.

"I didn't mean to bring that much attention to you. Honestly, when he first approached me, I had no idea who he was or what it was about. Then he said 'werewolf,' which confused the hell out of me. I approached your territory and realized what you were. Since I couldn't get close to learn more about you, I used him to get me basic information." Heath sipped his beer before continuing. "Has it gotten worse?"

"Yes, since Carey came down here," I answered. "It

used to be a joke, and now it's a bit of a game, but its frequency is increasing."

"Unless you want to tell him..." Heath's sympathetic look told me everything. There was no fixing it without dragging Joey into the supernatural world. Since neither of us really knew Joey that well, nor was he an employee, there was no incentive for it. Telling someone you can't trust led to disaster, and that was something I never flirted with.

Unless it's for Carey. Then I didn't just flirt with disaster, I took it out to drinks and asked it to fuck me on the first date.

"No, he doesn't need to know. It just started to make me uncomfortable, and..." I trailed off, realizing what I was about to ask. I was a werecat, and this was my territory, and I was about to ask a wolf to handle his previous spy and get him off my back. "You know what? Don't worry about. I'll start throwing him out of the bar if it gets too bad."

"Good. I'll finish my beer and get out of your hair early tonight, then." He nodded slowly, glancing over his shoulder. I saw Joey jerk his gaze away. "Your territory, your decision."

I didn't reply to that, quickly beginning to fill glasses as I saw one of my regulars stand up and walk over. By the time she was at the bar, I had three beers and a margarita waiting for her. She took them without comment, and I silently added the drinks to her tab.

It was another thirty minutes before Heath wandered out.

"Drive safe," I called after him. He waved over his shoulder in response and strolled out of Kick Shot like the night had been like any other.

For some reason, I had a suspicion it hadn't been. I glanced down at my phone, frowning, that sinking feeling in my gut setting off warning bells in my head.

No, it wasn't like any normal night at all.

2

CHAPTER TWO

I huffed as I realized I didn't know what to wear for the day. It was already three in the afternoon, and I was nervous as hell, although there was no real reason. It had occurred to me as I closed up Kick Shot the night before, that this was only the third time I had spent time with Carey and the two werewolves at the same time. I would babysit her, have girl days, play video games, and other things, but I nearly never hung out with her and her family. I saw Heath at the bar often, and Landon sometimes, but I'd only seen all of them together for an extended period twice since they moved into my territory.

This made me nervous, and it didn't make much sense.

"Therefore, I decide I don't know what to wear and have even more anxiety," I muttered to myself, staring at the clothes on the bed.

I looked back at how excited I was when Heath asked

me the night before. I had been looking forward to bowling. Now I was dreading being at some Everson Family outing where I didn't belong. The same thing had happened during the holidays. I felt so out of place, and no one knew what to do about it. Carey had tried so hard to make me feel welcome, but the problem didn't lie with her or her family, even if they were werewolves.

It was me. I craved community and having people around, yet ran from it. I could feel it trying to make me shift, walk out in the woods, and become unreachable. Carey was easy to manage. Heath was easy to manage.

But a crowd? More than one person at any given point? That made me wary and uncomfortable, and I couldn't fight it, no matter how much I wanted to.

"What did Hasan say?" I racked my brain for the advice he'd given me once. "When you feel like running, consider what you would miss out on and if you will be better off without it. If you know you'll miss it or regret losing the chance, don't run. Face it." It sounded like advice every parent would give a child, but it was honestly good werecat advice. We were very good at hiding from the world around us—very, very good. Hasan had disappeared from public life for a century until my fuck up when called to Duty. His mate walked away from their world so long ago, most didn't even know what she looked like, and that said something in a community of nearly immortal supernaturals.

I considered the pros and cons of skipping bowling, pleading for a day off.

Pro for staying: I get to see Carey and see how

competitive she is at something physical. I haven't been able to convince her to try sports because she knows she's around creatures she can't beat. Pro, I get out of the house and do something.

Con: I get out of the house and hang out with two werewolves. If people didn't think I was strange already, they'll see me with the Everson family and probably think I'm part of the pack...more than they already do.

I curled a lip at that thought. The idea of subjecting myself to an Alpha like werewolves did was completely against my nature. I knew if I didn't go, I would think about it all week, sad I didn't go. Half of that would be guilt over disappointing Carey after already telling her father I was going. If I canceled now, she would be upset, and I'd never canceled on her for anything else. I couldn't start now.

"But what to wear?" I mumbled, glaring at the clothes on the bed, back at square one. I finally shook my head, mustered my resolve, and grabbed a few items, deciding it didn't matter. A black t-shirt that wasn't old or dirty, a pair of decent jeans—easy, simple, relaxed, perfect for bowling. I dressed and stared in the mirror, nodding in appreciation.

Now, that wasn't so hard, was it, Jacky? See, you can do this. You can hang out like a normal person.

I hoped I could, anyway. There was a lot of evidence against me, but I could do it.

"Why is this so damn hard?" I asked myself, shaking my head in dismay. There was a time when I could jump up and go hang out with anyone. I loved to bowl, I loved to go to the park. I loved life. When did I become a shut-in who was scared to spend a few hours with people?

I knew the answer but didn't let it get to me as I stomped out of my bathroom, through my bedroom, and down to my living room. I could have gotten ready in the apartment over the bar but had decided to head to my house deep in the woods in the middle of my property. It was a sanctuary. Not even Carey and the wolves were allowed to venture deep enough into my property to get to my house. I needed a space that meant I was well and truly alone, *especially* since two werewolves lived in my territory, constantly scratching at my magical defenses.

I stepped out after pulling on my boots and swung my leg over my dirt bike, kicking off to head to the bar and my little hatchback. The weather was good with little rain, so I didn't have any puddles on the path between home and the bar. When I got to my car, I was pleased to find I wasn't half covered in mud.

As I started driving to the bowling alley, my mind continued to wander. Jabari's news weighed on me suddenly, trying to dampen the bright day and the good mood I was supposed to have. The problem was, the quiet drive gave me an open space to think.

Dead werecats—two of them in the same region. If I had truly shaken things up so much on accident, it could have been a purposeful attack on werecats. Would I get a text in a week saying more were dead?

Why now?

My mind turned it over for the short drive, my face stuck in a perpetual frown, still frowning as I parked and slid out of the car. I wasn't paying attention as I leaned on my hood and waited, staring at the bowling alley but not really seeing it.

"You came!" a young voice called out—energetic, surprised, and very much a change from the girl I had met at my bar's back door.

I didn't jump, not totally shocked by Carey's sudden appearance. I had known the wolves were getting close, half paying attention to them with my supernatural radar-like magic.

"I did," I replied with a chuckle. "I said yes to your dad last night. Didn't he tell you?"

"Yeah, he did, but..." Carey shrugged, a grin still on her face.

"Have I ever canceled on you before?" I asked, using a somewhat stern tone of voice, daring her to say I had.

"No, but I didn't think you would want to go bowling. It just doesn't seem like something you like to do." The girl's innocent smile and clean scent told me that she was telling the truth.

"Well, I would have you know, I love bowling," I retorted. "Or, I used to. I haven't been bowling in nearly eleven years, so we'll see. I'm probably rusty." I moved away from my car and raised an arm, ignoring the two werewolves walking closer. Carey ducked underneath my arm, I nestled it on her shoulder, and she wrapped her closer arm around my waist. It was a comfortable position. We did it whenever we went somewhere, just the two of us.

"So, you haven't bowled since before..." Carey's eyes

were wide, full of curiosity and questions. Unable to resist, and still ignoring the wolves walking behind us, I answered.

"That's right. Not at all. I haven't had anyone to bowl with so..." I shrugged one shoulder. "Thanks for the invite."

"Of course! I know we have girl night tomorrow, but I wanted to bowl, and three people can't do teams. I like teams because they give me a real chance of winning."

There it is. Just as competitive as always.

"Boys versus girls?" I asked softly, trying to sound mischievous. Carey began to nod vigorously, the grin growing wider. "We'll kick some ass."

"Watch your language with my daughter, please," Heath said from behind us. I ignored him as I got the door and held it open for Carey, him, and Landon.

"She's definitely heard worse from your wolf pack, but I'll try to behave."

By the look on his face he obviously didn't believe me but said nothing. I slid into the building last, realizing it was my last moment to get out of this if I had wanted to run. What I hadn't counted on was how much Carey calmed me down. Once she was talking to me, the anxiety disappeared. I smiled as I met them at the counter.

"What's your shoe size?" Landon asked me softly.

"Don't worry—"

"We're paying," Heath cut in.

I raised my eyebrows and stared at him, daring him to

try to say it again. It scratched at my independent nature to let this wolf pay for things I could reasonably afford.

His blue-grey stare back was even, not backing down. I held back a territorial growl, one I knew would remind him who was really in charge of the building, the land, and everything within miles of us.

"Jacky isn't some kid friend, Dad. She can pay for herself!" Carey groaned, pushing her father a little. "Hurry, or we won't get a good lane."

He finally broke the stare. With a sharp nod, I let him know that he'd done the right thing. He quickly paid for his family, and I stepped up next, telling the young woman behind the counter my size. Heath was eyeing me as I sat down across from him at our lane and didn't stop watching me as I put on my shoes.

"What?" I finally hissed out.

"Carey always wants me to pay for everyone because I'm able to," he replied calmly, but there was no missing the touch of confusion in his voice.

But she didn't want you to pay for me, and that's bothered you, huh? I shrugged. He didn't need an explanation right at that moment.

"I say we do teams!" Carey called out from the score screen, where she was done putting in everyone's names. "Me and Jacky versus you two! Boys against girls!" She was grinning, and I couldn't resist grinning back.

"I like it. We'll kill 'em." Holding up a hand for her, I kicked my shoes out of the way for her to sit next to me. She slapped my hand, a classic high five, and sat down with me, leaving her father sitting with a bemused Landon next to him.

"Carey...we're always on the same team," Heath said, obviously pretending to be more hurt than he really was. Oh, he was hurt, that I could smell, and if I could, Landon could as well, but he played it up to bother his daughter.

"Nope! I'm with Jacky!" The cheeky eleven-year-old grinned with all her teeth, obviously mimicking a more wolfy smile.

"Hear that? She's with me." I puffed up in fake pride at being chosen. "We're going to put these boys in their place," I said to her, grinning in the same overly excited fashion.

"Yes...The eleven-year-old and the thirty-six-year-old are going to put the over-century-old werewolves in their place...You hear that, Landon?"

"I do," the quiet wolf said, a small smile forming. "Little sister is competitive and so is cousin cat, it seems. I think we're in for a fight."

I jumped up to find a ball. Everyone except Carey needed a sixteen-pounder, and I wanted to laugh as I realized just how easy it would be to bowl. I wondered if the wolves were going to have as hard a time as I would with how light the heaviest balls felt.

"Does that feel good?" I asked Carey as she picked an eight-pound ball. "You can go down to six."

"No. This is good." She beamed at me. "I'm first, so you sit back and watch them. Make sure they don't cheat and mess me up."

"I don't think they will, but I promise to try."

When she walked away, I made an exaggerated effort to keep an eye on the werewolves. They tolerated it, and when Heath winked mischievously, I pointed at my eyes then his. It got a chuckle out of him, that masculine thing I hated since the first time I heard it—absolutely hated it.

The clatter of a ball hitting pins made us turn. I clapped my loudest as Carey jumped up and down, proud of her six and waiting for her ball to come back.

"Good job!" I called out.

"I'm going to get the rest, promise!" she said, grinning like a goof. It was infectious as I found myself giving her the same grin in return.

To anyone other than a werecat, the relationship would be strange. A woman in her thirties didn't become best friends with an eleven- nearly twelve-year-old girl. For a werecat, it was the only thing that made sense. There was a deep-rooted psychology to it Hasan had explained to me after I told him about the new living arrangements. Children were safer, easier to attach to, and less likely to become a threat, something werecats thought of any adult as.

"It's like introducing a kitten to an adult cat. I should have known you would have a problem letting go of her, especially since you didn't spend the proper time with me and the family after I Changed you. I didn't think you would let wolves into your territory, but I knew you would keep talking to her."

Safe social interaction. That's what Carey represented. I knew it and accepted it, just letting the friendship do as it wanted and lead me where it would go.

Carey knocked down three pins, and I cheered, taunting her family a little as we high-fived when she came back to the bench. Heath went next, landing a strike, and I joined Carey in booing the man. Landon was a complete failure, knocking down four pins, then guttering his second try.

"Can you not bowl?" I asked, genuinely confused. He was a supernatural. There was no reason for him to miss like that.

"I have a really hard time pulling back my strength and remaining accurate. It's always been a struggle for me." He smiled and shrugged, sitting back down next to his father. Landon was the one I barely knew, and I was always nervous to try to get to know him. Not because he was dangerous, but he was aloof, and compounded with my own need for independence and social anxiety...it just never happened.

I jumped up for my turn, grabbed my borrowed ball, and stepped up to the runway. I focused, taking a deep breath, settling into my stance. I had done this hundreds of times.

Just don't throw it, Jacky. People are going to talk if you toss this ball down the lane like a freak.

I threw, putting minimum power into it, holding my breath. At the last moment, I put a spin on it, like it was second nature. It flew down the center of the lane and crashed into the pins.

Strike.

I let out all that air in my lungs before I started getting lightheaded. Carey was cheering behind me. I smiled as the fallen pins were cleared away, and another set was put down.

"Good job!" Carey screamed. "We're totally going to win today!"

"You know how to bowl?" Heath asked as I turned to sit down as Carey started the next frame.

"Um..." To answer that, I knew I had to give him personal information. "I was part of a casual bowling league a long time ago."

"Oh. Well, shit. You two might actually win," he huffed, shaking his head. "Just what my daughter needs. A partner to help her win everything."

I relaxed and took my seat again, glad he didn't press or dig for more information. He had shown me the information he'd pulled on me. It was well-done but incomplete, and we both knew it. I had done well hiding some things about my life when I was Changed—not all of it, but some of it.

The first game, Carey and I did win. Heath begged for a team change, but we shut that down. Carey enjoyed winning too much to indulge her father, and I once again puffed up with pride that I was the chosen one.

3

CHAPTER THREE

I was waiting for my turn quietly when my phone went off. Everyone around me stopped and turned my way. Two werewolves and a human girl was a crowd I didn't really want for a phone call, so I held up a hand.

"Stop. Let me take this outside. I'll be right back."

"We'll wait!" Carey grinned and laid back in the seat. "Dad, go buy us a pizza, please?"

"I can, but you will clean up the trash when we leave. Am I clear?"

"Yes, sir!" It didn't perturb her in the slightest. I smiled to myself as I pulled my buzzing phone out of my pocket and walked away. Checking my phone as I walked out the door, I groaned to see Jabari's name on the screen, answering once I was outside.

"What do you need, Jabari?"

"You didn't call me back last night." His words were curt, a touch cold, but I didn't let that hurt my feelings.

He had once before, a long time ago, and I wouldn't let him do it again. I wasn't close to my siblings, and I used that as a shield from their attitude about me.

"No, I texted you like a normal person would when it's very late at night or one is working. Like I was. I was working." Did he forget that I owned a business I used to provide for myself? That I tried my best not to dip into the money Hasan gave me after I had everything up and running?

"Did you?" Now he was just confused. "Well, my apologies then. Anyway, there's an update. Hasan has decided to send me out to Washington State to check out what happened and investigate. I just thought you should know."

"Um...thanks?" I pulled the phone away and gave it a confused look. "Why did you need to call and tell me?" Jabari and I did *not* talk. We hadn't spoken since before I left Hasan's territory.

"Because...How do I put this?" He groaned softly on the other end. "We've all been talking about how we needed to try harder with you and let you know what the family is doing. That's what I'm doing. Letting you know what is going on with us and how we're stepping in, leading the rest of the werecats and being responsible. Since Father told Lani about you, about who you *really* are, that information has spread to every other werecat, and they expect you to be like us. Except you invited werewolves to live with you, which makes everyone wonder if we're going to open up friendly relations. That's not the point, though. You're a member of the family, so you need to know what's going on."

"Stop rambling, Jabari. I get it. News received. Thank you. I'll make sure not to die any time soon like those other werecats, and I'll make sure to continue to leave a good impression on the rest of werecat society."

"Good impression? Jacky, every werecat who's contacted us thinks you're an impulsive youngling who needs to be dragged home by Father and corrected. You let wolves move into your territory, an Alpha at that, without consulting anyone. You made a major political move without telling anyone until the news had already broken." I could hear his impatience and condemnation.

"I didn't know everyone felt that way..." I whispered. "Be safe in Washington."

"I will. Keep your nose out of any more trouble."

I hung up first, reeling at the sting Jabari had just given me. I was a shut-in. I kept my head down. I got roped into one damn werewolf turf war, had to protect one little girl, and I was an impulsive youngling? Me?

I growled at my phone before shoving it back into my pocket. Was that why Hasan was barely calling me now? Was he actually furious with me? He'd been shocked about Carey and her family, but I didn't think he was angry, not when I told him.

I walked back in slowly and stared at Carey, Heath, and Landon without approaching them. I considered Jabari's words for a minute before slowly walking toward the group, acting like nothing happened.

I'm not letting some old ass rivalry stop me from

having some damn friends. They all need to get over themselves, and Jabari can shove it where the sun doesn't shine.

"I heard pizza before stepping out. What did you order?" I leaned on the table, grinning as Carey pushed a drink in front of me.

"That's lemonade because I know you like it. Dad got two large meat lovers and a small cheese. The small cheese is for me, so don't even think about it. You have to share with them." She pointed at her family, both doing well to look innocent. That was how people could tell Landon was Heath's. They didn't look alike, not in the slightest, but Landon picked up some very obvious expressions from his father. The fake innocence was one of them.

I wonder if Richard looked like his father when they hung out as a family like Landon. I can't imagine being Carey and having to deal with three of these wolves.

I wasn't sure where the thought came from, but I let it pass, trying to not think any more about the fourth, very dead member of the Everson family. He was dead because I killed him, and for some unknown and illogical reason, they didn't hold it against me. Carey acted like that day had never happened, like her brother never tried to kill her over petty jealousy, fighting for their father's love.

It was odd, to say the least, but they never brought it up, so neither did I. It haunted me, though, seeing them over the holidays and remembering how I killed one of them.

On bad nights, I remembered the blood in my mouth every time I'd had to kill a wolf during that entire affair. I remembered the blazing pain of being shot with silver bullets. I remembered the wide, scared eyes of Carey and the clear snap of her wrist breaking.

I was never one for violence, and it had left its mark, even if I never told any of them.

"Jacky?" Carey's voice was soft and concerned. "Are you going to eat?"

I blinked, nodding quickly. *Shit, I can't zone out like that around her.*

"Yeah. Where's a plate?"

One was dropped in front of me with three pieces of pizza. Heath stood near me, watching carefully, close enough I could guess who had dropped the plate. Landon was across the lane on a bench, already munching on his share. He watched me just as carefully, though, with a hint more wariness than his father, a hardness in his eyes that made me stiffen slightly. Instinct made me recognize I had killed the weaker son. Landon was much more dangerous than his brother and maybe even his father.

"Calm," Heath murmured. "Both of you."

"What's wrong?" Carey demanded, picking up on her father's words.

"Landon," Heath snapped, turning away from me and toward his boy. "She zoned out. It happens."

I quickly realized the werewolves must have caught a scent on me they didn't like. I sighed, shaking my head to dismiss what was on my mind, trying to rattle the thoughts out.

"Nothing is wrong, promise. Just had an errant thought, and paired with that call, I was distracted."

"Yup." Landon took another bite of his pizza, breaking the eye contact. Heath visibly relaxed, and Carey smelled of confusion but didn't ask for anything else.

"What was the call about?" Heath asked blandly. "You were busy on your phone last night when I showed up, too. Something going on?"

"Nothing you need to know about. It has nothing to do with us." I distracted myself by grabbing the lemonade and taking a long sip before continuing. " I don't plan on telling you but even if I did, it can't be said here."

"Is it family stuff?" Carey asked, just as keen as her father was.

"If I can answer with yes or no, will that be enough?" I asked her in return. A child's curiosity should be nourished, at least I thought so, but I couldn't give her too much. I wasn't going to tell her how I was thinking of her dead brother and how I killed him or how my family was mad at me for what I did to protect her.

"Sure!" She beamed, and I knew she was going to use my weak will against me soon. She would try to learn more tomorrow during our game night.

"Yes and no," I answered, grinning as she fell into my trap.

"That doesn't tell me anything!"

"I'm with Carey. That's a shit answer," Heath said almost petulantly. Landon chuckled next to his father.

"I could have told you she would do that. She doesn't

tell anyone anything," he reminded his father. "I mean, how much do we really know about her? I certainly can't find more than what you and I dug up on her years ago."

I continued to grin at Carey as her eyes worked out the answer I gave and saw the wheels spinning as she formed her plan to find out more. I ignored the words of the wolves, not letting the slight touch of distrust in Landon's tone bother me, pocketing away the fact that Landon was still trying to find information on me. That was something I needed to snap at Heath for. He needed to keep his wolf in line.

"Fine. So, it's kind of about family." Carey leaned back in her seat, smiling.

"Kind of," I agreed. "Now, let's forget it and get back to food and finish our game."

It wasn't forgotten, but it was ignored. I inhaled my pizza and went for two more pieces before the werewolves could go in for seconds. I'd learned at Thanksgiving I had to get enough early or there would be none left. When the game restarted, Carey and I once again were driven to beat the men on the other side of the lane. Every frame, Heath grew more defeated, exaggerating that Carey was whooping his ass, while Landon remained his quiet self, not getting any better or worse at bowling.

It was nearly six when they were done, and Carey yawned, making all three adults watch her.

"This was fun. Can we do it again soon, Dad?"

"Sure. Why don't we try to make it once a month?" He smiled indulgently. I watched the interaction, my heart aching just a little. I had wanted to be a mom once and wanted my late fiancé to be the same doting father Heath was now.

It stung. For just a moment, seeing them, it stung.

"Jacky?" Carey turned her grey-blue eyes on me.

"Yes?"

"Once a month?"

"Oh yeah, I can come. Just let me know what Sunday you want me." I wasn't going to turn her down, that was certain. I also wasn't expecting a standing invitation to their family outings. By Heath's face, he wasn't either. He didn't say anything, but I saw a flicker of annoyance and could guess where it was coming from. He probably didn't want some werecat going on their family outings all the time, and I already had Carey every Monday after school until she had to go home.

"Well, it's time for us to head out," Heath announced. "I'll pay for the lanes, Jacky. Don't worry about it."

"I can help," I reminded him, knowing it wouldn't help but wanting to try anyway.

"Our group is bigger and dragged you out to this. We've got it." His tone was one I knew well, from men specifically. The 'don't argue with me' tone. I'd heard it from fathers, boyfriends, guy friends, even male strangers.

Brothers, too, if I can really call any of Hasan's older children my siblings.

I shrugged and hugged Carey, heading out before there was another lengthy conversation, or I got roped into anything else, like movies or dinner at their place. By the look in Carey's eyes, she was thinking about it.

"Drive safe!" she called after me. I gave her a small salute, our new sign for listening to each other. "I'll see you tomorrow!"

"Yes, you will! I'll pick you up at four!" I slid into my car before anymore could be said. It was hard walking away from Carey. The girl was chatty, always wanting to have the last word, always wanting to know more, know what was going on, being involved with the adults, or trying to make friends.

I drove off quickly, trying not to think about how I was possibly betraying my kind just by hanging out with her and her werewolf family. Jabari's words had hit home.

4

CHAPTER FOUR

I got home and didn't stop at my bar, instead jumping on my small dirt bike to head back to my house deep in the woods. I should have stopped in the bar, knowing I had work to do, but that sinking feeling was back, and thoughts were running through my mind I had to put to rest.

Am I really doing something wrong by hanging around the wolves?

I didn't think about it for a long time. They lived nearby, and I hung out with Carey, who was human. I kept my head down and didn't engage in politics and whispers.

Now, I was beginning to regret that. From Heath to Jabari, things were being brought to my attention I should have thought about months before. I should have paid attention to Hasan when he said he didn't think I made a sound decision about the wolves moving in.

There was only one person I could think to ask as I

pulled in front of my house. I sighed as I kicked off my shoes at the front door, wandering into my living room. For a second, I stared into the woods around my home, through the massive glass windows I had along one side of my home. My home was beautiful and modern, but I wanted a connection to nature even when I was inside it. The windows did that for me.

I dropped onto my couch and pulled my phone out of my pocket, considering my decision to make the call. Ever since Jabari texted me the night before, it had floated at the back of my mind. Heath giving me an update on the wolves, especially those trying to talk to werecats and become allies, only made the sinking feeling worse. Then Jabari on the phone? I hadn't expected that at all.

"I hope she has answers," I mumbled to myself, pushing the call button on Lani's contact information.

It only rang once.

"Jacky! Long time no talk. How're you?"

Normally, I would have immediately launched into whatever was going on, but something sounded nervous as hell about the entire line—anxious.

"I'm good, how are you?" I answered, posing the question back on her.

"Good, good. Just busy. You know how it is."

"I do. Life gets busy sometimes."

Right after that, there was an awkward beat of silence. There used to be a time when Lani and I could talk easily. That had changed after the Dallas incident. Calls with Lani died off as I realized the new awkward strain between us. I wasn't sure if it was my family in the werecat world or not, but something had strained the tentative bonds we had.

"What did you need?" Lani finally asked, her anxiety wearing off as she must have realized I was only calling because something was on my mind.

"Do you listen to werecat politics?" I asked, leaning back on my couch, trying to relax.

"Yes, I'm active in them, actually. Are you looking for some information in particular or...?"

"Information. I was recently told werewolves were trying to open more communication with werecats because of what happened last year. I then was told that a lot of werecats were mad about it, preferring to be left alone..." I trailed off, trying to ask the question on my mind. "There are two dead werecats in Washington. Is there a chance it's my fault because of everything that happened with the Dallas pack and the Tribunal?"

"A lot of werecats will think so as that news spreads," Lani answered, and I heard a touch of 'maybe I do too' in her voice. "Who told you?"

"Jabari," I informed her quickly. "Family, you know?"

"Hmm." That was short.

"You're mad at me."

"Maybe I am. For years, I tried to help you in our world, thinking you were a stray who needed help settling and getting adjusted to being a werecat. Instead, I find out you're the young, prodigal child of the most respected werecat in history. If we believed in Kings, Queens, and Alphas, you're the daughter of ours, and you just never bothered to tell anyone. Now, you get news from Jabari—"

"Jabari and I don't talk that often. This is the first time he's contacted me in over seven years, Lani. They let me walk away from the family—"

"And now, everyone knows you are part of that family, and yes, werecats are mad at you. Damn it, I have lost longtime friends for my minimal involvement in your Tribunal case, Jacky. There was a reason I was the only werecat there, except Hasan. They think you're young and refuse to follow the rules. If they didn't know Hasan was your father, they would just call you stupid and ignorant."

"You weren't pissy with me when I did it," I snapped, pissed off that she sounded like she believed how those other werecats felt. *God damn gossipy werecats. They never see each other in person, but they all have each other's damn cell phone numbers. They can never resist calling each other to pass along the news!* "You said you would stand with me! Did you think you would speak up for me, I would still be executed, and that would be that? There wouldn't be anything further from it?"

"Honestly? Yes."

Guilt. If she was in the room with me, I knew I would smell it just based on the tone of her voice.

"Damn, Lani." I resisted hanging up on her. "How do I fix this?"

"You kick those wolves out of your territory and keep out of trouble for a decade. Maybe a century. Depends on how long it takes us to go back to a nearly forgotten species. Do you know how many werecats have been called to Duty since your stunt? *Four.* That's more than the last *twenty years.* It hasn't even been a year. Thankfully, none of them have been injured, but it's only a matter of time."

"I can't do that. I can't throw them out," I mumbled, shaking my head. "There has to be something else."

"To win over other werecats? Not likely. You would have to curb any war you might have started rolling before it has the chance to start. Sadly, you stirred the pot, then walked out of the kitchen, leaving the rest of us to deal with your mess. The Houston pack refuses to leave me alone. They want to have dinner, get to know me, discuss protection plans for any of the humans in their pack, in case something happens. I finally told them to fuck off last month, and they've given me space again."

"I'm sorry." I groaned. "Lani, I am. I didn't think—"

"No, you didn't think. Your family is known for stepping in and correcting these issues. They help us stay alive. You just kicked a hornet's nest and—"

"I get it!" I growled. "I'm a fuck up compared to the rest of Hasan's children. I know! That has been made abundantly clear, damn it! I don't need you fucking rubbing it in."

"Sorry. I shouldn't be harsh with you—"

"No."

"But you can't deny you should have thought about all of this a lot sooner."

"I know." My anger deflated quickly. *I know.* "I'll...

figure something out. Some way to make a better impression."

Lani sighed on the other end. "If I have any ideas, other than the ones I've already given you, I'll let you know."

"Thank you."

I heard the call disconnect, defeat weighing on me. She hung up on me. Why did this become such a big deal? Why did no one tell me sooner? I would have tried something.

But would I have? Or would I have buried my head in the sand and bitched it wasn't my problem?

I didn't know. All I knew was that two werecats were now dead, Jabari was figuring out what killed them for Hasan, and fingers were slowly being pointed at me as the reason werecats were now being given so much attention. There was a chance this had nothing to do with me but learning that would come too late. The accusations were already apparent.

Did I get two werecats killed by doing whatever I wanted?

The idea plagued me as I left my living room and went upstairs to my home office. I never worked in it, instead slowly letting it become a small library and relaxation room with a computer to play games and a few large bookshelves to read. There was a small desk, a recliner, and even a couch if I just wanted to have a nap. I never got to use it often enough. I had so much house, no one in it, and no time to enjoy it.

Could solve that by hiring people for the bar...

I shook my head. The last thing I needed was more people in my life bothering me, up in my space, trying to learn my secrets.

Half my problems were because I didn't want to deal with more people than necessary, even at the expense of my own ability to have a life. I knew that. It didn't mean I was going to change any time soon, but I knew it.

Except, normally, my lack of involvement only affected me. It didn't seem like that was the case anymore.

"Fuck. Where do I even start with this?" I fell onto the recliner and curled my legs in. I contemplated calling Hasan but decided against it. If he honestly wanted to yell at me, he would have already. Unless he was waiting for me to go to him with my proverbial tail between my legs. He hadn't been very angry with the wolves moving into my territory, so I was at a loss. With him, I didn't know.

"I can't deal with this," I finally mumbled to myself, shaking my head. Why was it anyone's business I let two wolves live in my territory? What was the problem with fighting to protect and save someone I was charged with? Why did this have to be a mess? "I shouldn't have to deal with this."

I had the strong urge to stomp my foot and say anyone could live in my territory if I wanted them to. That nothing else outside my territory was my business, and they could all shove it. They could deal with their own wolves and werecats, and that was that.

But if I got two werecats killed...

45

I sighed, rubbing my face. I played with my phone and finally decided to call Hasan. He picked up halfway through the first ring.

"Jacqueline. How are you this evening?" he asked gently.

"Jabari called me. I got my ass chewed by not only him but Lani as well. When were you going to tell me how much trouble I've given you?"

"I wasn't going to. I knew what trouble I was asking for when I walked in front of the Tribunal that day." He sounded bland like the conversation bored him. That wasn't a good sign, actually. It meant something had annoyed him by whatever I said.

"Are you mad I let the werewolves live in my territory?" I asked softly. "I know that's given you even more—"

"I despise werewolves, but you like Carey, who is very human. The wolves are just an extension of her, and it's a mutually beneficial relationship. You have something to cling to in the real world while they have a built-in guardian. They aren't giving you a hard time, correct?"

"No, and other wolves don't come visit them. I just... heard things recently."

"The two up in Washington. Yes...that's concerning. It could very well be a reactionary attack from me stepping into the limelight and the small evolution of the Laws. I've already taken that well into account."

"Will you keep me updated on what's going on?"

"I can do that. Are you worried?" I could see him

mentally perking up. I was so known for staying out of everything and not wanting to know. This was a big change.

"I am. I don't...want to be the cause of werecats dying and another war starting."

"I'll do my best for that not to happen, daughter. So, how was talking to Jabari?"

I groaned and replayed the conversation for him. Jabari was Hasan's biological son, and their relationship was close, very close. Hasan didn't make the distinction between biological and Changed when it came to those he considered his family, but Jabari was considered his heir. There was no denying that bond.

"They did tell me about how they would try harder with you. Part of that is my fault. I didn't introduce you into the family the way they're accustomed, meeting you before you were Changed. Jabari and Zuri have seen everyone grow up except you. When I did Change you, none of them were home, and I was still...withdrawn from the world." He sighed on the other end of the line. "I was accused of Changing you to replace Liza. They didn't like it. They were gone so much to punish me, and your possible relationship with them suffered because of it. From my understanding, they weren't particularly kind when they were around, and I thought their distance was becoming a good thing. It gave you a chance to flourish."

"Ouch," I mumbled. In a half-joking tone, I asked the stupidest question I could. "I'm not, right?"

"No," he snapped. "No, Jacky, you aren't a

replacement. I Changed you because I couldn't imagine a world without you in it while you were there dying in that twisted hunk of metal. It was impulsive, something I had never done before, but that was it." I could hear him grumble and growl on the other end. I shouldn't have asked. I knew better, honestly. He never compared me to her, never made it seem like I was a replacement.

"Back to your siblings. I knew they were going to try speaking to you more, and I'm glad Jabari is using this to kick things off. It's important. I hope you accept it and let them make their attempts. Try opening up to them. You'll be less lonely if you start talking to other werecats more often, others who truly understand you."

"Did you encourage them, or was this their decision?" I wanted the truth. "Hasan, I don't want family who don't want me."

"Jacky, they were willing to expose our kind to keep you alive. You are their younger sister. They mean what they say. Now, what Jabari said to you? He's used to things being done a certain way and having a certain amount of control, something he doesn't have with you. To him...you're a rebellious teenager."

"I'm thirty-six and just like to live my own life," I reminded him.

"Yes. A child in our world. Don't take his harshness to heart. You might be a well-balanced, functioning, *human* adult, but to a werecat, you're still young. You try to live life by rules that no longer apply and cannot continue to apply."

"You would tell me if you were angry, right? About

everything?" It was complicated between Hasan and me. It always would be, but I had the same attitude with him as I did my human father. I got angry with his secrets, I craved his pride, and I wanted him to leave me alone. I leaned into his affection and snapped at his hand when I didn't want it.

"You'll know the day I get angry with you," he whispered. It sent shivers down my spine. Oh, yes, I would. He would make sure everyone within a few hundred miles knew he was angry with me.

"Thanks for talking to me. Keep me updated?"

"I said I would. I'll put you on the list of calls I have to make every time one of you is out getting into trouble." He chuckled softly. "Sadly, being the youngest, you are last."

"I figured. Did they all get calls from you about me?"

"I call them about you more than you can imagine," he said with a bite. "But yes, when you were called to Duty, and everything happened, they all heard about it as I did."

I wonder why else he calls them about me. It's not like I do much of anything.

"All right, well, I have to go. Bye!" I hung up as he replied with his own goodbye.

I felt a little better, glad to know he didn't blame me and wasn't angry like so many others. That was enough to put me at ease to take the nap I had been craving—social activity took it out of me.

5

CHAPTER FIVE

I picked up Carey promptly at four in the afternoon at the family's dark brown brick, two-story farmhouse. She had just enough time every Monday to do two things—eat a snack and do her homework. She wasn't allowed to come with me until the homework was done. The snack was just her preference.

"Stay out of trouble," Heath said to her as he walked her to my car. "And don't give Jacky a hard time."

"I never do, Dad!" Carey rolled her eyes at me as she stepped in front of her dad and grabbed the door. Months before, she had let him open the door for her. Now, she was doing it herself, and every time Heath tried to do it, he felt the sting of his little girl not wanting his help. How did I know? I could see and smell it, but past that, I was once the same little girl, rejecting the help of an adult because I could do it myself.

The poor man is never going to survive her teenage years.

"So, what are we doing today?" Carey grinned at me as she put her seat belt on. I lowered her car window so Heath could say something before we drove away.

"I was thinking we would try baking that cookie recipe. The one I told you about last week."

"The strawberry ones?" Her face lit up like the sun.

"Yup. What do you need, Heath?" I looked around her and smiled at her father, knowing he was probably getting annoyed with waiting.

"I want her home by nine tonight. You can feed her dinner. I've got calls to make, it seems, and she's better off with you while Landon and I work."

"A whole extra hour..." I sighed. "Fine." I dragged it out, smirking at Carey, whose laugh echoed around my car.

"Funny." Heath shook his head in disapproval before kissing his daughter's forehead and stepping back up onto the dark wood, wraparound porch.

"He loves you," I whispered to her, closing the window. "Let him open the door sometimes."

"It's weird. I can open the door by myself."

He's trying to teach you what a gentleman does. I didn't say that to her, but it ran across my mind. How many times had I talked to Shane about that? How women looked to their fathers, who were great or terrible examples of men. Heath was a great father, there was no denying that, and I knew Carey wouldn't recognize how good for at least another few years. Maybe when a boy breaks her heart for the first time or hurts her feelings.

"Just do it. He'll appreciate letting you remind him you're still his little girl."

"No one opens your doors. Or pays for you. Or anything like that." She shrugged like that was explanation enough.

"Because I'm an adult." *And I would love a man to open the door for me if he wants to sleep with me, but that's not something I can tell you.* "And he's not my father. My father will still try to open the door for me." I pulled out of the driveway and began the short drive home with her. She had this intense look of concentration on her face for a moment then popped a question I was expecting.

"Your human dad or your werecat dad?"

"Both," I answered, trying to sound nonchalant. "But my human dad doesn't know where I am or can't see me anymore."

"Could he find you? If something bad happens?"

"No," I murmured, shaking my head. "I took the last name, Leon, right after I was Changed. It's common for our kind. Not that last name specifically, just a new one. I thought I was being funny."

"What's your real name?"

I gave her a side-eyed expression, letting her know she wasn't going to learn that *ever*. Heath knew and he'd been able to track down my human family. When I thought about it, it was funny. He could back track my life to humanity and learn about me, but he couldn't find anything about my werecat life. Oh, he'd found fake names and bank accounts, which had taken him years to put together, but he couldn't connect me with Hasan or the rest of the family, something the family took a lot of care with, not only for my privacy but also for theirs. Unless someone knew beforehand, they weren't going to find out without someone in the family telling them. Since werecats never offered that information to outsiders, the secret was safe.

"Why are you so nosy today?" I asked as I turned down the highway to get to my bar.

"Because I can." She gave the same nonchalant shrug from earlier. "I like hearing about you. You're my friend."

"Thank you." I smiled down at her. "Cookies and cards tonight, though. I'm not up for a lot of heavy conversation."

"Okay." She smiled back and pulled her legs up to her chest, sitting in a little secure ball in the passenger's seat. "You know my birthday is next month, right?"

"Yup. It's marked on my calendar. Twelve years old. You excited?"

"Not really. It's another year closer to sixteen, though, when I get to learn to drive."

Priorities. Carey had the right priorities.

"Well, what do you want this year? Twelve is important, too, you know."

"Not really!" With a huff, she sagged into the seat. "I don't know what I want. Dad's been asking too, and I just don't know what to tell him. What did you want for your birthday?"

"I..." I realized that I couldn't remember. Damn dead spot in my memory. Part of me wondered if it was from the car accident. Hasan didn't know of anyone else who had lost so much of their memory during the Change. It was common for werecats to lose bits and pieces, but I lost nearly six years of my childhood. "I don't remember, actually."

"Then it can't be that important." Carey crossed her arms. "Maybe I'll ask for a dirt bike like the one you have."

"Oh, I'm sure he'll love that..."

Carey laughed, but I could tell she was strongly considering it. Amazing. Heath was going to be so mad at me for that if he had a problem with dirt bikes. He'd bought a large piece of property between Tyler and Jacksonville, so maybe he would be fine with it, but I knew his property was so he and Landon could shift during the full moon, not for Carey to run around and get bitten by snakes or break her arm on a dirt bike.

I pulled in front of the bar, closed on Mondays like normal, and unlocked the door for her to follow me in, climbing the back stairs together to my small apartment. I pointed to the table, a silent order for her to park her butt in a chair while I got stuff out for cookies. It was ritual now. Monday was the day she came over, asked me girl questions, or just wanted to talk to an adult who wasn't her father or brother. We cooked, baked, played video games, anything either of us was interested in. Once, I took her walking on some of the trails behind the bar, keeping her away from my house.

"Any cute guys at school? Or girls?" I asked, pulling out everything we needed from the fridge and pantry.

"No. They all know my dad is a werewolf which means they think I might be a werewolf—"

"We've already established you go to school with shit kids," I reminded her. "But not all of them are shitty. Are there any you like at all?"

She shrugged. "Dad says I need to hang out with other kids my age, but...I've always hung out with werewolves and werewolf families. Normal kids are... boring. And scared of me. And my dad."

"Yeah, I know." I tried to give her a sympathetic look as I put two bowls down on the table. "Is anyone teasing you?"

"You can't tell Dad," she said pointedly.

"I don't tell your dad anything."

"Then, yeah, there are a couple of boys who tease me. Never enough to tell the teacher. A few of the girls move away from me when I try to sit with them. It's not a big deal. My old school was like this too, and it's okay. I still see my tutors on Tuesdays and Thursdays, and those kids aren't as smart as me."

"If it becomes more than teasing, you'll tell me or your dad," I ordered.

"I know," she huffed. "You know, he was annoyed with you yesterday."

"You know, I think I got that impression," I said, thinking back. "What's his problem?"

"You don't tell him anything. Dad is used to people telling him *everything*, and he doesn't like that you don't. He knows it's because you're a werecat, but he's a control freak. He likes to know everything, and now he doesn't. He says you keep secrets."

"I do. More from him than you, actually." I sat down and cracked open the cake mix that was the base of the cookies. It was a recipe I had found online when I was human and loved so much, I tried it with every cake mix I could find. I didn't bake often, but this was my go-to baking project. "He didn't like how you didn't make him pay for me at the bowling alley."

"Oh, because I know Alphas pay for their wolves when they do things together. It's an Alpha's way of saying he'll take care of you. But you don't want anyone to take care of you, and...I know if he acts too much like an Alpha, you'll want him to leave. Then I have to leave too, and that would be awful."

"You're perceptive. Maybe you should tell him everything I've told you about werecats. It might help him." I raised an eyebrow. "Why haven't you?"

She gave me a sly smile. "I like finally knowing more than him."

I laughed, shaking my head with dismay for her poor father. "I think he might like to hear things I'm telling you. It'll help him."

"We've been doing this for months, and he's only getting...weirder," she said, her face screwing up in confusion. "Like, every week he's asking more questions and getting nosier. I don't get it."

"Let me talk to him. It's not like I'm going to make you a werecat or anything."

"No, you just like having someone safe around," she whispered, giving me a look.

I had explained to her she was always welcome and why months before. We fulfilled each other's needs in that way. She wanted a woman to talk to, that was obvious. One who knew everything, both girl problems and supernatural problems. It helped that she felt safe with me. And I needed someone I could safely share with, who didn't threaten me or feel threatened by me. We were symbiotic, Carey and me. It wouldn't last forever, but I started treasuring the Mondays we shared after only a few short weeks, something that only began to ease her nightmares. The feeling I would burn down the world to make her smile never faded. It was always there, ready for something to spark it.

"So, cookies," I declared, showing her everything I set out. "This recipe is so easy, you're going to die. Promise."

"Are we just doing strawberry?" she asked. "Can we put chips in it?"

"We are going to do plain strawberry, and I was thinking..." I had a surprise up my sleeve. I grabbed another box and a bag of chocolate chips. "Yellow cake, whatever flavor that is, with chocolate chips. Like how yellow cake almost always has chocolate icing."

"I love yellow cake!" She made one of those high-pitched girl noises, grinning. "And then we're going to play something while they bake."

"And after, I'm going to order us food. If I'm going to bake, I'm not going to cook."

"That's cool." She was still beaming as I sat back down.

Together, we poured, mixed, and stirred. I grabbed two cookie sheets and taught her how to roll the right size balls for good cookies as the oven preheated. Once it dinged, we had two full trays of cookies and extra dough for another batch. Once the cookies were in the oven, we played solitaire together, me teaching her the rules. I had already taught her spider and hearts but figured poker of any sort was off the table for at least a couple of years. Solitaire was easy and would give her something she could do when she was bored.

"You can always download it onto your phone," I reminded her. "You would learn faster."

"I like learning from you."

I wanted to melt. I liked teaching her.

When the first batch of cookies was done, I pulled them out and placed them on racks to cool and put the second batch in. Carey wandered off to my bathroom. Leaning on the counter, I began to think about how awful it would be to kick Heath, Landon, and Carey out of my territory. It would hurt not to see her so often, and I couldn't imagine how she would feel if she suddenly had to move because I didn't want them around.

I can't do it. Not to her. There had to be another way to make everyone out there calm the fuck down. There had to be a way to appease the insular natures of the werecats without throwing her out just to get rid of Heath and Landon. I could always tell them they just needed to move out of my territory, but would Heath trust me with her after that? It would be a major inconvenience and could give him the impression they weren't safe around me.

And they are. They are safe with me.

Carey walked back in, but I busied myself with checking my phone, seeing if anyone had texted me. By now, Jabari would be in Washington, maybe talking to other werecats in the region about the two who were killed. I didn't know if there were bodies found or not, or how everyone even knew they were dead. There was no news, though. Hopefully, Hasan would keep in touch, and Lani would call me back.

The alarm for the oven made me jump. I quickly turned it off and removed the cookies before anything was burned.

"Are you okay?" Carey asked softly.

"I am," I lied, smiling easily at her. I wasn't. I wasn't normally so jumpy or distracted, not with people around —never with people around. This was the second time in front of her I'd lost track of my surroundings. Including Saturday with Heath made it three times. Three times in three days. Unusual, to say the least, but the recent news had me distracted. I grabbed a plate and two glasses. Carey couldn't walk over to me fast enough as I swiftly poured the milk, moving too quickly, and over poured. She grabbed the glass before I knocked it off the counter as I cussed darkly.

"What's wrong, Jacky?" Her words sounded woeful and sad.

"Nothing. There's just a lot on my mind, and I was

rushing to get you milk and..." I shook my head. "Go sit and I'll—"

"I got it!" She smiled and ran to grab the paper towels. I snatched them from her and pointed to the table. I was too edgy now, especially since she was noticing something was off. I cleaned up as she sat back down. I put her milk and the cookies in front of her, grabbing my glass last.

"Why don't I just turn on a movie tonight?" I suggested, smiling weakly.

"Okay."

Turning on the most recent superhero movie, we watched from the table, eating cookies. I ordered Chinese food absentmindedly as the movie played, and it got there fast. I made two plates of Mongolian beef and fried rice, making sure I fed her before shoveling the rest onto my own plate. I could easily eat it all, but I always made sure Carey had enough food. There were even a couple of days when she had told me to stop giving her food. When the first movie was over, I turned on another. It was a good distraction for her, something to keep her eyes off me while my mind continued to wander.

The other werecats could force me to give up Carey. My palms grew sweaty. If they hated that wolves lived in my territory, they could force the issue. They had to see it wasn't so bad, they could work with their wolves.

Unless their wolves wanted to kill them because they were possible threats.

What if Carey was in danger? Or Heath and

Landon? What if a werecat decided to try to claim my territory to teach me a lesson?

The very idea paralyzed me for much of the second film. When it was over, Carey jumped up and took our empty glasses to the sink.

"Jacky..." She touched my shoulder when she got back. "It's nine thirty." She yawned, and I groaned.

"Sorry. Let's get you home. I wasn't the best company tonight."

"It's okay. We all have bad days." She didn't seem sad, but I felt guilty. "You'll be better next Monday."

"Yup." I smiled and herded her out of my apartment and back down to my car. She texted her dad with my cellphone as we got into the car. What amazed me was he didn't call, not that he ever had before. Normally, when I was a little late getting her back, we told him, and he just said it was fine.

"He's not mad," Carey finally announced next to me. "He says he got caught up with work. Who's Jabari?"

"My brother," I answered quickly then clamped my jaw. "Don't..."

"Tell anyone? Okay. I don't like people meeting Richard and Landon either. They just...scare people off. Big brothers, right?"

"Right," I agreed. "He's a very private man, and if Heath learns about him, you know your dad is going to look up everything he can."

"Oh yeah, he is that nosy."

I let the conversation die out until we were in front of

her house. "Be good for your dad. Tell him I'm sorry for being back late with you."

"He'll understand." Carey yawned as she slid out of my hatchback. "Good night, Jacky."

"Good night, Carey."

I watched her walk inside, her dad meeting her at the door. He tilted his head at me, leveling me with a confused stare. I wasn't normally late. I just drove off, hoping he would forget about it.

6

CHAPTER SIX

I spent the week constantly checking my phone. Hasan was true to his word for the first few days, but Friday came and went without a call or text from him. It was already late Saturday and still no word.

Really? Did he forget about me already?

"So, Jacky—"

"Not tonight, Joey," I snapped, putting my phone down, cranky there was still no contact. *I'm going to call him tonight, and he better pick up. He promised to keep me in the loop. If anything happened to Jabari, I deserve to know.*

"Whoa. Okay..." I heard him back away from the bar. Before he got too far away, I slammed his fresh drink on the countertop and stepped away so he could get it without being snapped at by me. I continued to pour drinks and line them up, ready for my regulars to come get them. Without Joey bothering me, there was no one speaking to me at all. The news was playing softly on the

TV in the back corner, and country music was a bit louder, but I naturally tuned it out. I could feel Heath's approach, like every Saturday. Again, he was coming without Landon.

I hadn't talked to anyone from the small werewolf family since Monday. I was plagued by the idea I was doing something wrong or would get them into trouble—improbable, fear-driven thoughts, but once I had started to think them, I couldn't stop.

So, I tended my bar and avoided them all week—two missed calls from Carey, three texts from her, and one call from Heath.

Now, the wolf was coming to the bar.

I shined a glass impatiently as I felt him draw close and enter the parking lot. I got annoyed as it felt like an eternity for him to get out of his car and walk into Kick Shot. I made his drink and set it in his favorite spot as he came inside. Grabbing it, he moved further down the bar toward the back, near the emergency exit and the back staircase. He didn't say a word to me, but the hardness of his eyes told me I was in trouble.

I followed him, and he bared his teeth.

"We're talking after you close," he said with a snap.

"Fine," I snapped back, continuing with my job, turning my back to him.

For most of the night, I flat out ignored him, checking my phone when I had time. Nothing happened until nearly midnight when Joey, drunk as he normally was on a Saturday night, walked up and looked between us.

"Aww, trouble in paradise between the Alpha and the bartender? What happened, J—"

"Shut the fuck up, Joey," I growled, unable to hold back the very real animal sound that came with it. Out of the corner of my eye, I watched Heath stand up quickly. If the stool wasn't bolted into the floor, it would have fallen over. "He's not my Alpha, and my personal business isn't yours. Go fucking play pool or go home. If you want a drink, let me know. Other than that, get away from me."

It was the harshest I had ever been with any of my customers. People looked over at me with wide eyes, staring until they realized I knew they were.

All was quiet for the rest of the night. The people who normally told me goodbye, didn't, instead scurrying away like misbehaving children, hoping not to catch their teacher's eye. I held the door open for them, locking it once the last of them was gone, glad to be done with another week. It wasn't completely over, not yet, but it was close. I just had to deal with the wolf behind me.

"Heath," I greeted, turning on him. "What do you want to know?"

"Where have you been all week? Carey said something was wrong on Monday, then you avoided her all week. I promised to find out tonight."

It sounded simple, but it wasn't. He was eyeing me as if he was sizing up a possible threat, something he hadn't done in a long time. He couldn't beat me and knowing that kept the more predatory behavior at bay between us.

"I..." With a sigh, I realized I needed to tell him. For

Carey's sake, he deserved to know what was going on. "Two werecats were killed up in the Pacific Northwest. It's made me edgy."

"I didn't hear about that. Do you have any idea who killed them or why?" His temper deflated, but only a little.

"No. Someone is checking it out, but I haven't heard an update in a few days. It's just had me distracted. That's all." I tried to wave it off, not wanting to realize just how badly it distracted me.

"You're not allowed to be distracted around Carey," he growled softly. "You're a dangerous predator, a monster, even stronger than Landon and me. You have to be ready for anything when you're with her, including your own urges. If you're spacing out, I don't trust her near you."

"That's ridiculous, and you know it. I'm *never* going to be a danger to Carey." I growled back, the rumble building in my chest as his accusation I was somehow a threat settled between us like a thrown gauntlet.

"Then why, even distracted, have you avoided her all week? And I've heard—'Dad, Jacky didn't respond to my text yesterday,' or 'Dad, Jacky hasn't been answering my calls, and I really want to talk to her about something,' and 'Dad, did we do something to Jacky?'" He slid off the bar stool and crossed his arms. "So, did we do something? Or are you finally tired of dealing with a pre-teen?"

"Carey is the only person in this damn state that I like right now," I snarled viciously. I shook my head, biting my bottom lip hard as I considered what to say to him. "I'm in trouble with other werecats. I've lived on the outside of werecat and supernatural society for so long, I naturally avoid it and don't engage. I should have died, guilty as charged at the Tribunal—"

"Don't ever say those words again," Heath roared, kicking the barstool next to him hard enough that he ripped it out of the floor. "My family and my pack worked our damn hardest to get you out of that. You deserved to be a fucking hero for stepping up and helping us protect and save Carey."

"Thank you for that, but every werecat in the world would have rather I died instead of shaken up the status quo!" I flung my hand toward the outside world. "All except..." I wasn't ready to tell him that. "Hasan is the leader of our community, and if it weren't for him, I would have died, and there wouldn't be any werecats grieving over me. You know what they're doing, though? They're getting pissed werewolves are bothering them. We *love* our privacy. We don't want to be tossed into problems and used as a meat shield for people we don't know. It's all we have, but that doesn't mean we *want it*. Four werecats have been called to Duty in the last six months, Heath. *Four*! And it's my fault!" I was yelling by the end. "They're furious I let you live here with Landon just so I could see Carey. And it probably hasn't escaped them that I swore an oath to protect Carey while you're here! That's un-fucking-heard of!"

"Who told you they all wanted you to die?" he asked softly, my words obviously making an impact.

"Lani," I said, my voice breaking for a second. "My

only friend for six years thought she was going to defend me like a good friend should, but I was going to die...and that would be that. Weird werecat without a family would be out of the equation, everything would be normal, and werecats would keep their private, nearly-forgotten lives." I'd tried not to think about it all week, but telling someone else, my vision blurred as I blinked back tears. "Then I got thinking if they were all so damn mad at me...what if they came here? What if an older werecat challenged me for my territory, and I *lost*? You would be at their whim unless you ran, and Carey doesn't deserve to be running for her life again..."

"What does this have to do with the two dead werecats?" He kept his voice just as soft as it was before my rambling spiel.

"They might be my fault," I answered, swallowing the lump of guilt in my throat. "What if those two werecats weren't considered possible allies by their neighbors? What if they only thought they were threats? Heath...I could have started another war, and I don't know yet if I have or not."

"*We* could have started a war," he whispered.

"No—"

"Yes." He nodded slowly, enforcing his idea that somehow it was both of us. "You would have never been involved with Carey or my pack if I had been a better Alpha. Even then, I should have sent you away from Dallas, but I didn't. I let you make the decision, knowing full well where it could get you. If I had been considering the politics and not just my daughter's life or my own pack, I maybe could have seen how this could go wrong."

I shook my head. "They aren't going to care about that. I'm the failure to my species, apparently," I mumbled, walking back toward my bar. "My own brother..."

"Brother?" He perked up quickly, and I mentally began a string of cusses that weren't appropriate for the public.

"Nothing."

"You said brother," he pressed. "You have family?"

"Drop it."

"No."

I growled, looking up from my bar to stare into his grey-blue eyes. He and Carey both had this stubbornness to them, and it was in their eyes.

"Yes, I have a...werecat family. I don't talk to them that often, and there are reasons I live out here alone. Drop it."

"How do they feel about everything?" He leaned on the bar, all his heat gone. I sighed, watching him. It wasn't over yet. I had made the foolish decision to open up, and he was going to find whatever scraps of information he could about me.

"It doesn't matter. They can't protect me from myself, and I have to take full responsibility for the can of worms I've opened. I just need to figure out what I'm going to do about all of this, which meant I wanted some space away from everyone. I need time to think." I touched my phone, where I left it on the counter. Still no word from Hasan or anyone else from the family. "Lani says I should throw you out," I said softly, feeling guilty even if they weren't my words.

"That...I would have to move Carey into another new school. Landon and I—"

"I told her that wasn't an option," I cut in before he started going off about how bad that would be for him. I tried not to think of him as selfish, jumping straight to how bad that would be for him. Well, not straight to him specifically. His first worry had been Carey and school. "I'll figure out something else. Some way for me to calm the werecats down about this. A lot of them, roughly half, are survivors of the war, so it's a tough battle, but I'm not going to toss you all out. I made a promise, and I plan on keeping it."

"So many?" Heath frowned. "Really?"

"Werecats grow older far easier than werewolves, mostly because we don't have as much infighting. Rogue werecats roam, looking for a territory of their own, answer to other werecats, or just don't want to settle down yet. I've fought a few of those when they got curious about someone's territory and needed to be chased out. Those were never fatal, though. Territory fights are nearly never fatal. It's frowned upon." I was rambling again now.

"Have you gotten into any fights since we've been here?"

"No. I would have told you there was trouble just so you wouldn't go near the border."

"So, to recap, you've been avoiding my daughter,

which hurts her, because you are...busy considering how to stop any possible wars that may have started thanks to our actions."

"And how to keep out of trouble with other werecats. Or, I don't know, make them see I don't mean anyone harm, and neither do you. You better not mean my kind harm. If you do, you won't make it out of my territory alive."

"Understandable. No, I don't mean any of your kind harm. Most of the time, I'm curious. Vampires, fae, werewolves, and werecats. Nagas, kitsunes, and more. I like to meet others from different species and get their perspective. You give me a close eye into the world of werecats. I don't plan on using it against you, and I'm not spying under false pretenses."

"You say that now, but if I threw you out or a werecat attacked, you would use everything you could to protect yourself and Carey," I pointed out. "I'm not stupid."

"Like you don't know more than you let on about werewolves," he reminded me with a small smile. "Some were very surprised by how much you knew about us, me included."

"Touché." And I was willing to use it all to survive, even if the urge to survive surprised me because before I met Carey, I didn't have all that much to live for.

"Can I admit something since we're doing this sharing thing tonight?" he asked, looking down at his hands, considering them. My thoughts wandered to the memory of how warm and calloused they were when he helped clean and re-bandage my injuries in that warehouse in Dallas. They were nice hands.

"You can say whatever you want."

"I was mad at Carey for being so upset by you."

I raised my eyebrows in surprise until he looked up. He chuckled sadly.

"Not to her face. Just privately annoyed by it. I thought...I thought she would be over you by now. I figured the first few months, her attachment would be understandable. You protected her, she was having nightmares, and being able to talk to you...helped her. She refuses to talk to me about Richard. So does Landon..." He groaned. "Yet she's more in love with you now than she was six months ago. I wasn't expecting that."

"Are you uncomfortable with it?" I asked in a small voice, knowing it was strange. A thirty-six-year-old shouldn't be the best friend of an eleven-year-old, not to humans, and maybe not to werewolves. Werecats were different.

"Jealous," he said, leaning down to put his forehead on the counter. "I'm jealous. Does she talk to you about him? My *son*, her *brother* tried to kill her. Wanted to kill me and Landon...and I don't know how she feels. Part of me knows if she ever told anyone, it would be you, and that irks me. She used to tell me everything."

"No, she doesn't talk to me about Richard. None of you have since that night," I answered, swallowing my guilt over killing his son. Richard refused to stop fighting, and I had to protect Carey, but it still didn't wash all the guilt away. A man had to bury his child. His asshole child but a child, nonetheless.

"You understand her. Every female in my pack... either I didn't trust them as much as I should or had reasons to keep them away. Every human woman who ever tried to get close to the family was looking to turn her into a princess, and she's not that girl, will never be that girl, no matter how much *I* tried. You understand being a tough woman in a world of monsters and...I'm jealous it makes you special to her."

"There's no reason to be. She's your daughter." I shrugged, trying to play off how uncomfortable this conversation had turned.

"Just promise me one thing. Even if you do need to have us leave, keep talking to her. I don't care what else you do, Jacky, but if you hurt my daughter, I'll hunt you down and give her your hide."

"I would give it to you," I murmured. "I don't agree with hurting kids, and I'll do everything in my power to keep werecat drama far away from her. I can't promise to keep it away from you, but then, you're an adult werewolf. There's not much I can do for you or Landon. She's human, though. *No one* should try to hurt her." I frowned. "You never answered my question."

"No, it doesn't make me uncomfortable," he replied, looking up again. "I've seen it in wolves, too. An adult will take someone under their wing, mentor and guide them to adulthood. Protect them. Not as...privately as you, not for the same reasons, but I don't think anything weird is going on. I'm just jealous."

"She's a great kid," I said, smiling. "I'll keep you updated on this. You can't share what I told you tonight, though. It could seriously harm me and other werecats. Please."

"It's safe with me. There's no reason to tell anyone about what the werecats are dealing with on their own." He checked the time. "Thank you for talking to me. Don't ignore her anymore, please. If there's something on your mind, tell me, then talk to her about whatever. She's been a mess since Tuesday."

"I'll text her tomorrow and apologize." Carey was probably already in bed, so there was no way I was texting her tonight and waking her up for Heath to deal with when he got home. "Do you want one more drink?"

"No, I'm fine. Landon is probably prowling around the house, wondering if he should come get me, or if I'm alive. He doesn't trust you very much, which is typical for Landon. He'll warm up, eventually."

"Is that why he used to come in with you but not often? Because he's worried I'm going to attack you?"

"Yes and no," Heath answered with a small smile. Pushing off the bar, he adjusted his light jacket, making sure the zipper was exactly halfway up. The longer I looked at it, the more I began to think he must have ironed it. Did he iron his casual clothes?

Weird ass wolf.

He started walking toward the door, and I took the last chance I had to say something.

"Look, I am sorry for the cold shoulder all week. It was nothing personal, really."

"Just remember to tell her that," he replied, pulling open the door. "I like you, but if you disappeared tomorrow, I wouldn't be hurt. I would just be angry that my daughter would lose you and not understand why."

I tried not to take that personally. No love lost between us, he walked out. After he was gone, I did take it personally.

He wouldn't care at all? Really? After everything in Dallas and the last six months living in the same area, seeing each other every damn weekend? Then why is he at my bar all the fucking time?

CHAPTER SEVEN

I waited until midafternoon on Sunday to make any calls. Or I told myself that. Really, I slept until one in the afternoon and realized I couldn't put off calling people for the rest of the day. I had to apologize to Carey for ignoring her, yell at Hasan for ignoring me, and maybe try Lani again. She hadn't contacted me all week, though that could just be a sign she really didn't consider me as much of a friend as I considered her.

I went to the safest option first, hitting Carey's name in my contacts.

"Hello?" she said, cautious. "Jacky?"

"Hey, Carey. I...I wanted to call to say I'm sorry. It's been a bad week for me, and I didn't want to take it out on you." *I'm trying to find a way to protect you because I'm paranoid, scared, and hurt by what I heard other werecats say.*

"Yeah, Dad told me this morning you were just really busy with werecat stuff," she replied.

I closed my eyes in dismay. Heath and I gave her two different explanations, which meant she knew one was lying. Honestly, the two explanations only explained half the issue each. The truth was in their totality, but Carey would probably not see it that way.

"We're still on for tomorrow, right?" I asked her, hoping she would agree.

"Duh. I would have had Dad drive me over if you didn't show up."

I didn't like the sound of that. It was serious. The girl threw it out like an obvious fact of life and a threat at the same time.

"I'll remember that." *If I want to skip a Monday with Carey, I would need to hide better than her father can find me.* "So, what can I do to make the last week up to you?"

"We're going out to see a new movie. No more movies at your apartment. And I want to see your *real* house."

"You're playing hard ball. I'll take you to a real movie at a movie theater and out to dinner. Not my house."

"Done. I'll find some movie times for tomorrow, and you'll feel better after a good movie away from your bar." She sounded so mature like she couldn't possibly be wrong. Half the time, she was too mature. The other half, it was obvious she was only just about to turn twelve. "Dad says getting out of the house is good for you."

"Does he mean for people in general or just me?"

"I think he meant in general, but you never leave your house, so it must be good for you." I could hear her smile on the other end. I wondered if Heath was listening in and had fed her some lines this morning, knowing I was going to call.

"Tell your dad I said hello. I'll be there at four tomorrow, don't worry."

"Hello, Jacky," his smooth, scotch voice said from the other end, further from the phone than Carey. He sounded pleased, probably because I called—just like I promised him I would—and was in the process of groveling for ignoring her for nearly a week. "Carey, let her get to work. You have a science project to be working on."

"I'm going! Bye, Jacky!"

"Bye, Carey," I said and heard her hang up. For a moment, I just smiled at the phone. Talking to Heath the night before had made me feel better. Not completely better, but at least someone on the other end of the phone knew what I was trying to deal with. He would keep her safe if I couldn't, especially now that he thought I believed there might be a threat. He was her father, after all.

Letting them go, I immediately dialed Hasan. He hadn't answered at three in the morning before I went to sleep, and it was close to two in the afternoon now.

Maybe if I blow up his phone, he'll call me back.

It was strange, actually. Anytime I contacted him first, he was quick to answer or get back to me. One would think because I was showing some interest in the family's business, he would call frequently. Instead, he missed three days of calls when he promised to call every night with whatever Jabari reported.

He didn't answer, and I growled at the phone. Pondering, I tried for someone I hadn't spoken to in nearly eight years, Jabari's twin sister, Zuri.

The only reason I had her number was Hasan didn't let me leave without making sure I could contact any of my siblings. He wanted me to have options if I needed help. Zuri was even less close to me than Jabari was and was always the one who maintained the most distance when I was Changed, and Hasan brought me to his home. The only reason she was the one I wanted to call was because she was his twin. She would be the first to know *any* news.

"Jacqueline. To what do I owe the pleasure?" Her voice was cool, crisp, much like I remembered her entire demeanor. Jabari and Zuri were essentially royalty, thanks to being Hasan's children and their age. It was Zuri who embodied that ideal. Regal and beautiful, it was said she looked like her mother, Hasan's mate. She was intelligent and ruthless, cunning and vicious, all wrapped in beautiful traditional African garb I didn't know the name of or couldn't pronounce. I couldn't even tell someone what region it was from. She once said I was 'too American' as she laughed. I had tried my hardest to pronounce what it was when she told me. It was the only time I ever saw her laugh.

Looking back and not being able to remember, I felt a little bad. I never gave any of my new siblings much of a chance either.

"Um..." Nerves hit me quickly. "So...I asked Hasan about knowing what—"

"Yes. Father said you were going to be brought into the loop about Jabari. Why are you calling me?" The coolness turned to boredom. She was already done with the conversation, and whatever confusion she had about my calling was carefully masked by her attitude.

"He hasn't called me in a few days. I just wanted to make sure I wasn't missing anything. I'm getting worried and—"

There was a soft laugh on the other end. "He always said you would grow to care, learn to join the family if we gave you a chance. Looks like he was right. I'll tell you what you want to know, but understand, none of us are very worried yet. This kind of thing happens."

"Okay."

"Jabari hasn't called in since Thursday evening. He said the local wolf pack was being stubborn about speaking to him, unsure of where he came from or who he was. They weren't helpful, so he went out to investigate the territories our lost brother and sister lived in. He said something about a park, but I don't live in the United States. Please forgive me, I don't really know where he was talking about." I heard cushions sink under weight, the unmistakable sound of fabric rubbing against fabric and a small squeak of springs. She must have sat down or gotten comfortable. "Now, under these circumstances, we don't worry until one of us goes a week without reporting in. There could be a number of reasons he hasn't gotten in touch. Father probably didn't tell you because he knew you would begin to worry."

"So, ignoring me is helping me not worry?" I asked dryly.

"Ignoring you means he's not giving you information you can act rashly with. I don't have the same problem though, little sister. You want in, so I'm going to treat you like our brothers and sister. Jabari handles work with Father, and I handle the rest of you."

"You never handled me..." I muttered. 'The rest of you' sounded like an insult, but I didn't take it that way. Zuri was the big sister who made sure everyone ate dinner. She made sure everyone lived in a good home and had everything they needed. If she was royalty, and you were related to her, that made you royalty, and she expected you to live like it, to act like it.

I never gave her the chance to do that, hence my comment. She never tried to either.

"No. Father wanted to deal with you on his own. You're his first rebellious American child. The first one in the family at all. That being said, here you are calling me. I always thought he handled you with...what's that saying? Kid gloves?"

"That's the one," I mumbled, leaning over to rest my head in my free hand.

"Yes. Like precious china or something delicate. After last year, though, I would say you are anything but delicate. Then again, Mischa always told him that very thing. The one thing she and I ever agreed on."

I snorted at that. Mischa was Hasan's Russian daughter. Born in the cold winds of the Siberian tundra, her werecat form was an unusual white and light grey with electric blue eyes. She was also loud, boisterous, and totally at odds with Zuri. They were from literally opposite sides of the world and acted like they were completely opposite people.

"If Hasan doesn't call me, can I call you?" I asked, letting the topic of Mischa and family dynamics drop.

"Yes, and I'll pass along what he says to me. He probably didn't think you would reach out, but I'll give him my mind over it. Everything aside, you are my little sister." There was a hint of something motherly and caring in her words.

"Hasan said you all...wanted to help me last year."

"Being called to Duty is awful, and I don't wish it on any werecat. When he told me you were, I was furious. You should have been at home, safe from that particular part of our life. Too young to handle something like that, in my opinion. When I heard you survived but were in trouble with the Tribunal, I screamed at him. Asked him what he was going to do to help you. It wasn't my best moment, but I only want you to know the truth."

"But you didn't talk to me for...years."

"Did you want me to talk to you?"

"Not really."

"There you go. Jabari and I once stopped talking for thirty years. Mischa and I regularly call each other only once a year if either of us remembers. The rest, I try to stop in and have dinner with every six months or so. Or we all meet at Hasan's for a holiday, whatever is popular with the humans at the time. You're young. I should have realized such silence would hurt you in ways it doesn't bother us. I never...lived in a time where a few short years mattered. I was never human."

"I forget that you've been a werecat since you were born," I replied.

"Well, if that's all, I'm going to let you go. There's a very beautiful man standing in my doorway."

"Male model or actor?" It was the only thing I remembered clearly about Zuri—her choices in men. She had great taste.

"Model. They talk less."

I snorted as she hung up.

With that handled, I tried one more person—Lani.

It rang into her voicemail. I didn't say anything, hanging up with a sigh. At least two of my four phone calls went all right. Carey wasn't upset, and Zuri told me what I wanted to know. Now, I just hoped nothing was wrong with Jabari. Two werecats were already dead. I wouldn't be able to forgive myself if it became three.

Lani sure wouldn't.

8
———

CHAPTER EIGHT

I waited impatiently by the phone Monday and Tuesday morning. When Carey came over, she proved to be the only temporary distraction I would get, graciously not asking too many questions about what was bothering me. Once she understood it wasn't her or her father, she wasn't concerned, demanding I take her to a second movie next week with another dinner at a proper restaurant.

Kid knew how to bargain.

Work wasn't a better distraction, mainly because the weeknights were always a little slower than weekends, and business was never what one would call booming. I was pacing behind my bar after my early opening with only two patrons inside when I received a text from Hasan. Zuri had told me Monday there was still no word. My heart started to race as my phone buzzed with the new message. For the first time, I was in a group text with

Hasan and the rest of the family. Whatever he wanted to say, he wanted to make sure everyone saw it.

Hasan: Family meeting tonight. No contact from Jabari. Jacky, it will be at seven in the evening for you.

Hisao: I had a date, but fine.

Davor: Why can't Jabari just use the satellite phone I got him? Did he forget it, then realized he was out of cell phone reception? He's normally not so dumb.

Zuri: He didn't forget the satellite phone, little brother. I watched him walk out the door with it.

Mischa: Should have sent me.

Zuri: We learned nine hundred years ago never to send you anywhere.

My eyes were wide, watching the texts continue as my siblings ribbed each other. Hasan never commented again, and Niko, the last of the males in the family, never commented at all. Gathering my courage, I started to ask what was probably a dumb question.

Jacky: Do I need to shut down the bar for the night?

The quick replies died off. I felt stupid. Of course, I should shut down the bar for a family meeting, and the full moon was Wednesday. I would be closed for two nights, which would kill my weekly revenue, but I could afford it.

Zuri: Ask a manager to watch the bar for a few hours.

Jacky: I don't have a manager.

Mischa: Of course you don't...

I groaned. *Stupid, stupid question.* There was no taking it back now, either.

Jacky: I'll be fine. With the full moon soon, no one will notice.

Davor: Such faith in your customers. Do you even get business in that shithole area of Texas?

That one hit me in the chest. I looked up at my two customers, debating if I should snap a picture to tell him to fuck off. I took the picture, neither of them looking up from their drinks. I sent it into the chat, knowing it wouldn't make too much of a difference.

Jacky: Look at that, jackass, I do!

Davor: You do us proud.

It didn't take a genius to read the sarcasm there.

Zuri: Ask one of your dumb wolves to take over. I'm sure they know how to pour a beer. They're male and canine.

Hisao: Yeah. If they're going to live in your space, you might as well put them to work.

Niko: Leave her be.

Niko's comment killed the entire conversation. My face was red with embarrassment as I put the phone down to find my 'Full Moon - CLOSED' sign. Part of the embarrassment was I felt like an idiot. The other part was Niko only spoke to defend *me*.

Niko was an anomaly. From what I could remember about my first four years as a werecat living with Hasan, he was even more standoffish than the rest of them and avoided everyone. He would come in, talk to Hasan, then leave, and I was never told where he would go or what he would do. He just disappeared. He was the youngest son, but for some reason, he garnered a lot of respect from the others, even if they weren't always sure what to do with him. The longest conversation I ever had with him was a simple greeting and exchange of names. After that, nothing.

I'm an adult with a respectable business and once had an amazing, balanced life. How is it they make me feel like a child with all of ten words?

It was a frustration I'd dealt with since the morning I woke up to my new world of supernaturals. After nearly seven years not speaking to them, that hadn't changed at all.

As my customers left, my phone buzzed again, and I checked it, frowning.

Niko: Are you okay?

Jacky: Fine.

Niko: Good. Remember, family meetings are video conference calls.

I didn't remember that because I had never been in one. Well, that was about to change.

I WAS at my computer five minutes before the family meeting, setting up my headset and web camera. Since I never used a webcam for anything, I had to kick out my patrons due to a 'family emergency,' run to the store, buy it, and now I was fighting to set it up. I had no idea what the older werecats would be doing. From memory, they were pretty comfortable around technology, but I didn't know what kind of setups they had or how this normally played out.

Or they just pay one of their staff to set it up. That's a possibility.

I was told to download a program and install it, something I had also done earlier in the day. I opened it up to find I was instantly logged into a private server. I'd never seen or heard of the program before, and the file had been emailed to me. It wasn't something I could find online.

Did one of them hire a programmer to make this? Probably Davor.

It logged me in as Jacqueline, of course. I couldn't find a place to change it to Jacky, glaring at the name as I admitted defeat. Soon, other names were popping online. Zuri, Hasan, Davor, Mischa, Hisao, and Nikolaus. Once everyone was on, I winced as a ring came from my headphones and quickly turned the volume down before hitting Answer.

My thirty-two-inch monitor was suddenly covered with different video feeds. I could see a preview of mine on my second monitor and adjusted the webcam just a little.

"Don't fiddle with it," Davor grumbled. "There's no fixing it now. Did you buy it from the discount section?"

"No, asshole," I snapped, growling into my mic. "I just set it up and haven't been able to test it."

"Davor, she doesn't have staff, and this was short notice," Zuri reminded him with a touch of boredom. "Leave her alone. I'm sure by the next time we have a meeting, she'll have a nicer set up."

That was the line being drawn. Zuri would only let me be a technological pauper in their eyes once. Hopefully, it also got Davor off my back for the night.

"Let's get to business," Hasan said softly, a command no one fought back about. Davor's mouth shut before he could make another comment, and I watched as my siblings straightened up. Hasan tapped a pen on his desk, sighing. "Normally, these meetings are called when someone is out on assignment and hasn't called in for a week. Tomorrow is a full moon, so we know Jabari won't be reporting in, and none of us will be able to answer the call. I would like to discuss what we should do come Thursday when his week is up. If we can start the plans tonight, we can have a plan ready to go into action by then."

"I can't go this time," Zuri said, sighing heavily. "He and I live so far away, it was already a pain to get him to America."

"Where are you right now?" I asked, frowning.

"South Africa."

That took me by surprise. Their numbers weren't international. I didn't comment, though, keeping my mouth shut after that.

"They also have homes in Morocco, Egypt, Ethiopia, and Nigeria. There's not a single werecat on the continent who doesn't know them." Hasan seemed focused on business by his tone. There wasn't a lot of the honey or fatherly nature coming from him tonight. "And you're right, Zuri. I would have to fly you out too soon after a full moon, and it would be a long trip. Did he take the private jet?"

"Of course, he did, which means I'm grounded unless I use commercial." By the curl of her lip and scrunched face, commercial flying was downright unacceptable. So soon after a full moon and for so long? It was.

"I would have the same problem. I'm in Moscow right now," Mischa said, shaking her head. "I do have a jet, but do you know how hard it is right now to fly into the United States from Russia?"

"I'm closer in Sweden," Davor said quickly. "Less human issues to get around to get into the country."

"I'm in Germany," Niko threw out his positioning. I had already known they generally lived around the world. Niko's territory included the Black Forest.

"I'm in Japan," Hisao snorted, cutting off Niko. "It would be much easier for me."

"I could fly to Washington state in an afternoon," I said softly. "Two-hour drive to Dallas and a four-hour one way commercial. I can go and be there without any problems. I'm also American. I won't seem like a foreigner."

Davor was the first to start laughing, followed by Mischa, and Hisao. Hasan didn't say anything as even Zuri snorted, covering her face.

"You? Oh, Jacky." Davor slapped his hand on his desk as he bent over to laugh harder.

"Yeah, that's what we need. The fucking American," Mischa tried to say clearly, her fits of mad giggles making it nearly impossible to understand what she was going for.

"I can! I'm really close and..." I looked desperately at my camera. "I'm part of this family, aren't I? I didn't get invited to this meeting as the kid sitting with the adults, right?"

"That's exactly what you are," Hisao said, his laughter dying but the smile not leaving. "Sorry, Jacky, but there's too much swirling around you to make this any better. If you show up outside your territory, you could very well start a damn war with your luck. Hopefully, you've heard everything that's been going on since you decided to throw caution to the wind and risk it all to save some werewolf's kid."

"Carey is human," I snarled with a viciousness no one was expecting. Some werewolf's kid. She deserved better than that. "The consequence of her parentage doesn't make her less human or less innocent, god damn it. And if you had a fucking feeling bone in your body, you would care too."

There was silence on the call. I dared to glance at the video feeds. Hisao's eyes were wide. Davor had leaned back from the camera, wary of something.

"Yes, she is," Hasan agreed, the only one not shocked into silence. "But I'm not sure I'm comfortable sending you to Washington after Jabari. We don't know what's going on up there. If something is a risk to him, it's very much a risk to you."

I bit my lip hard, thinking of anything I could say. Then I remembered what Zuri had said on Sunday. "There was a cold shoulder from the werewolves up there when Jabari had tried to talk to them. I could—"

"The last place you need to be is in werewolf territory," Zuri snapped. "You weren't supposed to let everyone know what I'd told you."

"When did you two talk?" Mischa asked, frowning. "Why didn't you come to me, Jacky?"

"We're not getting into this," I said quickly. "I don't have to go alone. I could ask Heath for a favor. He just needs to introduce me to—"

"You are not getting that wolf into our business," Hasan snapped.

"She has a point," Niko said softly. "Hasan, listen to her. Heath owes her for a lot. If that means we can use him to find out what happened to our werecats, we can use it."

"You trust wolves too much sometimes," Davor growled.

"You trust them too little," Niko retorted. "Things have been changing. There's no avoiding it. Werewolves aren't ignoring us anymore, and we need to have one we know is our ally."

"I can't...promise that with Heath, but I'm pretty sure I can ask him to introduce me to the pack up there."

"That's all we would need him for this."

"That's it, then. You will go up, do some minor investigation to make sure the wolves aren't involved.

Stay in the area until Jabari contacts you and wait for him to leave."

"She can use this as a vacation from that—"

"Don't talk shit about my bar, jackass," I snapped before Davor could finish. "Look, I know this could be retaliation from...whatever. I just want to help fix it, all right? I don't want anyone else hurt because I—"

"I'm amazed you have a single ounce of personal responsibility."

"You know what, Davor? Fuck you." I couldn't believe the kind of shit I was getting from this guy. He was like a thousand years old and was talking to me like a high school bully. "I'm not sure what the fuck I ever did to you, but I'm really damn tired of this."

Someone clapped, and I rolled my eyes at Mischa, who had her hands right in front of her camera.

"Get him, girl. Father, when are you going to let me leash his misbehaving ass?"

"There's a reason Davor keeps skipping holidays home," Hasan said mildly, annoyance written plain on his face. "Davor, you'll be nice to Jacky, or I'll come get you and remind you who the biggest cat is in this family. Are we clear? She's your sister and doesn't deserve your abuse."

"She—"

"It doesn't matter," Hasan growled loudly. "Leave it."

"Father—"

"Jacky, be ready to fly out of Dallas by noon on Friday, with or without your wolf. Let us know as soon as you can if he will be going with you." Zuri shifted into the leadership role as Hasan and Davor both dropped out of the call.

"What's Davor's problem with me?" I asked before anyone else could hang up. "I mean, except the obvious problem that I had issues with Hasan."

"To put it lightly?" Zuri sighed. "He considers you an abject failure and thinks Father Changing you was a waste of time, energy, and space. He thinks you have no drive, no real education, and no goals in life."

"Oomph." Once again, I was hit directly in the chest by my siblings' words. "Waste of time, energy, and space. I got the entire trifecta of being wasteful."

"Well, he missed resources. At least he feels you need money and food to survive," Mischa said blandly. "That's something. He thought we should let Niko starve or hunt for himself for a long time. He loved Liza..." Mischa trailed off. "He's just cranky with you. He doesn't know how to deal with you and believes we have expectations to live up to, and we do. We're all college educated and work with werecats around the world to better our lives and theirs. We manage rogues when we see them, and if we can, get them to settle down."

"And we kill anyone who breaks our rules," Hisao added. "Then, *you* broke our rules."

I winced. "Yeah, I know."

"Obviously, we couldn't kill you, so we're adjusting." Zuri tapped her nails on the coffee table in front of her. "This could go wrong if you screw up, Jacky."

"Or it could go very right," Niko retorted. "They're all mad at her and us because of her. Western European werecats call me once a week to bitch about their werewolves, who have started this insane global effort to talk to us. The London vampire nest is also trying to talk to a werecat nearby, and that has *me* worried. We can't change that, but..." He tilted his head, thinking. "If we show Jacky is just as invested in our safety and prosperity as a species, the others might not see her as such a problem child."

"I'm not a problem child. I protected one little human girl!" I grumbled softly. "I did what any rational being would do, and that's it."

"And we need to show them you didn't mean to cause as much trouble as you did," Niko said softly. "This is a great opportunity, Zuri."

"I know, and I know how you feel about the possibility of real, lasting peace with the wolves." Zuri gave him a small smile. "Too bad you could never lead the cause."

"I did what I could when I could." He shrugged.

"There's a chance this had nothing to do with the wolves," Mischa reminded everyone. "But yes, Niko is right. Do you think Father considered that before he went to take one out of Davor's hide?"

"Probably," Hisao mumbled. "Keep in touch with us, Jacky."

"I will," I promised, swallowing. "Thanks for trusting me."

"You're family," Zuri said, still smiling. "Stay safe. Family meeting adjourned."

The video feeds all cut out at once.

Leaning back in my desk chair, I considered my next move. I was being entrusted with helping Jabari once the full moon passed, and I would be able to help fix the problem that could very well be my fault. I was going to help get justice for two dead werecats.

It felt like a win-win in my book.

Now, I just have to convince Heath he owes me enough to help me out.

9

CHAPTER NINE

The full moon was coming. I could feel it in my bones, ready to answer the call but not yet, not just yet. I had a few more hours before it became pressing. That meant I had time to call Heath, who would have already locked Carey away for her own safety, the same way I had done. If it were any other night, he would let her pet him. I knew, like me, they shifted more than just on the full moon; there was just more control on every other night. Tonight, there would be little control. It was the most dangerous time of the month for any of the humans in my territory.

I dialed him up, hoping he was calm, not already edgy from the coming night.

"Jacky. What can I do for you?" His scotch voice was easy on my nerves, soothing. I could recognize the Alpha talking and figured it had to be the upcoming full moon that made him channel such a calm.

"I wanted to ask you a favor to think on tonight," I

answered. "I told you about those dead werecats, right? Well, the werecat who went out to investigate has now been declared missing as well. Due to...things, I'm heading up there to check it out without getting into trouble. The problem is, we already know the last werecat had a hard time talking to the local werewolf pack..."

"What do you need from me? It sounds like an introduction." He didn't sound annoyed or surprised. If anything, his calm seemed to grow deeper, more patient on the other end of the line.

"That's exactly what I need. I've been told to stay out of any immediate trouble and danger, so it should be an easy trip. With our...obvious public connection, it might be easier for you to get me in to get some answers if the wolves know anything."

"Or they could be the problem, and I would literally be throwing you to the wolves," he replied. "Have you or whoever you're talking to considered that?"

"Sure." *Kind of...not really.* "Look, once you introduce me and I get a chance to talk to them, you can head right back home. Wouldn't be longer than a weekend trip for you. I'm supposed to stay in the area in case anyone needs me or until we have the answers we need."

"I'll think about it," he finally said after a long silence. "Will you owe me a favor in return?"

"No. Let's say this makes us even for last year."

"What about information?" His voice stayed calm, but there was no missing the edge of excitement.

I should have known. He was an Alpha wolf and never did anything for nothing unless it was for a treasured member of his pack—politicians, the lot of them.

"Depends."

"I want to know more about you. I won't ask for anything that could put anyone at risk. I just want to know more about the woman my daughter is so taken with."

"Done." I was willing to give up some of my own secrets if it meant helping Jabari and getting justice for two dead werecats. I could handle that. As it was, I didn't have that many secrets left. Every werecat in the world knew who I was now, and my peaceful, ignored existence was no longer a viable one. Now, I was going to give up those secrets to a werewolf. "I have to fly out of Dallas by noon tomorrow. We'll be landing in Seattle—"

"There's only one werewolf pack in that state, and Seattle belongs to them. I can give them a call ahead of time before we get on the plane tomorrow. They don't like surprises. The Seattle Freeze is not a joke."

"The Seattle Freeze?" I frowned. "What?"

"The idea that Seattle doesn't welcome outsiders. They won't throw you out, but they can be a bit cold and selective. It's not so bad. I spent a year up there once. The werewolf pack up there takes it to the extreme and doesn't talk to outsiders at all without an introduction from someone else, not on their home turf." He chuckled. "Don't worry, I know their current Alpha. I'll tell you more on the plane tomorrow."

"So, that's it? You're going to help me out?" I was a little shell-shocked. I had figured I only had a fifty-fifty chance of him saying yes. It seemed too easy.

"Yeah. I can take a trip for the weekend and help you out. I'll leave Landon and Carey here, and they'll be grateful for a weekend away from me. This doesn't sound like it'll be more than a social trip for me."

"You're a lifesaver, Heath." I let out a breath of relief, glad I would have something my siblings wouldn't—a wolf who was willing to help. "See you tomorrow once we're showered and clean."

"Come run with us if you want," he said lightly. "I'm sure you get lonely running on full moons."

"I like being alone on full moons, sorry. And it's safer if you stay on your property while I run my territory."

"Can you run your territory?" he asked, his voice making me wonder if he was frowning. "It's...forty-five miles in diameter now? If you run the edge..."

"It's one hundred and forty-one miles, give or take a couple. I can do it in a night, don't worry. I should if I'm planning on leaving. A werecat never makes a territory bigger than it can run in a night. Remember that."

"I will. Well, see you on the other side."

"You too." I hung up on him, antsy. If nothing went terribly wrong during the full moon, he and I were going to help my family out. I already knew what some of his questions would be. Who Changed me was probably going to be the first. I sent the family group chat a text, telling them Heath was in, so getting into Seattle and talking to the wolf pack wouldn't be a problem. None of them responded, but thanks to time zones, many of them were probably already under the spell of the moon.

Soon it would be me too, then Jabari right after me, wherever he was—hopefully, alive.

I stripped and stepped out onto the front porch of my gorgeous, hidden home. The night air in March was still cool. It couldn't be more than fifty degrees outside, and it licked at my skin as a breeze kicked up. I looked up to see the sky turning darker.

And waited.

My body wanted the call. I hadn't shifted in weeks, for whatever reason. Maybe it was because I was distracted. Maybe it was because my dirt bike was working, and I was lazy. I hadn't let the instinctual werecat come out to play in too long.

I growled as it began, taking over my body swiftly. Bones cracking and breaking. Hands and fingers growing and changing in shape to paws with deadly claws. My canines grew and grew, hanging over my bottom jaw. Fur exploded out of my flesh, and I dropped down to all fours as the change continued. Finally, I shook, adjusting to the feeling of being a large cat.

The first thing my brain had to deal with was the presence of werewolves in my territory. The werecat and I fought to hold the leash back on the need to drive them out. Every full moon was like this, a silent war not to attack predators who weren't supposed to be there. Other nights, it wasn't so bad, but tonight was the night I was in the backseat.

Finally, the cat scented deer on the wind, diverting our focus. It was a safer, more acceptable quarry.

By dawn, I was bloody, full, and tired.

It was a sluggish climb up my front steps, but I knew I couldn't sleep. The first thing I did was check my phone to see Hasan had been glad to hear I would be going north with some sort of back up. Hisao wanted me to promise to tell him if he needed to fly out in his jet. I didn't reply to either of them, heading for my shower. I also needed to pack quickly and hit the road if I wanted to make a flight out of Dallas.

I MET Heath at his farmhouse, where I could see him talking to Landon and Carey on the front porch. Parking behind his massive pickup truck in his giant driveway, I stepped out, walking closer slowly, making sure they knew I was there. With the intense, concentrated look Landon and Carey were watching their father with, it was possible they missed me driving up.

"Carey, please behave for Landon."

"I will! Keep Jacky from getting hurt, please."

"I will."

I smirked, stepping up behind him.

"You hear that?" he asked, looking over his shoulder at me. "I'm to keep you from getting hurt."

"I did." I reached around him to high-five Carey. "Kick Landon's ass at bowling while I'm gone. Or kick him when he tries to cheat at video games."

"Will do!"

"Head inside while I talk to your brother," Heath said kindly, though the order couldn't be missed. Carey jumped forward to hug him, then grabbed hold of me before darting inside. "Landon, you'll keep a close eye on her."

"Yes, sir." Landon's eyes shifted onto me. "Are we sure we can trust this?"

"He's only going to help me with Seattle's pack. Everything after that is his own choice. He should be coming home soon and well away from any possible danger...unless it's the Seattle pack that's the problem. Then who knows?"

"It's fine, Landon. We owe her one. This is simple compared to last year." Heath didn't seem worried in the slightest. "Plus, I can see if Emmy is doing all right."

"Ah..." Landon snorted. "Emmy is a dangerous bitch, Dad. Be careful."

"No more dangerous than the one behind me," Heath retorted. I jerked back, confused, making both men laugh. "She's an old acquaintance. Left my pack for Seattle when she and I had a bit of a falling out."

"Old lover," Landon clarified. "But then she fell hard for the Seattle second, and the rest is history...or so they say."

"What was the falling out about?" I asked curiously, eyeing Heath.

"I wouldn't marry her," he answered mildly. "I didn't feel for her like that. This was all about forty years ago."

"And you didn't get her pregnant? Color me shocked."

"Very funny." He shook his head in disdain for me. "Are we heading out?"

"Ready when you are. We can talk about what I know about this on the drive. Then we're in for a pretty long flight."

"I know. I resisted calling the Dallas pack for the use of their jet because it would be improper without clearing it with you, but...I can call them."

"No, we're fine. I checked flights already. We might not sit next to each other, but we can get there on the same plane." And I was going to fly first class. I had booked my ticket right before walking out the door.

"Be safe," Landon said with urgency. "After last year, I don't know what I would do if you didn't come back, Dad."

"I know. This will be a quick trip, Landon. I promise." Heath hugged his son tightly. When he released, Landon ducked back into their house. I eyed Heath, wondering where his bag was when Landon came back out with it. "Thank you."

"Have a good flight, Alpha."

"Hold down the fort." Heath gestured to my car when he dismissed Landon. "And this is our chariot? Your tiny Nissan Versa?"

"It's a hatchback. Plenty of space in the trunk." I shrugged and started walking toward it. I popped the trunk and helped him put his suitcase inside next to my two bags. I also had a carry-on laptop, but he carried nothing else. "Do you have a problem with my car?"

"Not at all. Functional, not very flashy. Very...normal. That's the impression I get every time I see it. It's very normal."

"That's exactly the impression I want to give, so it's working." I smiled at him, slammed the trunk closed, and went to the driver's side. Buckling in, I started the car and proceeded to wait on him.

He entered slowly, and suddenly, he felt too big. I had grown accustomed to Heath's height, a touch over six feet tall and built to match, but seeing him bend into my car was strange. He didn't fit well, and his classically handsome and chiseled face seemed too regal to be sitting in my car—an image that felt out of place.

It was kind of attractive how he didn't complain as I pulled out of the driveway. He did move the seat back as far as it would go but never opened his mouth about it.

"I'm going to call the Seattle pack in about an hour," he announced as I got onto the highway that would take us straight to Dallas. "I didn't want to drop it on them right before the full moon."

"You said as much yesterday," I reminded him, keeping my eyes on the road. "Do you want to know what I know? Or do you want to grill me before we get on the plane?"

"Let's discuss your predicament first, then I'll grill you." He smiled and shifted in the seat, angling his body toward me. I glanced over at him, seeing his dark hair fall over his mischievous eyes.

"Two werecats were reported dead in the Pacific Northwest. Their territories are in Washington, specifically, partially in at least one of the national forests of the area. Um..." I tried to remember my notes. The names were strange to me. "The Lake Chelan National Recreation Area, the North Cascades National Park...I think one of them covers over a place called Glacier Peak, and the other covers Mt. Baker? That's what I know about where. Apparently, it's a popular hiking and camping place with many remote areas. It's a massive area if you check the map I have in my laptop bag."

"Hm. Not based in a town like you and a lot of other werecats are."

"No, not even a farm, another popular werecat home base." I wondered how much he really needed to know. Hasan had sent me a small run down of what he knew about these two, and none of it seemed very helpful, so I omitted it for now. "They were found dead by humans," I said, shaking my head at the thought. "They had some humans in on their secret. A few park rangers, actually. The rangers were performing a simple check on them and found their bodies. When they found the first, they rushed to check on the second."

"And the second..."

"Had been dead a day longer, by preliminary estimations. In his home, same as the woman." I frowned. "They were a mated pair..." Heath's blank face told me he didn't know what that meant or why it was important. "Their territories naturally overlapped, and they had a cabin in the zone they overlapped, a place where they could be a couple. Neither was dead there. Both were killed in their private homes where they would go to be alone and get away from each other."

"Interesting. Someone would have had to know where to find them and how to kill them."

"Yeah. Apparently, that was why someone was sent out to check into this already. Now I'm going out to learn whatever I can and provide backup if necessary."

"How did this fall to you?"

"Is that pertinent to the situation, or is this where you get to grill me?"

"This is where I grill you. For six years, you did nothing and went nowhere. Now, after everything last year, you're being sent to back up someone investigating two dead werecats. It feels like you got some promotion or punishment I missed."

"Some werecats take on a responsibility to the werecat community to lead from the shadows," I explained. "Hasan and his children. All seven of them."

"That's a lot of kids."

"I know. I'm the youngest of them." I threw it out there like it was unimportant, but I knew it wasn't. I could smell his shock, the deep surprise as if I had just rocked his world view, then wariness. He was suddenly wary in the same way Landon always was.

"He said...at the Tribunal, he said..."

"That he considers all werecats as his sons and daughters. I remember. He was respecting my privacy because knowing who he is...and my place in the world of werecats..." I shrugged. "I was never comfortable with it. I'm not comfortable with it now."

"So...who is missing? Who went to investigate the deaths?"

"My...well, in werecat terms, my older brother, Jabari, son of Hasan. The General." I used Jabari's war title for a reason. He was feared by wolves old enough to remember who he was and what he represented during the war between our kinds.

"Who is the Assassin?" Heath asked softly.

Shit, he does know his history well. I didn't know if he was testing my knowledge or if the names and titles were lost to time. There was a time when someone would say Hisao and every supernatural knew exactly what he was and what he did for Hasan. Or they would say the Assassin, and everyone knew it was the Japanese werecat that was Changed by the oldest werecat alive.

"Hisao, Hasan's second oldest son," I answered just as softly. Because the identities of Hasan and his children were public, I ran down the list. "Davor the Genius, and Niko the Traitor are his most recent sons." I took a deep breath. "Daughters, Zuri the Negotiator, Mischa the Rogue, and finally, me. I wasn't around during the war, obviously, so I never got a fancy title. Did you know, the family didn't give themselves those titles? Other supernaturals coined the terms. The family doesn't use them privately and never claimed the titles publicly." I didn't tell him about Liza. She was long dead, but not long enough for Heath not to know about it. I wasn't sure about the situation concerning her demise, only that werewolves were the ones who killed her. It was easy to see why the family didn't like wolves too much.

"And you've spoken to all of them?" His eyes were narrow, still watching me with care.

"I did just a couple of nights ago when we were discussing what to do about Jabari not reporting in for nearly a week. Actually, a week as of the full moon. That's why I'm heading out there so fast."

"Why you? *Any* of them would be better choices, no offense."

"I'm close, and...I have you," I answered honestly, trying not to be stung by his honest assessment of my siblings and me. They would all be better choices in their own ways. "I'm sorry. I'm using you. Between two dead werecats, the current unrest with werecats, and the activity of the werewolves, I'm in trouble. I've...stained the family's reputation, to be honest. So, this came up, and I offered myself...and you. I'm using you, Heath. If you want me to turn the car around now and take you home, I can do that."

"No, it's fine," he was quick to say. "Jacky, daughter of Hasan."

"Jacqueline, daughter of Hasan," I corrected. "He refuses to use a nickname. He only calls me Jacqueline. Zuri sometimes uses it, but she'll slip to Jacky most of the time. Depends on her mood. Same for Jabari."

"This is the family you don't want to talk about? I can't say I blame you."

"It's a lot to live up to, and I never asked for it." Again, I shrugged. "It's what I got, though, and now, I need to step up. If Jabari has gotten hurt or killed, none of them will forgive me. It would spark a war, the likes of which would make the last one seem insignificant. Add in we're in modern times, and there would be no way for the rest of the species to stay out of it or stay secret. We would all be exposed."

"Something Hasan threatened the Tribunal with," Heath pointed out.

"Yeah, because he was about to see his daughter executed," I countered. "He's...vicious when it comes to his children."

"What if one of them betrayed him? Niko the Traitor? How did he get the title?"

"I don't know," I answered honestly. It wasn't something I gave much thought and not something I cared to think about. I had other shit to deal with.

"So, there you have it. That's how I got roped into this. I'm expected to get roped into these things. I'm the daughter of the only leader the werecats have, and that comes with responsibilities I've been ignoring for seven years. Ignoring them hasn't played out too well for me, so I'm going to take the reins and deal with this."

"And use me to achieve your goals in the process." He shifted in his seat, turning his body away from me and looking ahead.

"Think of it this way. You're the only wolf who can be considered a friend or ally of someone close to Hasan. You even live in my territory."

"Is Carey safe?" he asked, obviously holding back some thought. I heard the hint of a growl in his voice.

"I..." I considered my answer carefully. "I'm not safe, but any werecat that goes after a human child is signing their death warrant. If a werecat were to attack me and win, *you're* not safe. Neither is Landon...but Carey would walk away completely unscathed for as long as she's human. If you Change her into a werewolf one day, she'll play by the same rules as the rest of us."

"I don't want that for her. I don't want this world for her." Heath was shaking his head as he talked, and I wondered if his precocious daughter was already asking about it. "Thank you for reassuring me. If you die, then Landon and I die, but that's all okay because Carey will just...go live with her mother, I guess."

"Or Hasan would take her in," I said, trying to be light about it. Heath growled.

"Why?"

"I was kidding," I said quickly, sharp enough it made him pull back. "Mostly. Hasan likes to think I've half adopted your daughter. If he felt her mother wasn't good enough, he would take her in to honor me, knowing I would want her taken care of." I never asked Hasan, but I knew the man well enough. He wouldn't let someone important to me disappear—not again. "He owes me."

"That scares me, the idea of him owing you."

"You have no idea," I muttered, refocusing on the road. "Anything else you want to know?"

"No...not right now. We'll see." He sounded like he was drifting into his thoughts.

"Oh, joy," I mumbled under my breath.

10

CHAPTER TEN

We were able to get onto a plane without major incident. Heath made two calls before we entered the city, one to the Seattle pack, letting them know we were on our way, and one to his old pack, just letting them know we were passing through. That led to some of his old pack members waiting for us at the airport where they took our bags and tried to ask some invasive questions about why we were headed toward Seattle. I didn't answer, and Heath took my example and did the same, claiming it was something minor to throw people off the scent. For him, it was minor, a simple introduction, so no one could pick up a lie on his scent.

Security had been a hoot. I was thought of as human and got through without incident, but TSA stopped Heath and gave him the whole pat down treatment. It was funny, stupid, and sad, all at the same time. Funny and stupid because a werewolf didn't need illegal weapons or bombs to hijack a plane. There was nothing they could find to deny his right to fly. Sad because it was a classic sign of how fearful humans really were. I was roughly eleven years from humanity now and being on the other side really showed me just how scared humans could be about everything. Once he was through, I made sure to laugh at him, trying to make him a little less annoyed by it, and it worked, getting a chuckle out of him.

We were given early boarding onto the flight, and I couldn't wait to watch him head to the main cabin while I settled. When I sat down next to a window in first class, I noticed Heath didn't walk past, sliding in and claiming the seat directly next to me.

"Is this why you refused to show me your seating when you asked to see mine?" I gave him the most annoyed look I could muster, which should have been pretty impressive since I hadn't slept. He just smiled innocently.

"They had a seat open in first. I wasn't going to pass that up."

I looked around first-class and saw two other seats open. He'd done this on purpose. When I looked back at him, he was fiddling with the arm rests, and slowly, my elbow was pushed off mine, and he took it. I roughly elbowed him off it and hissed softly, which only made him chuckle.

"I wanted to see how territorial you would be. Now, I know you're going to treat it like you do everything else.

Tell me, do you hiss at humans too?" He kept his voice low to keep the conversation private.

"I haven't been on a plane in seven years, so I don't know. Last time, I was on an empty plane and didn't have some damn wolf trying to claim my arm rest." Before flying into Texas to get away from it all, I had flown to an island on my honeymoon, and that hadn't ended the way anyone ever saw coming.

Needless to say, I didn't fly all that often.

"You need to get out more," he pointed out, smiling.

"So I've been told," I snapped. "By your daughter."

He leaned away from me, going from jolly to concerned in a split second. "Are you okay? Did I upset you in the car?"

"No, I'm just stressed out. Sorry." I wasn't handling any of this well. I wasn't fit company, and I was tired. "Do you mind if I pass out on the flight, and we do the whole twenty questions thing later at the hotel?"

"Definitely. I looked over your booking. It's a good spot, and I made sure our rooms were connected, just in case."

"Thanks. Appreciate it." I sighed, leaning back and closing my eyes. "Only one of my siblings will say it out loud, but they consider me a failure. I have to do this right. It's making me worried."

"Well, I'm going to help you as much as I can. After what you did for Carey and letting us settle in your home, it's the least I can do." He sighed as well, settling further into his seat. "I can't imagine being in your shoes. I was Changed by happenstance in the middle of a war. I never had anything to live up to, or history to worry about. Back then, packs in the United States were scattered, and most werewolves were rogues."

"What are you getting at?"

"I'm saying I understand why you're feeling pressured. Maybe I wouldn't have when we met, but..." He trailed off.

"What sucked was I understood him, and part of me hated him for that. I disagreed, but I understood," I whispered as everyone was finally done boarding the plane. "At the time, I thought of my twin—my human, perfect twin. She became the doctor while I became the EMT. That's just one example, but she was always more perfect than me. Now, I'm very much reminded of why I spent seven years or more not talking to my other siblings. They're all perfect, all do something important."

"You're young and have different goals. You obviously have a different vision about what having a good life means."

"I like normal, and they don't know the definition of the word. I never thought I would own a bar, but when I left them and started out on my own, it was the best thing I could think to do. It would keep me busy and teach me new things." I looked out the window as the plane started to move. "It was also so different from the rest of my life... or what used to be my life."

"What really convinced you to do this? Is it just trying to live up to them?"

"No. I feel guilty..." I yawned. "Might be my fault."

"Ah."

We went quiet, and slowly, my eyes drifted closed. The plane was compact, meaning it felt safe to me. Heath's scent was familiar now, leaving me unbothered, and I was so tired, staying awake and on edge was practically impossible.

～

"Jacky, we're landing," he whispered to me. I groaned and growled, not thinking for a moment. "We're on a plane, Jacky, and everyone thinks you're human."

"Humans can growl too," I mumbled. I was glad he and I were able to talk low enough that no one would overhear it. After months doing it in the bar, it seemed like second nature, but planes were much smaller than my bar. I yawned and lifted my head, bleary eyed and annoyed. "What time is it?"

He checked his phone, not the watch on his wrist. "Nearly two in the afternoon. We moved back two time zones, so we have plenty of hours left in the day."

"Did you get any sleep?" I asked, trying to show him I wasn't the worst traveling partner ever.

"I did, thank you for asking. I was able to get a solid nap. The announcement woke me up."

"Better you than me," I said casually. "Let's hope the landing is smooth."

"Let's hope," he agreed. "Weather app says it's just over sixty there right now. And partly cloudy. Hopefully, we don't have to deal with this area's reputation for pissy, shitty rain."

"Don't like the rain?"

"Have you ever smelled a wet dog?" he asked back, grumbling. "I like thunderstorms. This area doesn't have those. It has perpetual drizzle. The annoying rain where the lowest setting on your windshield wipers is too fast but leaving them off makes it hard to see."

I chuckled. "You should have remembered all of that before agreeing to come up with me."

"It's not a big deal," he huffed. "They're going to pick us up at the airport."

"That makes things easy. Hopefully, I'll live long enough to check into the hotel and tell my family I've settled in to wait for Jabari."

"You might want to text them once we land."

"No shit." I turned slowly to give him a look.

He chuckled this time.

The landing wasn't rough, and we were able to get off the plane without a problem. He grabbed my bag and carried it for me, and I wondered if his old school manners had finally come back to the surface after months of me forcing him not to try it on me.

I have to admit, it's kind of cute.

I nearly shuddered at the idea of Heath being *cute.* There were adjectives one could use for the Alpha werewolf, but none of them were *cute.*

Attractive. Broad. Tall. Annoying. Exasperating. Aggravating. All better words than cute.

We tried to get to baggage claim quickly, avoiding humans as much as we could. From there, it was the long wait for our things, knowing any moment, a werewolf could walk in looking for us. I started feeling itchy, so far from my territory. So far, in fact, there was no way for me to run home if something went wrong. How did Jabari do it? He traveled the world when Hasan needed him to. Mischa was a rogue werecat. How did she live without a safe place to go?

I crossed my arms tightly across my chest, trying to feel safer. I tried to hold off any jumpiness, knowing it would bother people around me and make Heath worry more than he always was. I knew he could smell my anxiety because I could already smell the concern on him.

Bags started to drop out, and we found ours quickly, not bothering with a cart. I threw my duffel on top of the rolling suitcase, letting Heath keep my laptop bag for now. If he had it, maybe this other pack wouldn't take it and dig for information. Maybe he had the same idea. He wasn't a stupid wolf.

Walking outside together, all I could smell was oil and gasoline off the cars driving by to pick up those riding with them. Heath, however, snapped to attention, looking over my head.

"Over there," he whispered, nodding his head to my right. I turned to see a large, black SUV parked with its warning lights on. It couldn't have been there for very long because no one was telling it to move along. To the side, there were two big men wearing black. A few steps closer, and I could smell the werewolves for what they were. Their heads snapped to us as we got close enough. We had been downwind and nearly snuck up on them.

"Alpha Heath Everson?" one asked brusquely.

"Just Heath Everson now."

"Certainly, Alpha Everson. I'm Ryan. And this is Jacky Leon?" The wolf nodded at me, sizing me up quickly. I watched him visibly relax at whatever he saw.

"Yup. I'm here to introduce her to Alpha Lewis. Let's be polite, wolf." Heath stepped a little closer to me. "He said we would have no trouble from him."

"Of course. Your bags?" Ryan extended a hand and snapped his other, making the other wolf jump into action.

"I'm going to keep my laptop on me in case my son and daughter need me for anything," Heath said quickly before the second wolf could take it from him. "You can load the rest."

Apparently, he is thinking the same way I am. Damn, he's good.

"Yes, sir," the wolf said quietly. I handed over my bags to Ryan, letting him deal with them.

We were ushered into the SUV with the quieter wolf driving. Ryan sat in the passenger's seat, looking at us in the back.

"It's good to see you again, Alpha Everson."

"Ryan, just call me Heath."

I snickered, causing the Seattle wolf to direct his gaze at me.

"What do you call him?"

"Heath," I answered quickly. "Because I'm not a wolf, and he doesn't have a pack."

Ryan's eyes narrowed. "You tolerate that, sir?"

"I live in *her* territory," Heath said mildly. "Even if I was still Alpha in Dallas and Fort Worth, I wouldn't press the issue. I was never a stickler for those sorts of rules."

Ryan's mouth opened and shut quickly like he was going to say something stupid and rash, but some decent part of his male brain figured out not to be totally stupid. The drive was quiet, and Heath kept my laptop bag in his lap. I tried my best not to feel anything. Heath was very good at not giving off any scents to let anyone know how he was feeling. I tried to channel that, so as not to give away my anxiety at where I was or my gratitude Heath was looking out for me.

Seattle's airport wasn't in Seattle proper. It was the Seattle-Tacoma International Airport, between the major city and its smaller companion. The drive into Seattle wasn't a long one, but it was noticeable. When the quiet wolf took us off an exit, I noticed how hilly the roads were, often finding us stopped at a red light on a steep incline.

Seattle was called the Emerald City, and as we drove, I could almost see it. There were a lot more trees than I was used to in cities. As we neared the Puget Sound, the smell of sea water and fish hit my nose, just underneath the scent of industry and cars. The roads were congested, but nothing like I hadn't seen before in a city. It was familiar in the way men with brown hair were familiar. Lots of men had brown hair, but they didn't all look the same, and sometimes, the differences were the important parts.

Seattle wasn't a city I knew, and it only drove home how very far from home I was.

We parked at a tall building that was obviously either offices or condos. We were directed into the building and passed a large front desk area, where two men worked security, and guided to elevators.

"This is the pack's headquarters," Heath whispered to me. "They own the top five floors for pack business and living arrangements for some."

"Interesting," I mumbled.

"They turned the roof into a garden. Maybe you'll get to see it today." He smiled, obviously more comfortable with this entire affair.

A ding announced we were at our floor. I never got the chance to see what floor we were headed to, squished behind Ryan, probably on purpose. He stepped off first with Heath, then me following, the quiet wolf taking up the rear. Our things weren't brought inside, left inside the SUV downstairs. Was it going to be parked? Was our stuff going to be searched? Heath kept a tight grip on the laptop, and I had my cellphone. There was nothing embarrassing except my underwear for them to find in my other bags.

I hope they like cotton.

_____

CHAPTER ELEVEN

W e were ushered into a large condo with floor to ceiling windows looking out over the Puget Sound, a beautiful and clear view. One could even see a hint of mountains on the other side of the water. I stepped closer to the window, a bit awestruck. It wasn't my woods, which I was biased toward, but it was a gorgeous view.

"Heath," a rich, masculine voice said loudly. "It's so good to see you, my friend."

"Geoffrey!" Heath laughed. "Alpha Lewis, rather. You know, your wolf, Ryan, is a stickler for the rules."

"He is. It's why I sent him. I wanted to make a good impression on..."

I was still staring out the window, just listening to the two wolves greet. When it became apparent I was the person he wanted to make a good impression on, I turned around slowly, my eyebrows going up.

"Really? I'm not all that special." I offered him a tight smile. "Really, the less activity, the better for me."

"Ah, I'm sorry, then." I didn't believe his apology. "When Heath said he was flying up with you, I expected...something else."

"I was only asked to make an introduction. Jacky would like to ask you some questions, and none of it should endanger your pack," Heath explained carefully. "If they might, she'll drop it." He gave me a pointed look.

"Of course," I agreed. "I'm not here to cause any trouble for the Seattle pack."

"Please tell me what the most famous werewolf and werecat could possibly need from me. Have a seat." Geoffrey pointed to his couches, smiling, but it didn't reach his eyes. I had a feeling he'd either figured out why I might want to talk to him or thought I was there to cause trouble. My siblings were right. Showing up outside my territory made others wary.

We all sat down, and Geoffrey made a show of making sure we all had something to drink. I asked for water and made a show of sniffing it before sipping it. That made the Alpha pause, and Heath coughed.

"He's not going to poison you," Heath whispered to me, though everyone in the room could hear it.

"After the introduction I had to your pack, I would rather be safe than sorry. Easier to ask for forgiveness for offending someone than dying." I shrugged. I was too edgy, far from home, and whether I wanted to admit it or not, scared. "Geoffrey, another werecat passed through here recently. Did you speak to him?"

"How..." The Alpha frowned deeply. "How did you know?"

"Because werecats, contrary to popular belief, talk to each other," I explained. "I'm here to continue the investigation he was on and find out what the fuck is going on in this neck of the woods."

"Heath," Geoffrey snarled. My attitude had apparently struck a nerve with the Alpha. "Leash your feline."

"Fuck me." Heath shook his head. "Jacky, maybe you should explain to him what is going on. He might be willing to tell you more."

"First, I want to know why he didn't talk to the previous werecat," I snapped.

"Because we're having problems with our two local werecats. Why do I want even more of you around?" Geoffrey growled as he spoke. "I'm only giving you a moment of my time because Heath is vouching for you."

"Problems?" I snorted. "Alpha Lewis, your two local werecats are *dead*. Now the question is if you killed them, and after you firmly shut down speaking to the previous werecat sent here to find answers, the outcome doesn't look good for you."

Every word that came out of my mouth made the wolf more and more pale. I played hard ball. Maybe it was my anger, not knowing where Jabari was. Maybe I was too edgy and frustrated from being away from home. Whatever it was, it had me on the offensive. I was pissed off now.

"Dead?" he asked softly. "Titan and Gaia are dead?

We're talking...we're talking about the two old cats that lived in the park, right?"

"Yes," I snapped. "Jabari was sent to—"

"That male was Jabari?" The wolf sagged back into his couch. "Heath..."

"Jacky." My wolf looked over to me, pleading with his eyes. "Tell him who you are and everything else. He obviously isn't part of this."

I knew that. I could smell the honest shock off the wolf.

"Jabari, son of Hasan, was sent here by Hasan to find out what or who killed Titan and Gaia," I explained, taking a deep breath to relax and loosen my muscles. "He said he met a stone wall with you when inquiries were made, then headed off toward their territories to discover more. He hasn't called in or reported in a week..." I sighed. "I'm Jacky, as everyone calls me, but to werecats, I'm Jacqueline, daughter of Hasan, and Jabari is my older brother. I'm here to assist him as needed or finish what he started if necessary. Heath agreed to help me talk to you because Jabari wasn't able to."

"Fuck. My friend, why doesn't everyone know you have a direct line to fucking Hasan himself? And the General walked through my fucking city without me even knowing! He called us and just said he was a werecat interested in finding out more about our relationship with the two cats who lived in the state!"

"Yeah, Jabari wouldn't have told you too much over the phone because lies are too easy. Because of...Heath and me, things have been tense between our kinds," I tried to say without getting snappy.

"I can agree to that. Some packs have found werecats are growing hostile if they enter their territories to talk."

"I can admit, werecats are upset with the sudden attention they're getting, and a werewolf should *never* enter a werecat's territory without permission," I added for him. "I understand you wolves want allies and a better relationship, and what I did in Dallas was..."

"Impressive," Heath filled in for me. "Who wouldn't want a werecat defending their family now?"

"Yes, and who would care if those werecats die for it? We're a small species, and we're defensive because of it," I reminded him, trying for diplomatic instead of cranky. "So, when two werecats show up dead—"

"You looked at the closest wolf pack because of our history," Geoffrey said, cutting me off. "I understand." He rubbed his face, looking over to his windows, staring over the water. "Gaia and Titan weren't friends, but they weren't enemies either. They allowed werewolves to camp in the park if it wasn't during a full moon. When I said we were having problems with them? Four of our wolves went out on a week-long trip, trying to get out of the city for a little while. They never came back."

"How long ago?" Heath asked sharply.

"A month ago. We contacted a park ranger who often carries messages back and forth between me and the cats, but the ranger couldn't find or get ahold of them. We... thought they might have killed our werewolves for some slight." He sighed heavily. "When did Gaia and Titan show up dead?"

"Nearly two weeks ago," I answered. Fuck. Now it wasn't just two dead werecats, but four possible dead wolves as well. Unless the pack was playing me, but I didn't think so. Geoffrey looked like death warmed over, and I couldn't smell a lie in his words. "Did you or any of your pack have any idea of their deaths? Or maybe help kill them?"

"Not that I know of, and I'm the Alpha. I'll begin an investigation immediately. Gaia and Titan were...fine. We never had problems with them until this." He nodded over my head, and I heard footsteps. I'd known Ryan was standing behind me the entire time, choosing to ignore him. The pack was trying to be safe, and I was an immediate threat to that. "Call my inner circle in for an immediate meeting. Let word out to the pack that they will all report to me within twenty-four hours or be hunted down. Their choice."

"Yes, sir." A door closed across the room.

"Thank you," I offered him sincerely. I could see, smell, and hear how genuine he was.

"If any of our wolves killed your werecats, they'll be dealt with. Swiftly," he growled. "Have no fear on that front. The last thing anyone wants is another war. I'll say it now. I was scared when your...father stood in front of the Tribunal and threatened to make everyone public. Afterward, there was some talk about killing him and his children for doing it. A war is the same problem— revealing those who don't want to be revealed."

"You're already out, though," I pointed out. "Would it really upset you?"

"If, say, vampires were revealed, imagine the public outcry. Or the fae who in some of their cultures are gods. Werewolves, we can blend, act human because most of us once were human, and if we're not perfect, we're wolves. We're the progenitor to man's best friend," Heath explained. "But the repercussions of the fear humans have for others would rub off on us. We're still trying to settle in our new place in the world, and we had to go public because it was too hard to hide anymore. Our numbers were too strong, and being revealed without a plan would have gotten us killed."

"So, if a bad apple is revealed in another species, everyone freaks out and kills everyone," I inferred. "Hence, why Emma was just an upstart wolf to the public and not a half-witch mad for power."

"Exactly," Heath said, nodding. "Honestly, Hasan was right about werecats. You protect humans by our own laws. You would come out strong and on their side, at least in the beginning."

"Until they have no one else to shovel their fear on," Geoffrey mumbled. "That was the fatal flaw with his bluff."

"It wasn't a bluff," I whispered, looking down. "He would have done it for me. Just like he would kill everyone who might have a hand in the death of any of his children. He would start another war if he had to. If he lost a second child, he would do it." That was an undeniable truth no one should ever take lightly about

Hasan. Not me, not my siblings, not any supernatural who may ever cross his path or the path of anyone in the family.

"Does he still hold a grudge over his daughter?" Geoffrey asked carefully.

"He hid from the world for a hundred years because of her death. Whatever the reasons, he decided to withdraw and grieve instead of burning the world down to its foundations. I don't know much about what happened to her, but I promise, he won't tolerate it a second time."

"Then why does he let his children run off into dangerous situations? Why are you here? Or Jabari? If either of you..."

Heath started to chuckle, but it was somewhat sad. "Because children don't listen to their parents."

Geoffrey growled. "No, they don't."

"Moving on..." I leaned back, finally showing a sign I felt comfortable. "We have to figure out what's going on here. I'm going to check into my hotel and consider what to do tomorrow. Can I have the contact for the park ranger you get in touch with?"

"Of course," Geoffrey answered quickly. "You both must be tired. The full moon, then a flight. I can't imagine it's been a good day. Heath, can I ask you a favor?"

"Certainly." We all stood up together, and Heath kept his eyes on Geoffrey, not paying me a lick of attention. I wandered back to the windows to look at the view as they talked.

"Because you know...Jacky here, I was hoping you could look into what might have happened to my wolves. If the werecats killed them, and some of my pack killed the werecats, I'm going to call eye-for-an-eye to the Tribunal and hope it stands. I'll keep my wolves in holding, I'm not going to hide them away or let them run, but if this was revenge for an unjustified killing, I'm going to fight for them."

"I don't expect otherwise," Heath said quietly. "I'll find out what happened to your wolves. I was planning on flying home Sunday, but I can stay if it's needed. Landon is keeping Carey under lock and key while I'm away."

"You mean while her bodyguard is away," Geoffrey countered. "Your old pack has some gossips. Everyone knows that werecat is your shield to protect your daughter."

"I'm a smart old wolf, Geoffrey, and I just gave away all the power and protection I had to be a simple family man. Of course I found outside help. Carey adores her, too. It would kill my little girl if I told her she couldn't see her Knight in Shining Armor anymore."

"Aren't those normally boys who are looking to take daughters away from their fathers?" Geoffrey chuckled.

"I know I'm lucky. Hers is a standoffish cat and female. I think I'll be able to keep Carey through her teenage years. Maybe even her twenties. She's not even twelve, so there shouldn't be a boy problem for at least a few more years."

"One would hope."

I smirked, knowing my reflection might be seen by the wolves behind me. The rest was interesting to hear. I couldn't blame Geoffrey for looking out for his pack if it came to it. He would help me, and other things would be decided, depending on the outcome of Jabari's investigation...and my own.

No, I smirked because I loved hearing how Heath talked about Carey and me. I also appreciated his honesty about our relationship, the one between him and me. We weren't so much friends as allies. Allies who saw each other once a week, oftentimes for no reason other than he wanted a drink and a moment away from his life, and I didn't mind the company.

"Which hotel are you staying at? I'll get my wolves to give you a ride." Geoffrey smiled toward me as I could see in the glass.

"That would be nice, but..." Heath gave me an unsure look.

"It's fine," I said loud enough for the entire room to know exactly how I felt. "I don't expect any trouble. Heath?"

"No, there shouldn't be any trouble," he agreed, though I watched him look at Geoffrey for more confirmation.

"I swear to you on my pack and honor, none of my wolves will harm you during your stay in my city."

"In your city? Or your state?" I asked softly. Hasan would kill me if I agreed to such small terms that were easy to break. If he promised the state, harming me would be too much effort. He would never come for me in

Texas, as an example. He would either run into Heath's old pack or onto my territory, where I would win. "And I want no harm from wolves, yours or otherwise."

"In the state of Washington," he corrected. "I swear to you on my pack and honor that no wolves will harm you during your stay in the state of Washington."

"If a rogue attacks us, we'll kill him," Heath said quickly. "And I won't check if it's a rogue beforehand, Geoffrey. If it turns out to be one of your pack, there will be repercussions. I'll take it to the Council and let them handle it."

"I know what I'm swearing to," Geoffrey snapped. "Stop being so paranoid."

I raised an eyebrow at Heath. He was fighting on my side. Maybe he didn't want another wolf pack to cause problems for him or make a bad impression. Maybe he didn't feel comfortable. He knew Geoffrey much better than I did, for obvious reasons. I was just using every lesson Hasan ever taught me. Heath was going by experience.

"I don't mean any offense, Geoffrey," Heath said quietly. "I'm just trying to make sure this goes smoothly. We don't need any more dead bodies."

"Of course," Geoffrey said with a sigh. "Hearing those two are dead...It's not what I was expecting."

"Of course, it wasn't. Now, Heath, I want to get settled in. You can stay here and hang out with an old friend, but I'm going to head out." I was tired of the activity. I was tired of being far from home, listening to two wolves posture, and tired of politics.

"I'm going with you," he said, stepping away from Geoffrey. "We'll meet your driver downstairs."

"He'll be waiting for you."

"It was a pleasure to meet you, Alpha Lewis." I extended a hand as I passed in front of the wolf. He shook and offered the same courtesy. Heath gestured for me to walk out first, and we got into the elevator together. Heath leaned over to me, chuckling.

"You're not too shabby a politician, you know."

"Bite me," I growled softly.

12

CHAPTER TWELVE

It was the quiet wolf, who I now knew was named Mickey, who gave me the contact information for the park ranger. He was waiting downstairs at the desk with the two guards, which I could now smell as wolves as I drew close to them.

"I'll be your driver as well. If you would like, we can get you a rental or a vehicle loaned from the pack for the duration of your stay in Seattle," Mickey said as we walked out of the building together. "Alpha has already let me know what's going on. I hope you two can find the answers we're all looking for."

"We're hoping so, too," Heath replied, sitting in the front seat beside Mickey this time, leaving me to the back seat. He even handed me my laptop bag, and I pulled it close to my chest. Mickey didn't miss that, looking into the rearview mirror and meeting my eyes.

"Smart," he mouthed, looking away so we would miss it. I didn't really see it so much as hear the air that passed through his lips, making the mouthed word into the softest whisper I had ever heard. Heath missed it completely. My hearing, as many people forgot, was more sensitive than a werewolf's. While we all had advanced senses, werewolves had the better ability to smell, but my hearing was much better than theirs.

I didn't comment on it, though. I planned on letting Heath know what had just played out when we reached the hotel. Heath gave our driver the name of where we were staying, and he got us there quickly, helping us unload and waiting for us to check in before leaving. I was grateful he didn't try to walk up with us to our rooms. I didn't want to have to turn down hospitality and look like an ass.

"He knows our room numbers," I pointed out as Heath and I stepped onto another elevator. "And thank you for coming with me and helping. I needed you in there with Alpha Lewis."

"It's no problem. It seems fortunate I came because now Geoffrey gets a mostly impartial wolf to help out instead of leaving it to werecats he doesn't know. Jacky...if Titan and Gaia killed those wolves, I won't hide it for you or your family."

"I know." I wouldn't have asked him to. If our cats killed the wolves first, there were even more questions to ask. Like why, especially since there seemed to have been communication and peace between them long before Heath and I rattled the scene. "What do you think is going on here?"

"Who knows? Maybe those four wolves threatened

your two cats, and they were dealt with. Maybe they went missing outside of the werecat territories, and the wolves reacted poorly by killing them. There are a thousand possibilities." He sighed, leaning against the wall.

"Yeah, there are," I agreed softly. Jabari had walked into a bigger mess than our family had realized and was missing now. "I hope they didn't go after Jabari."

"Geoffrey wouldn't..." Heath groaned. "If he has wolves acting without his permission, maybe some followed Jabari out there, probably thinking they were fixing a problem before it became bigger. Tomorrow, we'll go talk to that park ranger and see what he or she knows. What's the person's name?"

"Haley," I answered. The elevator stopped on our floor, and I started off, taking the lead to find our rooms. I stopped at mine and pointed Heath to his. "I'm going to call my family and let them know what I learned and what I'm planning from here. They might have some advice."

"I'll be available if you need me," he responded before going into his room. I stumbled into mine, tripping over my bags. With a growl, I threw my duffel across the room and kicked the rolling suitcase after it. I wasn't really angry, only frustrated. The entire situation was a powder keg, and I didn't know who was about to strike a match. If Jabari was already dead out in the woods, there was no hope for the Seattle pack if they tried to harbor his killers. Hasan would call the entire family down to take justice.

Including me.

I sat on the bed and pulled out my travel laptop, opening it and frowning as I saw none of my family was online on the unique little program they used. I needed to report and I wanted the feedback of the family without having to send several dozen texts. I sighed and tried messaging Zuri, my safest option to see if she could get the family together. When she didn't reply, I admitted defeat and grabbed my phone to dial Hasan.

"Jacqueline, how was your flight? Have you met the wolves? Were they hospitable? Do I need to send Hisao—"

"Everything's fine!" I said quickly. *Dear god, he jumped straight to sending Hisao. I really hope it's because Hisao's the closest and not for his other apparent talents.* "So far, everything with me and Heath is fine. I got a bunch of information, but I think we're going to need everyone for this."

"Hold on." Further away, I heard him talk more. "Send my children word we're having a family meeting in one hour."

"Yes, sir," Hasan's butler answered.

"Jacqueline, still with me?"

"I'm here."

"Tell me what you know first," he ordered.

I launched into it, giving him the replay of landing and what I'd learned since. I explained to him what Geoffrey said and what he meant and how Heath was now working for the wolf pack to discover their own lost members. That part made him growl, but he offered no comment, letting me continue.

"He's currently pulling in his pack for questioning. From scent, sight, and tone, I believed him to be serious. I don't think the pack knowingly caused us any problems. Now we have to hope they listened to their Alpha and haven't gone after our cats."

"So, my son tried to play this Alpha like a fool." Hasan sighed.

"I don't think so," I countered. "I think Jabari just didn't want to play his hand over the phone and didn't want to wander the city looking for the home base of the pack. It's not his fault Alpha Lewis stonewalled him. He tried the safest option he could, then moved on."

"You're pragmatic, daughter. I can agree with what you say, but Jabari—"

"Isn't the politician Zuri is, or you are. It was one of the first things everyone told me about him."

Hasan was silent for a minute, then started to laugh.

"You're right, you're right. He's not a politician. Zuri took all the talent and drive for that sort of work in the womb and left Jabari with the ruthless nature of a warlord. He's good at physical problems."

"He can't get physical with the wolves anymore. Well...he *can* but..."

"No, you're right. I'm proud of you. What else did you learn?"

I glowed for a second. *He's proud of me!* I wanted to shout it from the rooftops. After all the trouble I had given him and the family, I could still salvage something and prove I was a functioning, useful member of werecat society. Before everything, I had wanted little to do with him and even less with the rest of them. Now, that was the most important thing I had heard all week.

The shift in my feelings made me pause for a second. Was it because I felt guilty about this? Or was it something I never thought I wanted until I had a real chance of getting it?

"Alpha Lewis gave me contact information for a park ranger who knew the werecats, the one he used to pass messages along. They had a deal that werewolves were allowed to go camping out there, so keeping in some form of contact would have been important."

"Jabari was also going to hunt down the humans who knew about the werecats," Hasan said, giving me another important piece of information. "We found out because both Gaia and Titan had Zuri's emergency number for werecats, and the humans must have been told if anything happened, she would be who to call. They didn't know who they were talking to if I remember right from Zuri."

"So, they left something in place in case there was an accident or something terrible happened. Smart of them. I was planning on questioning the ranger tomorrow."

"Just...don't wander off into the woods, Jacqueline. Do you understand?"

"Yes, sir," I promised. I didn't want to go out into the woods until I knew the danger that was in them. With two werecats confirmed dead and Jabari missing, whatever was in there was more than I could handle.

"Be ready for a family meeting. I'm sure they all have opinions."

"I don't really want to deal with Davor," I said, moaning with childish annoyance that did nothing for my case of being a thirty-six-year-old who could handle her own life.

"Davor will take time to get used to you, and he was close to Liza. Closer than any of us saw coming when I adopted and Changed her."

"Will you tell me what happened to her?" I asked softly. "Or tell me about her? It would be nice to know this woman I'm supposed to live up to."

"One day, but I have never expected you to live up to her. I just expected you to be you and happy with it," he promised.

"Okay. It's just sometimes, I feel like so many other people know more about what happened to her than I do. You never told me werewolves killed her. I learned that from someone else."

"I'll give you the basics, then. She was killed by werewolves who were sport hunting. She was young, only out of my household about forty years. They had heard stories from an old werewolf about the war and wanted to see for themselves what kind of dangerous beast a werecat can be. The problem was, Liza was never violent or on guard the way many of us are. She didn't have it in her. They caught her by surprise on a full moon, right at the edge of her territory. She had no idea they were there, didn't think to scent the wind. She killed three before the injuries, and the remaining four finished her." Hasan took a shaky, deep breath. "I remember receiving word. The surviving wolves had gone to their Alpha, thinking they would be heroes."

"And?"

"And to make sure I didn't rain destruction on his pack, he and his inner circle swiftly executed the young wolves after they gave their testimonies to him before reporting to the Tribunal what happened. Because he did that, I decided to step away from the Tribunal for a sabbatical and grieve instead of going after him." I heard a chair squeak, envisioning Hasan sitting behind his desk, leaning back with a tired look on his face. "Davor was heartbroken, Jacky. It's not uncommon for the unrelated children of a werecat to fall for each other thanks to the closeness a family can sometimes share. While many of you have seen each other as siblings, Davor and Liza saw each other as possible mates and danced around it for years. Zuri spent years teaching Liza how to woo him while Jabari and I tried to teach Davor how to approach her with his feelings."

"Then, she was gone. And now I'm her replacement."

"To him, yes. One he thinks can't live up to what she was because he doesn't care for you in that manner. The rest of your siblings don't think that way anymore. Niko, for example, has quite enjoyed hearing about your adventures these last several months with werewolves living in your territory."

"Want to tell me why he's called the Traitor now?"

"No. That's his to tell."

"I tried." Shrugging, I laid back on my bed. "And the rest of them?"

"Zuri's been mildly impressed with you this last week. There's not much I can do about their behavior toward your chosen profession, but eventually, they'll come around. I did, so they're bound to."

"How often do you talk to them about me?" I demanded, realizing it was more often than I thought it was.

"Does it matter?" He chuckled. "I'll see you for the family meeting. You probably want to relax and settle in at your hotel."

I grumbled as he hung up on me. The conversation had felt much more relaxed than I thought it would be.

I rolled off the bed and went to the adjoining door between Heath's room and mine, knocking once. I heard his side unlock, so I unlocked and opened mine. We stared at each other for a moment. I didn't know what he was staring at, but I knew what I saw.

Heath looked like he had laid down for a nap, wearing only soft pants and nothing else. His broad, tanned chest was completely on display, and I realized he had a touch of chest hair, just enough to be masculine without feeling like I was looking at a gorilla. And his pants were too low. He worked out. There was no way werewolves were naturally that cut.

He had three kids with three different women, Jacky. Of course, he's good looking enough to get women out of their clothes.

"Can't say I blame them," I muttered.

"What? Jacky? What did you need?" I blinked and looked up at his face. I didn't know how long I had been staring at his abdomen. A frown slowly morphed into a predatory grin as he looked down at himself. "Can't blame who for what?" he asked softly.

"No." I shut the door in his face. "Absolutely not." I locked it and walked away, heading straight for my bathroom. I had thirty minutes before the family meeting. I could talk to Heath when he was decent.

"Jacky!" Heath was laughing. "I'm sorry! I put on a shirt. What did you need?" The fact that he was talking through the door made me glare at it.

"You're an attractive man, Heath Everson, but I will not get teased for noticing it."

"Of course not! If I teased every woman who noticed, I would have no female friends. Please. You knocked. What did you need?"

"I was going to tell you how my call to Hasan went, but I think I'm going to shower and get ready for a family meeting. I'll update you later."

"And if I call Carey, what should I say? It's going to be her lights out time soon."

I cursed and stomped back to the door. "Call her right now so I can talk to her."

He hadn't lied. He had thrown on a shirt.

"I'm sorry, I am. I forgot how fun it was to make you flustered. It's been months."

"I think you like the attention," I growled softly.

"I do, actually. Remember what I said. I have three kids, and I'm a werewolf. At the time, I was an Alpha. It's nice to be seen as just a man sometimes." He was still grinning. "Come on, Jacky. I didn't even know you found me attractive."

"I have eyes," I snapped. Also, I could smell the lie. My glare didn't stop until he sighed.

"Fine. I've smelled it on you before but never paid much mind to it. I wasn't trying to bother you when I opened the door. I was thinking I could get in a little more sleep before grabbing some dinner, but then you knocked." The goofy grin faded to a somewhat arrogant smirk. "Who would have thought that a daughter of Hasan himself would find a werewolf attractive?"

"I have blood that pumps through my veins," I hissed. "I bet my sisters would also say you're a looker if I asked them. Admitting you're good to look at is different from sleeping with the enemy."

He shook his head, his smirk refusing to leave. Instead, he started to chuckle—that damn chuckle.

"If it helps, you aren't a bad thing to look at every Saturday night yourself, Jacky."

"No, it doesn't help."

13

CHAPTER THIRTEEN

The call to Carey went about as one could have expected. She was glad we were safe, and Heath was very careful to make sure nothing about what was going on in Seattle was brought up while he talked to her. I followed his lead when I was on the phone, then handed it back to him for his time with Landon. He would tell his son everything, including about me, so I walked out. There was nothing he could say that would surprise me. He'd learned a lot over the course of the day, and I had to give up a lot of information about the world of werecats to get through my meeting with Alpha Lewis. He would probably repeat all of it.

I locked my door when I was back in my room, making sure the damn wolf couldn't sneak up on me. I was annoyed by his attractiveness, his arrogance about it, and the way he thought it was a good laugh to tease me about it.

I'll just have to make it a point to completely ignore him now.

I moved my laptop to the small desk in my hotel room and found I had barely enough time to open it and get into the video conference program for the family meeting. Videos began popping up, and I sighed, seeing the quality of my laptop's camera.

"Sorry, using a shit laptop for this trip," I said quickly before anyone could call it out.

"It's fine. We're just glad to see you made it there safely," Hasan said, almost a dare for any of my siblings to say anything to the contrary. "Now, everyone, Jaqueline has already given me a progress report. The Seattle pack isn't hiding our killers."

"Knowingly," I added. "The Alpha is going to commit to a round of investigations into his pack to make sure."

"What would have caused this?" Zuri asked quickly. "Is there any reason to believe the pack might be hostile?"

"Four wolves went missing in or near the werecats' territories," I explained. "They had a long-standing deal that werewolves were allowed to visit and camp when it wasn't a full moon. Those wolves went missing a month ago, and two weeks ago, Titan and Gaia were found dead. There's some reason to believe the werecats may have died in a revenge killing."

"Do we know anything about the bodies?" Hisao asked softly. It sent chills down my spine.

"No. They were cremated per werecat custom by the

time Jabari arrived," Hasan answered. "That's why I never brought them up. Complete dead end."

"Maybe not," Zuri countered. "Is there any way to speak to those who saw the bodies?"

"Jabari met with the park rangers who found them and had nothing special to report. They were human. They don't have our sense of smell or anything to help them without contacting the authorities, which we're lucky they didn't do." He sighed. "Jacqueline, please be careful."

"I always am," I cheerily responded, feeling my gut sink. By the looks of everyone on screen, they didn't find my cover attitude funny or reassuring. I sagged, letting it go. "This is a clusterfuck up here. If Jabari and the Seattle pack had talked, we could have avoided some of this, and he might have had backup out there."

"You will not go looking for him, Jacqueline. Do not make me say that more than once."

"I won't!" I growled. "I'm pointing out the obvious. If the damn wolf pack here had given him a meeting, they would have been able to exchange this information. As it is, they had no idea Titan and Gaia were dead. The damn rangers at the park didn't even tell them, probably worried it was the wolves who did it. Their lack of intel was the first thing I fucking noticed while I was there. I also noticed *my* lack of intel. They've lost *four* damn wolves. Heath is planning to extend his stay to help them find answers." I leaned over and rubbed my forehead. They didn't need to know about my embarrassing moment with the wolf, though it was partially why I was already a touch frustrated with the trip.

"This is bigger than expected," Mischa commented lightly. "Well, we take the punches as they're thrown. Are you worried about Heath's loyalty? Are you in any danger?"

"No," I mumbled. I quickly explained what I heard Geoffrey say. "On top of that, for helping me, I agreed to let Heath get to know me. That's my problem, though, not any of yours."

"How much have you told him so far?" Hasan asked carefully.

"That poor bastard," Davor mumbled softly, earning a growl from our shared werecat father.

"Just who I'm related to by werecat standards, though I used my position with the Seattle Pack too. Needless to say, it came as quite a shock for the wolves." I chuckled dryly. "We'll see what else he comes up with to ask. He promised it wouldn't be anything that can be used against me or other werecats."

"Then buck up and start talking to him. It sounds like you need him to remain in our corner, even though there're other wolves involved. If that's all he wants, give it to him," Zuri said with all of her regal nature. Ever the politician, just like the wolf next door.

"He promised to help, so he will. Wolves are like that." Niko was leaning back haphazardly in his chair. "I don't know much about Heath Everson, though."

"He's..." I tried to find the best words, something that wouldn't put my family on guard. I didn't feel the need to protect myself or be protected from Heath, but telling them *that* would be going too far. "He's a typical family man with sharp canines. He jokes about how having kids and sometimes being furry has ruined his dating life. He's also a natural politician who can read a room well. He honors his word, so far as I can tell. He promised me in Dallas that his pack wouldn't give me trouble, and when one tried, he shifted and handled it, putting an older wolf in his place." I smiled a little. "He comes in and drinks a beer, or several, every Saturday night and is protective of his daughter. He trusts me with her, so I trust him with this."

In one second, I realized I actually enjoyed the man's company a lot of the time. I liked his visits to my bar on Saturday and thought they were a nice addition to my week. A time when I could talk to an adult supernatural about supernatural things or just bitch about work.

And I was glad to have him on this trip.

"Hmm," was all anyone had to say, and it came from Zuri.

"Uh huh," Mischa replied with. "Well, now we know more about this Heath."

"If that's all, I'm tired and hungry," I told them, hoping to cut the conference call short. "There's really not much else. I'm going to question the ranger the pack uses to contact the werecats and maybe the others as well. I'll have more to tell you tomorrow."

"Of course. Keep a close eye on that wolf," Hasan ordered. "Be safe."

"I'll try," I promised. "I really will try."

"Try your best," he said with that stern fatherly tone. "Go find something to eat."

I hung up on them before anyone else could talk to me. Davor hadn't been an asshole, for the most part, something I wasn't going to test by staying on any longer than necessary. I was sure if they thought of anything important, they would text me. At least, I was hoping they would text; I didn't want to answer the phone while trying to eat.

I shuffled over to the adjoining door again, unlocking and opening it without so much as a knock. I didn't look in, though, just called out.

"I'm ordering room service! Do you want anything?"

"I can pay," he quickly offered. I heard the bed creak, and he showed up in front of me, with a shirt on, a second later.

"I have money," I reminded him. "Plenty of it."

"Really? I had no idea," he said, smirking. I rolled my eyes. "How were your calls?"

"Good. They reminded me I should ask about the state the bodies were found in. Jabari had probably asked already, but maybe I can get new information. I was told to stay out of trouble." I shrugged, stepping back from the doorway. I nodded my head to let him know he could come in. If I was going to order in, he could eat in my room—as long as he remained clothed. "How was yours?"

"Landon was interested in what I had to tell him," he answered without telling me anything. "So, do I get to restart my twenty questions now?"

"Let me order some damn food," I muttered, shaking

my head. I grabbed the hotel phone and the little menu propped up next to it. "I'm getting us burgers, steaks, or whatever I can find that's meat."

"Thank you." That sounded sincere.

I swiftly ordered four ribeye steaks, all with hearty vegetables as the sides. Then I added a dessert for myself, looking at him to see if he wanted something specific. He shook his head, so I finished the order with drinks.

"Want to hit the hotel bar later tonight?" He sat on my desk chair, ignoring my laptop. I sat on the bed once I hung up and sighed.

"Yeah. Alcohol might soothe my aching nerves. It's not easy being so far from home."

"I can't imagine being so connected to the land you live on, then having to leave it. I hate being away from Carey and Landon like this, but I promised to help."

"And now you're roped into the local pack's problems. How long do you think this is going to take? I'm praying less than a week, but who knows?"

"It could take a month," he whispered. "Landon was upset I offered myself for the job of investigating the missing wolves. His words were something along the lines of how bad the Alpha here must be if he can't do it himself."

"Really?" I raised an eyebrow. "I do remember a wolf or two needing help in Dallas with a certain half-witch."

"You were there to help Carey. I could have handled Emma, Dean, and Richard on my own with my own wolves. I didn't have you track my people down."

"Touché." I couldn't argue with that. "I hate this

waiting shit. I don't want to be out at night, and it's swiftly approaching, but fuck, waiting until tomorrow to talk to more people sucks."

"And it's only going to get worse for you if you're going to wait on your brother to come out of those woods." He leaned back and kicked his bare feet out. Catching me looking at them, he laughed. "Don't tell me those are nice to look at too."

"Oh. Ew. That's disgusting." I gagged. "No, I just noticed them. And can you please stay serious? You always do this. You always find some way to..." I waved a hand at him. "You did while we were in Dallas, too, when someone was trying to kill you and had kidnapped your daughter. What is with you?"

"I've lived long enough to remember I need to laugh sometimes," he countered, the pleasure of teasing falling from his face. "I've seen enough people die at what felt like random times. I know what it means to take a chance to smile with a friend when there might not be many chances left."

The words hit me like a wrecking ball. I stared into his grey-blue eyes, wondering what was torturing him at that moment.

"Who didn't you smile enough with?" I asked softly.

"Everyone, so far," he answered, taking a deep breath. "You?"

"Same." The word didn't come out of me without a fight, but I knew it was the truth. "There's never a good time to lose them, is there?"

"No, there isn't. So, I take my chances and try to have

good moments during the bad ones. I'm sorry if it gets frustrating."

"No...I'm sorry," I murmured, looking down at my hands. "You wanted to play twenty questions?"

"Why don't you tell me about you? I know...a lot already." He sheepishly smiled at me.

"Well, I told you about Hasan and the family. My family...I guess. There's something. I have a hard time thinking of them as *my* family. My human family is still alive out there, and it just feels wrong sometimes to think of others as my family. I can see why werecats do it, though. Why they make these attachments..." I sighed. "There's no one else. We can't go home. We can't...meet new people very well or anything like that, so we treat those we can as a family. I understand that, it's just hard to do sometimes."

"It's a hard world to join," Heath agreed. "It's the same for a lot of wolves. Many walk away from their human families entirely because it's easier in the end. You don't watch them grow old and die. You don't have to watch them try to Change and die in the effort. Before we went public, it was the life of many wolves. We learned to make bonds away from the human family we built and walk away from the mortal life."

"I rejected my new family for a long time," I admitted. "I still do, in some ways. Some core piece of me fights it while other parts of me...really want it. You know, I've gotten into so much trouble with the werecats out there, I was convinced my siblings were going to hate me forever. It's been strangely relieving for them to just welcome me back in and give me a chance."

"Why did you run from them and Hasan to begin with? You mentioned you left the werecat who Changed you much earlier than most werecats." He tilted his head in that confused dog look.

"I...learned something," I whispered, looking completely away from him. "That's too personal."

"All right."

We sat in silence until the food arrived. He answered the door and brought it in. Grabbing another chair, I sat at a small table with him to eat. I considered telling him more about my problems with Hasan but couldn't bring myself to continue the conversation.

"What's your favorite color?" he asked softly. I snorted, nearly dropping food out of my mouth. When I looked at him, he shrugged. "Try."

"Uh...Orange. Sunset orange."

"Music type?"

"Rock, mostly." I shrugged. "Country plays at the bar because they like it." He knew what I meant by 'they.'

"Why do you like hanging out with my daughter so much?"

"She's safe," I answered immediately. I looked up from my food and saw his concentrated look. "She's not a threat. Physically or emotionally. And she's so goddamn unique. She's a great kid."

"Did you ever want kids?" He was hitting hard now.

"Yes. If my fiancé and I had been doing our job right, and what happened didn't happen, I could have had one roughly her age, maybe more," I whispered, knowing how it might look. "I knew when she showed up, she could have been mine. She was someone's. Nothing else mattered except someone's baby was there, she could have been mine, and I would want someone fighting tooth and fucking nail to keep any of my children safe."

"He died in a car accident, didn't he? Your fiancé?" Heath rested his arms on the table, ignoring his food.

"Yup. I should have, too, but the official report was that he was driving to meet me somewhere and went off the road. It was written so I was never in the car to begin with." I chuckled darkly. "It was eleven years ago. You would think I would be over him and it by now."

"No. It took me decades to get over the loss of my first wife."

"The one who chose to remain human."

"Yup, and when I finally did, I barely had any time with the second. She was in and out of my life faster than I could blink. She's the one I never really got over. I never had a chance to say goodbye."

"Same. There was no goodbye. We were having a good time, then...we weren't." I grabbed a napkin and pressed it to my eyes. I would not cry, not after eleven years damn it, and not in front of Heath Everson. "Change the topic."

"I think I know enough," he murmured. "You're never what I expect."

"Really?" I snorted. "To my family, I'm exactly the fuck up American some of them think I am. Both families. You did all the research on my human family, you can tell me what impression you got."

"Your twin is an overachiever," he commented, leaning back again and grabbing his fork and knife. "A huge overachiever. You know she's a heart surgeon now?"

"Of course she is." I resisted rolling my eyes. "Does she still look exactly like me?"

"Like you in ten years." I didn't know what that would look like. "You still look like the twenty-six-year-old you were when you were Changed, Jacqueline *Duray*."

I groaned. "I always hated that last name. It makes me sound like I should be buying bread at some bistro on a corner in Paris."

"It does, doesn't it?" He chuckled even more, and I wanted to reach across the table, take his knife, and stab him with it. "Why Leon?"

"It's French without being ridiculously obvious, and my family was always proud of our French heritage. I was going for a laugh, honestly. I needed a new last name, and I liked it. It's been my last name for...nine years now. It suits me, I think." I had already been planning on changing my last name once I was married, so my attachment to my maiden name had faded. While I never got the last name I truly wanted, I was at least able to give up Duray.

"So, you're Jacky Leon, the werecat from Jacksonville, Texas, daughter of Hasan."

"Yup. Write it down, and don't forget it."

"I think I like Jacqueline better."

"Oh fuck, not you too." I shook my head as he laughed and began to eat. Damn wolf. "Really, only parents call me that or grandparents. Don't categorize yourself in that group of people. You might be two hundred and fifty some odd years old, but please."

"It's a really nice name," he said between bites of his first steak. "But fine, Jacky it is and will stay." He chuckled. "So, what else..."

"There's not much to know," I reminded him. "Imagine my twin and put me a few steps below her for everything—heart surgeon - EMT, high school sweetheart with three kids - lonely werecat with a dead fiancé." I snorted. "I love her, though. I was always proud of her."

"Sounds like you resent her," Heath pointed out mildly, the accusation softened but not ineffective.

"I resent *me*," I explained. "I resent I never did those things. I was never...as motivated, as dedicated, as... perfect as her. No, *she's* an inspiration, and I resent *myself* for never pushing myself to her level."

"You have years to figure it out," he said gently. "More than her now."

"Yeah. That's something, I guess. Sorry, this went off the beaten path. I'm feeling a bit whiny and mopey recently, I guess." With everything going on, the concept of living up to my siblings and my family's reputation weighed down too heavily. "I went from her to...well, them."

His smile was friendly. "No, life didn't get easier for you, that's certain."

"Did you have siblings?" I asked, trying to push the conversation off my woes.

"I had a brother who died early in the Revolution. A sister who married and went to London. She was for the monarchy, and it caused a rift. I didn't keep track of her or her family, but I hope she lived a good life."

"I'm sorry for both of them."

We sat quietly after that, eating our food without bothering each other. As plates were cleaned, we stacked them up to keep the mess from becoming obscene. The steaks were good quality and a perfect medium rare. The veggies were fine, though I continued to think they needed more seasoning.

"Do you want to hit the bar? We can talk a bit about the area..." Heath sounded cautious, but why I didn't know. "You won't have to serve the drinks."

"Yeah, let's go." Shoving away from the table, he followed behind me. At least we could relax on the trip in the evenings. Too bad it didn't make me feel any less stir crazy.

14

CHAPTER FOURTEEN

The bar was damn near empty. Only two businessmen, I assumed by the suits, were sitting at the bar proper. I pointed to a small corner table. Between the distance and the music, our conversation would go uninterrupted and unheard.

"What would you like to drink?" he asked, leaning over me, his hand finding my lower back. I tensed, feeling the warmth through my shirt. Instead of removing the hand, he curled slightly, acknowledging he knew what he was doing. "Darlin', what do you want to drink?" His Southern accent grew heavier, and there was an intimacy in his tone.

I picked up on it quickly and hissed softly. "A whiskey, but this is completely unnecessary."

"I'm just trying to make the humans think we're nothing important."

"And if a wolf sees us? Or anything else?" I snapped,

stepping away from him. "Last thing we need is to give the impression we're something when we aren't."

"Fine." He raised his hands and walked to the bar.

I took my chance to get to the table and made sure there were only two chairs, and they were far apart. I refused to think about how his hand had felt...good. Warm and comfortable, just like when he tended my injuries. Gentle, just like every time he touched me, moments I could count on one hand and recall with perfect clarity.

I slid into my seat and sighed. I didn't need to get snappy with him. When he came to the table with our drinks, I took mine with a quiet thank you.

"Sorry," he murmured. "When I'm with other wolves, we try to act...like something human. Guys out to watch the game when we don't care. That kind of thing."

"I'm not used to being touched," I quietly explained. "It's not bad thinking, though. I just...I'm not a wolf, Heath."

"You're right." He sipped on his beer, and I reached out to pull my whiskey closer. For a while, we concentrated on our drinks. Heath shifted in his seat, and I wondered if his frame was too bulky to feel comfortable on the bar stool. I never saw him act uncomfortable at my bar.

"You okay?"

"Thinking. Seattle is like most big cities. It has a sizable werewolf pack, but there's other players in most cities that we didn't have in Dallas. Down South, we don't have much of a vampire population. Don't ask me why, but none ever tried to set up in my cities. Some cities have a gateway, a portal, to the fae realms. Seattle is one of them, which means there's a fae population. It's never very big since they don't often settle in this realm, but they manage their gates from both sides."

"Yeah, I know about the fae," I said softly. "So, you're saying there's a lot here, and possibly anything could be part of this?"

"I'm saying we have to keep our minds open," he replied, sipping his beer. "The likelihood something else is involved is slim, but it's a possibility."

"So, we have the Big Four in Washington. Werewolves, werecats, fae, and vampires. Anything else?"

"Possibly a coven of witches or warlocks. Outside of that, I have no idea," he admitted. "The smaller species don't announce their presence anywhere, kind of like werecats, though you are considered a big threat, and they're just considered...a possibility. An Alpha wolf should know all the players in his city, but some come in, passing through or working, and leave without us ever knowing."

"That's not helpful," I groaned. I took a long swallow of my whiskey, relishing the burn for a moment. It wasn't nearly enough alcohol to soothe my nerves, but it was a start. It tasted like home, at least. "We're in for a long day tomorrow."

"Yeah, it's going to be a long drive. I texted Geoffrey and asked him to have a vehicle ready for us by seven. We should be there by nine if we get out of here by then.

Faster, if we don't hit too much traffic and don't need to make more than one stop."

"Fuck." I leaned over and put my head on the table. "Why couldn't Jabari call in like he was supposed to?"

"You're fine with going toe-to-toe with an Alpha werewolf, but a two-or-so-hour drive is what kills you?" He was chuckling again.

"Yup, but it's not because it's a long drive," I retorted. "It's a long drive with you. Another one." We had just done a long drive that morning to the airport.

"What's that supposed to mean?" He was laughing now, that full thing that was probably making his chest and shoulders shake. He sobered, though, faster than I expected. "We have two confirmed dead werecats, one missing werecat, and four missing, probably dead, werewolves. We can suffer a long drive together."

"Yeah..." I leaned back again, frowning at my drink. "I was just messing with you. Trying to take your advice."

"We could leave earlier..." he suggested, pushing his empty glass away. "Get there by dawn. We'd have to get some shut eye now, though."

"And you would need to ask Geoffrey to bring us that vehicle sooner," I pointed out. "Do it. I want to be there at dawn if that's okay."

"Of course." He pulled out his phone and started texting.

I slid out of my seat, finished the whiskey, and went to the bar to order another one. The bartender didn't say much when I gave him my order and told him to put it on my room's tab. I got Heath a second beer because I was feeling nice, though it might have been my own natural bartender tendencies. People didn't sit in a bar without a drink unless something was wrong. A cellphone rang, and I turned to see Heath frowning. The drinks were slid in front of me, and I grabbed them quickly. I gave Heath his beer as he found himself on the phone, talking to someone. I listened in, tilted my head slightly to try to catch the voice on the other end.

"You're running around with a werecat, Heath. Geoffrey let us know. And yes, I know it's the werecat that helped you out last year, but it doesn't—"

"Harrison, it's Jacky, and she's up here trying to—"

"Oh, yes. Jacqueline, daughter of Hasan," the other wolf snapped. I recognized his voice now, thanks to Heath saying his name. "Wish we had known that last August, damn it. He should have told everyone during the Tribunal she was his actual daughter. How long have you known?"

"Less than twenty-four hours," Heath answered softly. "She's here, trying to find out what happened. This is not a big deal. I owed her, Harrison. I owed her more than she asked me for. She wanted an introduction to Geoffrey, and I got that for her. Tomorrow, she and I are heading out to find more about his missing wolves and her dead werecats. Considering Geoffrey told you who she is, he must have told you what was going on."

"Yes, but none of that is the problem. You are helping a werecat—"

"You've been trying to convince your local werecat for months to work with you and failing," Heath snapped, a growl ending it. "Maybe if you didn't give out several demands and tried to find something they need or want, you might have better success. Don't say I'm betraying our species for succeeding where you're all failing. You're pissing the cats off because you're bullheaded."

"So, what do we do? The Tribunal changed the Laws. A minor but significant change. We have to make sure these cats can't carve paths of destruction through our packs if we're at war without another pack and they get pulled into it."

"We won't," I snapped. Heath narrowed his eyes on me. "Oh, you knew I could hear," I told him, shaking my head. "Harrison, we won't attack you without cause. The only reason the Law was changed was to protect me because I did the right thing."

"You got involved," Harrison growled. "And fuck you, Heath."

"We were at the hotel bar together," Heath explained mildly, but his eyes were still narrowed on me.

"To protect Carey, a human innocent. None of you understand nuance." I shook my head, frustrated. "Don't use werecats as your family's personal bodyguards, and they won't need to kill anyone in their way of protecting someone. How about that? That solves all the problems you think you're having right there."

"She has a point," Heath said diplomatically. "Now, I'm not here to pick the werecat side. I'm here because a werecat needed my help. My favor to her is done. Now we're both trying to find out what caused all the deaths out here. I'm going to help Geoffrey with his four missing wolves while Jacky looks into what killed the two local werecats and finds her brother."

"Jabari the General," Harrison spat. "Geoffrey is a damn idiot sometimes. He should have gotten eyes on the cat or scheduled a fucking meeting."

"You can yell at him for that. You're not going to give me a hard time on this, old friend. I don't have a pack, and I don't work with or for any of you anymore. I'm my own man. If you need anything, you know how to reach me." Heath hung up, growling. "Geoffrey called the North American Werewolf Council, thinking they might like to know who you really are and how I'm helping you. He just so happened to call as I was texting Geoffrey about the car."

"They can shove it," I snapped. "They're reactionary assholes who are passing off their own traits onto the werecats near them. We're not going to jump up tomorrow and start a war because we feel threatened. Them, however...I could see them starting a war based solely on their own imagined slights."

"Like I said a couple of weeks ago, Jacky...a certain supernatural reminded us we aren't the most powerful or dangerous kids on the playground. We'd forgotten."

I grumbled and drank my whiskey. "At least you don't feel that way."

"Most of the Alphas don't, but you left quite the impression on Harrison just by telling him you were going to break the Law." Heath snorted. "They don't realize how different you are from the rest of your kind."

"They better figure it out quick," I said before tipping

my head back and swallowing the last of my whiskey. "Now, I'm off to get some shut eye."

"I'll come up later. I want to make sure Geoffrey gets the car here."

"All right." I slid off my stool and walked away, exhausted. "Good luck with the wolves."

"Good luck with the cats," he replied. I left the bar yawning. It was such a long damn day, and tomorrow didn't seem like it was going to be much better. I made it to my room, locked the door between my room and Heath's, then threw all my clothing on the floor.

A shower. I need a shower.

Turning on the water, making sure it was hot, I stepped in, sighing happily as it rolled over my shoulders. I hadn't expected what I found today. No one had expected this to be much bigger than two dead werecats, which was serious, but the idea it could be worse wasn't something anyone had really considered.

And now, my wolf is helping the other wolves. I can trust Heath, I know I can, but I don't think anyone else is going to. Hasan sure doesn't want to. Jabari is going to flip when he finds out I brought him. And my family has good reason not to trust wolves.

I would speak up for Heath for as long as he proved worth it. If he betrayed me, there would be nothing I could do to protect him from Hasan's wrath, but as long as he remained the Alpha I figured him to be, he was safe.

I scrubbed my face, thinking about him as the wolf I thought him to be. The image of him in those soft pajama pants flashed through my mind, and I hissed as shampoo dripped into my eyes, mimicking the burn I felt on my cheeks. Why did he have to look like that? Why hadn't I expected him to look like that? He was a wolf in his prime, one who would always be in his prime. He was an Alpha who knew he had to fight to keep his position, even if he had walked away from having a pack. Of course he would look like that.

It was a far cry from the beer bellies I saw every day at the bar. Heath knew how to dress to hide the real extent of his physique yet still look in shape. I hadn't looked past the suits or the simple button-ups and jeans. I should have. Maybe it wouldn't have been such a shocker to finally see those fucking things he probably thought were normal abs.

That man has children! Adult children, at that! He's not supposed to look like that!

Then again, Hasan has even more children, and he's an ancient male model.

I nearly gagged at considering Hasan gorgeous, but it was the truth. Both men were uniquely beautiful. Hasan had some ancient quality to him like he was from a different time. Someone who didn't have a proper vocabulary would call him exotic, but I spent enough time with him to realize he was some blend of ancient African and Middle Eastern, like he walked out of Babylon or Sumer one day as the de facto ruler of the werecats. Heath, on the other hand, was an almost typical American dreamboat, just a couple of centuries older. His face pointed to a purely European ancestry with the classical masculine jawline. The blue eyes, the black hair. It was all so typically gorgeous.

I wondered for a moment if supernaturals chose their children based on their looks sometimes. I looked down at myself—light tan, small curves, and scars, though I hadn't had those when I was Changed, boring brown hair, and hazel eyes—nothing extraordinary.

No, Hasan wasn't aiming for looks when he Changed me.

I finished washing up, then stepped out in front of the large mirror and sink, washing and lotioning my face before looking at myself. I had deep bags under my eyes, thanks to the full moon and not properly resting after.

No, definitely not for my looks.

I crashed that night in bed, my hair still wet and a weird thought continuing to pester me. Maybe it was because it was the only distraction I had from the shit going on around me.

Heath was fucking hot.

15

CHAPTER FIFTEEN

A cutely aware of the man next to me, I kept my eyes on my phone the next morning. It was early—very early. We left at 'way too fucking early' in the morning since the park ranger we wanted to talk to asked to meet in a little town called Darrington. Heath had never gone out that way but knew Seattle better, so he drove.

"You okay?" he asked. "I know riding with me anywhere must be awful, but Darrington is only an hour and a half away."

"No, I'm just distracted." I was playing Tetris. "Nothing new to talk about." I didn't want to look at him. Maybe I was a little *too* lonely because my mind had summoned all sorts of images it hadn't needed to during the night. It had been a very long time since my mind was capable of conjuring those sorts of images about anyone in my life.

"Well, okay, then." He sounded a bit off like I had

somehow hurt his feelings. I gave him a side eye, looking over his profile. There wasn't much light in the car, but there was damn sure enough for me to see him. He didn't look disappointed. If anything, he looked as tired as I felt.

"Did you get enough sleep last night?" I asked, trying to see how he was really feeling.

"Enough. I'll be fine for the day. You?"

"Yeah, I'll be fine."

The conversation died again.

I wish mind reading was a werecat ability. He never gives off enough of a scent for me to pick up what he's feeling. Probably useful in his world but downright annoying right now.

I saw his nostrils flare for a split second and knew I had just given him something in the air to smell. He didn't say anything, and I narrowed my eyes on him.

"What could possibly be annoying you this early in the morning?" he finally asked.

"Nothing important." I went back to my Tetris game.

"I don't believe women when they try to say that to me. What's bothering you?"

"Fine. Nothing I want to talk to you about."

"That I'll accept."

"I wasn't looking for your approval."

"I'm just saying you promised to open up to me because I want to know the woman who is completely and utterly idolized by my daughter. I figured knowing what annoys you might be a good thing to know."

"It's really not a big deal." *I'm annoyed because I*

can't figure you out, and my subconscious definitely wants to know a lot more about you.

He stopped trying, and we rode together in silence. When I saw a sign for Darrington, I sighed happily.

"Do you think she'll be there?" I asked. "Like on time?"

"I'm more hoping she brings the other two. She mentioned there were two other rangers who knew about Gaia and Titan. The more people we can talk to, the better."

"Of course."

He turned into a little place called Country Coffee and Deli and parked but didn't get out. I followed his lead, sitting up and looking around. It was already six thirty in the morning, and the sun was out, just post dawn. A large pickup truck drove in and parked across the lot from us, followed by a second. Three rangers in uniforms jumped out, and one of them pointed to our little rental.

I got out first, hoping I would be the least threatening one. It didn't matter, though, because Heath didn't bother to wait for me to make introductions. He jumped out as well and walked up beside me.

"Haley?" I asked, looking between them. Two were women, and I didn't know who was who. "Heath, here, called yesterday and asked to meet."

"You must be Jacky," one said, smiling. She had dark hair and eyes, giving us a wary smile. "And Heath." She looked over at the wolf. "You...asked some uncomfortable questions over the phone yesterday. Geoffrey also sent word you would be in contact."

"Then you know what I am," he said, eyeing her.

"A werewolf? Yes. Jacky..." Haley looked at me, frowning.

"Werecat," I said, looking over my shoulder to make sure no one was around. "You three knew Gaia and Titan." I didn't phrase it as a question. I *knew* they had contact with the deceased werecats, and there didn't need to be any beating around the bush about it. No one had time for that. "And you're all human. So, let's cut to the chase. Who found their bodies?"

"You're a lot like the last werecat who rolled through here," the other woman said. I raised an eyebrow. I was a lot like Jabari? He would have a hernia if he heard that. "I'm Gina. This is John." She motioned to the older gentleman, who had to be in his late forties. "And yes, we knew them. John and I found their bodies. Haley went with us to check on Titan after we discovered Gaia was dead."

"I'm sorry you had to see that," Heath said gently. "We're going to have a lot of questions for you three. Is there anywhere more private to talk?"

"Not really. We could drive further out, but there's no one here right now, so there's nothing to worry about." Haley's smile was tight.

She doesn't trust us. Can't say I blame her. There are probably too many supernatural strangers roaming through for her to feel comfortable.

"Fine." I sighed, continuing to look around. "We've

heard there have also been some werewolf disappearances. Do you have anything we should hear about that?"

"No. I try to greet werewolves as they come in. That was a typical group of guys, looking to drink beer and sit around a campfire for a week. They didn't seem more or less trouble than any other group like them. It wasn't close to the full moon. They were planning on leaving about three days before. When they didn't come back down by the full moon, I got worried. Geoffrey started calling me, but I couldn't find their campsite." Haley crossed her arms like she was scared of something. "I couldn't find Gaia and Titan to ask if they had seen the wolves either. The next time we saw them was...when we found them."

"So, first, the wolves go missing without a trace, and the only ones who could have possibly found them showed up dead two weeks later," Heath muttered, shaking his head. "We pretty much already knew that."

I had an idea, but I knew if I didn't get it done in one day, Hasan would be furious.

"Can you take me to the territory line? Drive me closer to where one of them lived? I might be able to learn something."

"The other guy, he had a weird name, asked for the same thing," Gina informed me, looking down. "We took him up there, and he seemed really spooked or something. He just started walking out into the woods with his stuff and hasn't...come back either."

"Yeah. His name is Jabari, and he's got a one-track

mind. I promised someone important not to go into the woods." I ran a hand through my hair, realizing my ponytail wasn't holding up. I readjusted it and looked at Heath. "What do you say? Want to check out something closer to the area?"

"We don't have much of a choice. At least, I don't. I'm going to have to go into the woods at some point."

"Yeah," I sighed. "You promised to find the wolves."

"Why didn't Geoffrey send anyone out?" John asked, shoving his hands into his pockets. "Are you one of his?"

"No. I'm a friend and came into town with Jacky to figure out what the hell is going on. He wasn't going to send anyone out until he knew what was going on with Gaia and Titan, and I can't blame him for that. Why didn't you tell him they were dead?" Heath eyed the group in front of us.

"We...we didn't know if he did it or not." Haley shrugged. "It wouldn't be hard for wolves or anything else to get out here, and we wouldn't have any idea. The last thing we wanted was for the wolves to overrun our mountain...Gaia and Titan were important to us. They helped rescue humans, brought them back if they got lost or hurt. They also kept other...things like you out. And sure enough, now that they're gone, we've had two other werecats and a werewolf show up, so far."

"I'm sorry," Heath said, calm and composed, nothing bothering him.

I wasn't calm or composed. These humans had enjoyed a very close relationship with two very reclusive werecats, who had been out there saving people. Did they make sure to do it in human form, or would I find some weird local legends about a big cat that was a benevolent spirit?

"Look, we can bust out some four wheelers and take you up to the trail we used to get to Gaia and Titan's shared home. Visiting their private homes...we normally park at their shared home and hike in opposite directions. It's not easy, but you can probably see one of their houses and get back before nightfall." Gina motioned for us to follow her, and the other two rangers backed off as we stepped forward. She pulled out a map from her pocket and began pointing at different areas. "This is where they would sometimes live together. This is where Gaia lived. Her territory included Mt. Baker. Titan held more territory, reaching down past Glacier Peak. He was a lot harder to visit."

"Let's just...get toward their territory." I was getting more of a feeling as I got closer. The set-up of the land and mountains made me wonder if these werecats didn't have circular ranges. It was entirely possible they'd had something a bit more unique. The only reason my territory was as clean of a circle as it was? I was lazy and didn't feel like finding better lines. Their centers would still be their homes, and it would be a sizable distance from any borders. I drummed my fingers on the hood Gina had used as a table for the map.

"I wonder how they used the natural geography when it came to marking their territories..."

"What was that?" John stepped closer, but I shook my head.

"Personal curiosity," I explained. I knew some werecats used cliffs, ravines, and bodies of water to help mark their territory. Hasan's island territory came to mind. He 'owned' it, beach to beach, on all sides, even though it definitely wasn't a circle.

"Okay." The human shrugged and backed away again. "Well, we can get moving when you want."

I nodded to Heath, who just jerked his head. I followed him back to the car, and we loaded up. Once Haley's truck started moving, we followed behind.

"They wanted to have nothing to do with this," I announced blandly. "They'll help us as much as they can, but they don't trust us."

"No, they don't. I think they want answers as well. Not a bad thing since it puts us on the same side."

The same side. I thought about it. Everyone seemed to be hoping they stayed on the same side now—the wolves, the werecats, and the humans. If any of this turned out that someone was at fault, the lines would start being drawn, and it was possible a war could break out. Sobering to think about, which was why I tried my damnedest not to think about it.

We followed behind the rangers for a long time until they stopped at a closed road. John jumped out, opened it up, and began to wave us through. We followed Haley, stopping for the man to jump back in the truck behind us with Gina after he closed the road again.

It was a gravel, potholed mess that ran switchbacks up the side of a mountain. I wasn't sure how high we were going, but I popped my ears once, at least.

The road seemed to never end, but Haley stopped at a clear opening, and we pulled up next to her, rolling my window down as she did.

"We have a small service building up here. There's no electricity, but we keep the four wheelers there, along with spare gas. I just wanted to check in on you."

"We're fine," I called back. Haley nodded and continued the drive.

It was another thirty minutes of potholes and tight turns before we reached the secretive little service building. Three ATVs were parked there, and one dirt bike that made me excited. I jumped out before Heath had the chance to turn off the car and walked quickly toward it. It was an older model, but the same brand as mine. I would be able to drive it.

"So, we can haul you—"

"I'll take this," I told Haley, pointing at the bike. "I own one of my own."

"You have no protective gear," she pointed out. "Just ride with one of us like the werewolf has to."

"I know how to use an ATV," he said lightly, walking over. "Why don't a couple of you get together, that way if we need to stay out longer, you aren't stuck with us."

Haley narrowed her eyes on him, then me. "When we come back, you are too. You aren't taking our gear out there completely unaccounted for. You could get us fired."

"Then we'll check it out today and come back if we have to on foot," I said, looking at Heath. "Let's not lose their jobs for them."

He shrugged. "I still want to drive my own. I don't ride bitch. Haven't in decades."

"But you did have a pack member act as your driver," I reminded him.

"I needed to concentrate on something else at the time." He looked me over. "Like the werecat who had come to my city."

I nearly blushed from the way his eyes trailed over me, looking away, hoping he wouldn't notice. Once again, visions of a half-naked Heath danced in front of my mind's eye. I shook my head jerkily, trying to dispel the thoughts.

"Fine, you two can do whatever you want." Haley stomped into the building and brought out keys. She tossed me one and Heath another. I swung a leg over the bike and turned it on, giving it a minute. It was an old thing, but it would work. Heath revved the ATV he had jumped on. Haley grabbed another with John helping Gina onto the back of his.

"You'll notice there's no cellphone service out here, so be careful," Gina called out from the back.

"We'll be fine unless we go over a cliff," Heath called back. Haley went first, and I took off to follow her. Heath, followed by John and Gina, was behind me. When we hit a bump, I lifted off my seat to better handle the landing, laughing when Heath cursed behind me at the same bump. Haley was right. It wasn't an easy ride and, while I wouldn't tell her, it was harder than I was used to.

No one else noticed it but Heath and me. I slammed

on my brake about ten minutes into the winding ride and narrowed my eyes at an invisible line.

"What?" Haley demanded from in front of us.

"This is a territory boundary," I said softly. I had expected to find it much earlier, like when we were bringing up the cars.

"And?" Heath pulled along beside me. "What's wrong?"

I shook my head. "Its placement doesn't make much sense to me."

"They roamed all of these mountains. There's no way this is the line," Haley snapped. "What are you talking about?"

"This is where their territories technically stop," I snapped back. "You're human, so you don't feel it the way I do."

"How big would you guess by the map?"

"Smaller than mine?" I sighed. "Where are we right now, technically?"

"North Cascades National Park," Gina answered as she and John stopped behind us.

"There's a chance they made multiple territories," I commented, still thinking about it. "Or smaller territories that didn't require much maintenance and commonly roamed outside of it. Jabari would have noticed this too. It's not common, but in an area like this, it makes sense. They wouldn't be too worried about another werecat coming for them. While werecats are reclusive, not many of us are *this* reclusive. We like to live on the border of human society, not completely removed from it. I'll have to explore more to figure it out, but by your description, their territories, especially Titan's, should have been passed into much further south. We should have noticed on that road. The 20." I tapped my foot. "Did Titan spend most of his time down South?"

"Yeah, but he came up here often to visit Gaia."

"Then we're visiting her territory and definitely not still in his own." I looked at Heath. "It's going to be a long day."

He leaned closer. "Are you avoiding crossing into the territory?"

"A little," I admitted. "I've only ever been in one werecat's territory, and that was Hasan's. There are... things I have to pay attention to."

"Is there a chance their territories have gotten smaller since they died?" He ignored the humans waiting impatiently around us. Haley perked up at the question. Part of me wondered if she didn't like not knowing everything about the werecats who had lived here. Now, she was getting the education of her life.

"No. The magic doesn't work like that. It fades with time, either because we're dead or not in it, refreshing our connection to the land, but it takes a lot of time or another werecat claiming it for the magic to truly disappear. And it's not a shrinking. It just fades and fades until it's all...free." I shrugged. "At least, that's how I was taught."

"I would trust your education on the matter more than anyone else's," he said with a small smile. "What are you looking out for? All I can tell is that werecat land is right in front of me. I know when I'm in your territory or when I'm about to enter it but that's it."

"The feel of the land," I whispered. "Let's get to it."

I slid off the bike and let Heath go ahead of me, pushing it along until I crossed the invisible border.

16

CHAPTER SIXTEEN

I gasped as I stepped inside the boundary. My chest felt like it was hit by the emotional currents of the area. An immediate hostility made me want to back out. This wasn't a werecat I wanted to challenge. This wasn't land I wanted. It wasn't mine. It belonged to someone else, and I had to leave. The feminine rage that filled my senses terrified me. I wasn't an old enough werecat to handle this fight.

She's dead. Gaia is dead, Jacky. This land is free. All I'm feeling is the residual rage she felt. This was her last moment. She was enraged at an intruder. It's not me. She's not coming right now to battle me out of the territory.

I took several deep breaths as my logical brain fought against my primal instincts. I had never felt this sort of anger in Hasan's territory when I had lived with him. His territory had been welcoming. His emotions toward me changed the way the land felt.

This was the kind of signal I would send to a rogue

who walked into my territory. Normally, it wasn't instantaneous. It took a moment for any werecat to feel something come into its territory and the mind to process the information. Then it took time for the werecat to send its message, warning off potential threats. By Heath's reaction, I learned something very important. Emotional currents were something wolves couldn't feel. This was werecat to werecat communication. This was our way of telling another werecat whether they were welcome or not.

"Is she okay? Her eyes went really big, and she looks like she's staring off into space." Haley sounded annoyed.

"Jacky?" Heath asked softly. "What are you feeling?"

"Gaia was pissed," I said as loud as I could. My instincts screamed for me to remain quiet, maybe she wouldn't find me. I had to get over it, but I was young, and a young werecat picking a fight was a dead werecat.

There's no fight, Jacky. She's not here. I'm safe. She's not coming to kill me right now for intruding.

Even if she was, this was not the same level of reaction a werecat would give to a rogue intruder. This was primal rage. This was more than facing a challenger. Unless she was unstable in some way, something no one had given me any reason to think. I got angry with rogues, but not like this. Never like this.

"How do you know?" Gina was behind me still. "What would she be angry with?"

"I don't know what, but I know because it's something werecats can feel. Territory magic is an intimate connection to the land. Everywhere that belongs to her will feel of her, however she's feeling. If she's angry, the entire territory gives off an angry message to intruding werecats. Heath, you don't feel it at all, do you?"

"Nope. I just know I'm in werecat territory. Not a place a wolf generally wants to be."

"You're in them more than most," I said with a weak attempt at a lopsided smile. "My brain is trying to convince my body Gaia isn't coming here to throw me out right now. Her rage is so...powerful. Something pissed her off before she died. Pissed her off big time."

"Good to know." Heath extended a hand. "Come on. Take a step."

I grabbed it and kept the little dirt bike up and rolling with my other hand. I was able to take a few steps and brave the anger. I couldn't imagine how Jabari must have felt if he walked into this. Was Titan's territory the same way?

"I'll be fine. Thanks for the support." I released his hand once I was beside him and his ATV again. "I've never locked up like that before, but then, I don't often wander into territories of other werecats." Shaking my head, I swung my leg over the dirt bike again. "Let's keep moving."

"Are you sure you're okay?" my wolf asked before moving as Haley started to leave us.

"I'm fine." I kicked off and left him. The dirt bike made travel easier, and I knew I wasn't headed into the center of her territory. It was a sixth sense. I would know how to find her den, her home. Some things meant the same thing to all werecats. The closest to the center of a territory was the safest spot and gave the werecat range of movement if any of the borders were trespassed. It was also our refuge. I never let anyone go to mine. Gaia hadn't let her mate go to hers if she had a second house for meet ups. Titan even had to leave his territory to visit her.

We were at the house soon enough, and I guessed right. It was on the border of her territory. If Titan wanted to see her, he probably had to come here and wait, feeling her reaction to his presence, which would tell him if she wanted to see him or not. It was genius, a nice trick to dealing with and loving another werecat.

When we parked, none of the humans left their rides while Heath and I jumped off without a second thought.

"No one goes in there," Haley told us as we walked by. "Hey!"

"We're going in. We can't upset the dead more than they already are," I said with a small snap. Haley's attitude was grating on my nerves more than I needed. She needed to remember who actually knew what was going on and what it all meant, not whatever she had guessed over the years. Gaia and Titan had obviously not told the rangers much and let the humans draw their own conclusions with the scraps of real information they did have.

I went in first, sniffing the air, with Heath following so close behind me I could hear him breathe. I caught whatever scents I could. Jabari had visited this place, and the other two werecats, definitely a male and female, had to be Gaia and Titan. There was no scent of wolves anywhere.

"Do you smell anything?"

"Two male werecats," he answered.

"One is Jabari. I would know his scent anywhere. It's like Hasan's." I walked past the living room into the very old-school kitchen. "They were living here two centuries ago," I commented, pointing at the oven.

"Out here, I bet there was no chance of them getting modern appliances, electricity, or gas. I bet there's a well dug somewhere nearby or a mountain stream where they got their water."

"Yeah..." I continued to look around. Only one bedroom, smelling of them both. Jabari hadn't gone in it. As it was, I just stood at the doorway, not wanting to disturb the private place where two ancient lovers once met together. It made my heart ache that there would no longer be clandestine rendezvous here. "I wonder how long they were together."

"Hm?" Heath walked up behind me, sniffing the space over my shoulder. "Hm...I have no idea. Sad to see it end like this, dead in their own homes."

"I wonder if there was a falling out..." I leaned on the door frame. "There's no smell of wolves here."

"I noticed." His voice went gruff and thick. "We'll figure this out."

I only nodded as we backed away from the private bedroom and left the house. There was nothing to find.

"How did the bodies look when you found them?" I asked the moment I was in the fresh air.

"Broken necks," John answered. I must have looked surprised because John's face went a bit pink. "Honestly. I think Gaia's back was broken too…It had the look of it."

"You've seen that before?" Heath was more focused than me now. I was still trying to comprehend seeing a werecat with a broken neck and back. In human form, it was possible but still difficult.

"Fallen climbers and hikers. You know."

"Sure." Heath nodded, his grey-blue eyes darker than I had ever seen them. "No blood or anything?"

"No…" Gina whimpered, then sobbed. "It was so awful."

I sighed, turning away to let the humans console each other. I felt bad for not helping, but I was spooked.

"I want to see Gaia's house. Where she was found." I pointed out. "It's that way."

"Um…yeah, we use a trail for hiking over there…" Haley pulled away from John and Gina to come close to us. "You might be able to get an ATV on it, but it won't be easy."

"A dirt bike?" I asked.

"It can make it, but you both won't fit, and I'm not sure anyone should be walking around these woods alone right now."

I looked up and checked the daylight. It had to be close to noon, but the afternoon heat wasn't close to settling in. "Heath, you up for a hike?"

"We can make it there and back, I bet. How long do you think it'll take to walk out there?"

"It takes us about three hours?" Haley shrugged. "Might be less for you."

"It will be. Let's go. You all can wait here or head back and meet us at the service shack but leave us an ATV to take back. I want to check out her home alone."

"Wait...how do you know where it is?" Haley was frowning again. "And be careful where you step. We cremated her there."

"I'm a werecat. I know." I smiled tightly at her. "I'll be respectful of the land."

Walking away, I let Heath follow behind me as I set the pace. I took the trail only for convenience. It was worn down just enough to be walkable without major tripping, but the humans had been right. An ATV would be hard to take because it was very narrow. Heath and I couldn't walk side by side.

"Can you really find the center of her territory just by feeling?" he asked about twenty minutes into the walk.

"Yup. It's like...a beacon. It's the *center*. If a werecat didn't meet me for a challenge, it's where I would go to make them pay attention to me, to make them see me and respond. We don't fight over pitiful lines. We fight over it all. It's useless to take a piece of land from a werecat who can just reclaim it the next night or full moon or whatever. You have to force them completely out."

"So, you gamble it all. Is it ever fatal?"

"No, not very often. It can be if the challenger wants it to be or if the defender refuses to concede, but most werecats will back off from a lost fight, and dying over territory is frowned on. Killing for it is normally investigated. We don't have the numbers, and there's a lot of space in the world. There's no reason to kill or die for something unless it's that important."

"Is there anything that important?"

"I would die before I let another werecat take my territory, but it's not because of the land," I whispered. I glanced over my shoulder at him, seeing the thoughtful and sad expression on his face.

"You've died enough in the name of my family," he said gently. "There's no reason—"

"Don't make the decision for me. Don't *ever* make that decision for me."

With that, I turned back and kept trudging. On the path, I tried to scent another werecat or anything else, but aside from Jabari's old scent, I found nothing. Heath must not have either because he kept walking in silence behind me.

I checked my phone, even though it had no service. I wanted the time. Unless we took naps at Gaia's house, we should have plenty of daylight to get out of the woods, get cell phone service, and call the people we needed to call.

"I still haven't smelled any wolves," Heath said softly. "It's worrying. I can smell werecats and humans on this trail, but neither of those is out of the ordinary from what we've been told."

"Same. Jabari, Gaia, and those three. Not even a hint of Titan." I paused on the path, looking around. "Do you think the wolf disappearances are actually connected to this?"

"My gut says so. While I would love to hunt them

down first, just to find out their fate, that's a harder chase than finding out what killed your werecats and could lead to the same answers. If those who know the land couldn't find the wolf campsite, there's not much hope for us. It's been a month, so the scents have probably died."

"Sorry. I know Geoffrey is hoping you can figure this out for him. Those werewolves deserve as much justice as the werecats."

"Thank you for thinking so." He smiled at me and continued down the path, leaving me behind him now. "Would your family think so?"

"I don't think they care past how it helps or hurts them," I admitted. "It's not that they're callous or anything with life, but they have a much-earned distrust for wolves."

"They're all from pre-War, aren't they?"

"Yeah." So far as I knew. From what little I knew about much of their lives, they all had experience during the War and had fought in it. "It's more than that. You know Hasan lost a daughter to werewolves. He told me what happened. It, uh, didn't look good on the part of the werewolves."

"Of course," Heath sighed. "There's good and bad in all the species, isn't there?"

"Yeah, I would assume so. With great power and all that shit."

He chuckled sadly. "And all that shit."

We made it to a small clearing with a cabin in only two hours. I kept walking, refusing to pause at the black section of the earth where they had cremated Gaia.

Once I was at the house, I pushed in, sniffing quickly. Heath caught up and stayed near me. It was one bedroom with a tiny living room and kitchen, even smaller than the romantic little house the two werecats met at to be together. Everything was skins and hand done.

"She lived off the land all year," I commented softly. "What do you smell?"

"You, me, Jabari, Gaia, and human. Still no wolves or anything else."

"Yet she was found right in the middle of the room with a broken neck and back in her human form," I growled. "Heath, it doesn't make any damn sense. She was a werecat. Anything in her territory should have been easy to—"

"What if the humans lied about her injuries?" he asked, cutting me off. I let it sink in, trying to approach it from that angle.

"Why? Why would they kill and cover up two dead werecats, then call it in?"

"Haley is nervous," he reminded me.

"Haley is a know-it-all, and this is her world. We're outsiders. Her behavior makes sense."

"I'm not disagreeing, I'm just saying maybe we're disregarding the humans a little too soon."

I growled softly, not at Heath but his point. "They would have to have a reason. From where I'm standing, they worshiped these werecats."

"Maybe they thought the cats killed the wolves," he suggested, shrugging.

"I don't think they liked the werewolves that much," I countered. Hearing his sigh, I bet he agreed with me.

"So, what can sneak up on a werecat?" He leaned onto the kitchen counter, frowning. "You don't feel humans."

"No, we don't. They're like any other animal unless they're a witch or something. They have to have some sort of...magical signature." I groaned. "Heath, there's nothing. Nothing I can think of, anyway. I think I need to talk to Hasan and the family about this. I...I just don't know. What sneaks up on a werecat, kills her physically like described, then walks away without leaving a trace?"

He shrugged, and I could see a deep sadness in his eyes. He had no idea either, and it was killing both of us. Standing in the place where she died, the weight of her death hung heavy, and the idea of catching the killer seemed like a long shot.

"If the wolves didn't do it and the humans don't make sense, then who?" I yelled at the end, kicking a piece of furniture and sending it to the wall. "God damn it!"

"We'll find out. I promise you, Jacky. We'll find out who killed those up here." Heath didn't come near me, not that I blamed him. Failure taunted me. "Maybe since we're not learning anything here, we can leave for the day, stay nearby, then head out to see Titan's home tomorrow. Maybe it'll have some clues."

"Sounds like a plan," I muttered, storming out. Sure, I had learned more about what was going on than Jabari probably had before coming into the mountains, but I was no closer to knowing the murderer than I had been on the plane to Seattle. "At least there shouldn't be a war. If the werewolves didn't do this, and the werecats didn't kill the wolves, there's no reason for a war."

"There would still be a war if Jabari is dead or if you die," Heath said as he walked out behind me. "Maybe we can try to track your brother. He was obviously here."

"He was, but scent tracking isn't my strong suit. It's yours."

"My nose is better as a werewolf and in my actual wolf form. The full moon was only a couple of nights ago. A Change will be fast."

"But...can you talk to me in your wolf form? I know about pack magic, but I don't know all the logistics of it."

"Should be able to. Your mind is receptive to it in ways another werecat probably isn't thanks to...that gift you have. Have you used it since that night?" When I didn't immediately answer, he stepped around me and met my gaze. "Your eyes are gold right now, Jacky."

"Yeah...I'm pissed off...and scared. I'm not an old werecat. I'm very young, actually. If something can...kill them and make Jabari go missing, I have no chance against it. None."

"And neither do I. Maybe we should head back and start our search fresh tomorrow."

"Jabari could be dead tomorrow," I mumbled, looking out into the trees. "Fuck, he could be dead now. I mean, he's...literally, a few thousand years old, much older than Gaia and Titan but still..."

"That's older than dirt," Heath muttered, shaking his head. "How the hell do you cats stay alive so long?"

"I think I've said it before, but it's because we don't fight each other as much as you wolves." I sighed. "Let's go. I promised not to go into the woods, and I don't want to push my luck."

We started walking away, probably both thinking about the mystery we found ourselves in. When we reached the edge of the clearing, Heath asked me one more question.

"Did Hasan ever teach you about anything that would fit this?"

"Not that I can remember, but it was four years of lessons. If I remember anything, you'll be the first person I tell."

If that was our only hope, we didn't have much to look forward to.

17

CHAPTER SEVENTEEN

"I'm going to Change," Heath said before we got too far from the house. "I'll feel better if at least one of us is in our more powerful form, and I have the nose to find older trails."

I looked around, not seeing anything. If anything, the surrounding forest was beautifully serene. When nothing seemed unusual, I nodded.

"I'll carry your clothing," I told him, keeping my back to him. I listened as he undressed, the sound of his zipper seeming too loud for the quiet world we were standing in. A weird thing to notice, no doubt, but I couldn't help it. I felt something hit the back of my legs and looked around to see it, catching a glimpse of bare legs as I stared at the pile of clothing. I picked them up, trying to fold them as I went so they would be easier to carry. I didn't dare comment on the soft boxer briefs with...well, I figured they were dog bones. Were those supposed to be a joke?

I'm not sure what to even think about them. Are they a

dick joke? Are they a werewolf joke? Did he buy them for himself, or were they a prank gift from someone? Who would buy this man patterned underwear?

Questions for another time. We had more pressing things to deal with, like getting out of the woods safely.

We have time. Keep calm, keep moving, and we'll be out of here well before nightfall.

I listened to bone crunching, grunts, and growls as Heath went through the fast but painful-looking shift from man to massive wolf.

"Can you hear me?"

"Yup. We're good," I answered. "Let's get moving."

He huffed and began to trot toward the trail back. I followed behind him as we entered the woods and fell into an easy formation. I walked the trail, keeping my eyes and ears out for anything. As a wolf, he sniffed around the trail sides, looking for any place where it seemed someone or something might have been following alongside the path or taken off in a different direction. We trekked for a long time, not speaking. It was odd for me to talk to a wolf, and he probably had nothing to say because he wasn't finding anything.

Either way, it was a silent walk.

We were nearly to the house when Heath whined.

"I smell something, and it's bad news, I bet."

"What?"

"Gasoline," he answered before taking off faster. I ran after him, unable to keep up.

"Heath!" I called. "Wait up!" I really didn't want to get left behind in the woods—not now.

I watched him slow down, and together, we ran at a reasonable pace to the place where the two werecats once met and where we left our ride. I was about thirty yards away when I could smell what he had. The gasoline was strong in the air.

"Oh fuck," I snapped. "No. No. No. No." I continued to run for the ATV the humans had left behind for us and snarled at the fuel line—severed clean, all the fuel poured onto the ground.

"Does it seem purposeful?"

"Yes," I answered, my hand shaking as I continued to stare at it. "What do you bet our rental is in the same condition?"

He growled. *"You think?"*

"They wouldn't be stupid enough to screw us here without fucking with the car. I don't smell anyone new. Just those three. Unless it's our scentless killer." I leaned over, holding my face in my clean hand. "God damn it. Even if we make it back to the car before dark, if it's fucked up, we'd have to repair it at night."

"Or we can fortify here and make a break for it at dawn," he suggested. *"I'll stay in wolf form as protection. We'll borrow their...home."*

I looked over at the house. *Hasan is going to kill me. He's going to send the entire damn family out here, and people are going to get hurt.*

I felt like a fuck up. I was a fuck up.

So fucking stupid, Jacky. I should have known better! Why didn't I know better than to leave my ride out unsecured?

"We'll stay the night here," I said, sighing heavily. "This is probably easier to secure than that little shack they used to hold this shit." I dropped the cut fuel line and stood up, shaking my head. "I'm going to need help securing if you're okay with changing back to human form."

"I *would rather you get into werecat form,*" he countered. "*We're both safer in these forms.*"

"That works, but I want to lock us in the building." I started marching to the door, Heath on my tail. Once we were both inside, I shut the door and locked it. It probably wouldn't be too much help, so I shoved the couch in the way of the door as well. Then I went into the bedroom and lifted the bed to block the window. Slowly, I made my way around the house, closing all ways inside. If someone wanted to get in, they would have to move shit out of their way, which would give us a sign to get ready for a fight.

Once I was satisfied, I checked the time. There were another four hours until nightfall. It was going to be a long night. I stripped and folded my clothing, putting it on the kitchen counter. Once that was done, I began my own shift, letting the werecat form tear through me at a speed that still surprised me and hurt—still so painful. When I was done, I looked over to Heath and found him watching me.

"*It irks my male pride that you're so much bigger than me.*"

"*Is now really the time to worry about your ego?*" I retorted without heat. "*We're ancient big cats in the same way you're actually a dire wolf. We've always been bigger than you."*

"I know. Have you ever wondered about the origin of our species? I have. No one has any answers."

"I haven't, actually. Next time I talk to Hasan—if I'm alive at the end of the conversation—I'll bring it up. If there's one werecat out there with answers, it would be him." I considered the fae too. They could also hold the key, but the cost of receiving the answers to those sorts of questions was probably high, too high.

"You don't have to. It's just a curiosity. I don't believe it changes anything for us in the end." He sounded somewhat defeated.

"Are you one of those who thinks we're all damned in the end and all that?" I didn't. I thought I was a monster, but I didn't really consider the afterlife. I had no choice in this life, and I did my best to do what I could with it. That had to count for something with whatever higher power was out there, right?

"Somewhat. I grew up in a heavily Christian society. Mind you, we weren't all Christians back then, or we didn't use that term. I was raised Protestant. My parents hated our Catholic neighbors." He rolled onto his side. "I lost that faith a long time ago. I've just always wondered if maybe our origins would hold the secret to removing the curse on us. And that's what it is, a curse."

"I know. I've been told other species of supernaturals call us the Moon Cursed Ones or just the Moon Cursed. It makes sense. We lose nearly all of our control on the full moon, and if we aren't careful, we can hurt someone." I gave an audible grumble. *"But many of us didn't ask for this."*

"I know. Neither of us did." He shifted and rolled to his other side as if he couldn't get comfortable. *"I'm wondering if we should try to sleep now so we can stay awake for the night."*

"You can nap, and I'll cover for now. You just have to watch my back tonight, so I can get some sleep in."

"Good idea."

Moments later, the wolf was snoring. I huffed and laid my head down on my front feet. I wasn't used to staying in this form for very long. Normally, I was very active while a werecat and shifted back into my human form once I was done hunting, eating, or checking my territory. The idea of staying in werecat form to sleep bothered me enough; any exhaustion I felt from the early morning was long gone. I was wide awake, alone with my thoughts, and had nowhere I could safely go. I couldn't even roam around to stretch my legs.

Already I was feeling cooped up.

This is what I get. Hasan told me not to go into the woods. I went without even fucking thinking about it. It was only supposed to be a short hike and back, and here I am. I know they fucked with the car. I just know it. Taking the risk to check on it and having to find better shelter than that shack was too much.

What could possibly be doing this? What's in these damn woods, killing people?

Who is helping them? I swear if those fucking humans cut the fuel line, I'm going to kill them.

My mind went to awful places while Heath slept. I bounced back and forth between killing and not killing the humans, solely based on their species status. The world could ignore several dead werewolves and werecats. Dead humans would bring the eyes of the local authorities. If answers weren't found, uncomfortable questions would be asked.

I groomed for a little while, trying to put the thought of killing humans off my mind. I tried not to think about the mysterious killer out in the woods.

Then I thought of something.

Heath was good at making sure his feelings didn't infiltrate his scent. I wasn't sure how he did it, though I figured a certain amount of self-control was part of it.

What if a wolf—or four—figured out how to hide their scents completely?

I narrowed my eyes on my wolf, sleeping soundly across the small living room. I was already planning my round of questioning as the sun dipped, and the rays coming through the windows began to disappear.

When I felt he'd slept long enough, I walked over to him and nosed his side, then jumped back as he woke up. A yawn revealed impressive canines and a clean, dangerous row of white teeth. I could have thought mine were nicer, but the reality was, wolves survived because their fangs made sense. Ancient sabertooth felines had a niche bite that might have contributed to their extinction. His impressive set was more useful and versatile than mine.

"Is it nightfall already?" he asked, his voice sleepy in

my head. I'd never heard him tired before, and it had a husky quality that I immediately wanted to hear more of.

"*Yeah. So, I was thinking—*"

"*I can't wait to hear this,*" he teased, something akin to a smile showing up on his face. His voice still had that huskiness I liked.

"*I noticed a lot of the time, I can't scent your emotions on you. What if the wolves learned how to remain unscented?*"

"*I have a large amount of self-control over my feelings, and even then, you can still smell me,*" he explained. "*There's no way to turn off the body's functions that produce scent. I'm alive, therefore, I smell. My emotions, however, can remain private if I can control myself.*"

I jerked my head up.

He's *alive*.

"*No. Oh, shit, I'm so stupid,*" I hissed into his head, making the same sound for his ears. "*Alive! Everything alive had a scent, Heath.*"

"*Yes?*"

"*But have you ever caught the scent of a vampire?*" I asked, growling. "*Probably not, because they're frozen. Their bodies don't function the ways ours do. They don't produce a scent! That was Hasan's first lesson on vampires! Fuck me! We might have vampires in the fucking mountains!*"

"*I never noticed that,*" he said softly as if he was cursing himself the same as I was pissed off for not remembering that lesson sooner. "*The only time I see* them is in company. I always assumed they smelled like humans."

"No..." I groaned mentally. "*Oh fuck, it makes sense in terms of the murders.*"

"Explain."

"Hasan told me that vampires rarely want to deal with a werecat because we're strong. Werewolves are slightly easier targets, but vampires generally stay in their nests and hunt their food source, humans, down without getting into anyone's way."

"It's easy to ignore them as long as they aren't killing people. I know it's an addictive rush for them when they do."

"Yeah, so we ignore them, and they want to be ignored. Do you know what creature on Earth has the best chance of pointing out a vampire in the crowd? Humans. They innately sense something is off with the thing wearing their face."

"Then how did they hide from Gaia and Titan?"

"They didn't. I've never personally felt it, but Hasan once told me vampires are hard to pinpoint once they're in your territory. They're slippery, elusive, there one minute and gone the next. He said he thought it was because of their closeness to humanity and the blood they drink."

"And their shadow magics could help if they're powerful enough to use them," Heath added. "I'm making a wild guess here, but they must have confused the werecats, and slipped in when their defenses were down."

"I think we're right. I don't remember shit about their magics if Hasan taught it to me. I never really gave them any thought because he made it sound like they would just...never be a problem. *A vampire isn't strong enough to kill us in this form, me or you, not alone, but they can easily kill us in our human form. They normally aren't stupid enough to.*

"They can..." Heath stood up, then sat back on his haunches. "*So, what do we do? We're stuck in this house until daybreak if that's the case.*"

"*Good thing we decided to hunker down. We would be easy prey if we were trying to fix our rental right now.*"

"*Very good thing, but they can break in. Those old human legends about doors and crosses aren't true.*"

"I *don't have* all *the answers,*" I snapped. "*I'm trying.*"

"*No, you this much remembering is great. It gives us something to work with, at least. If anything, we stay in these forms and hold out. If one attacks, we're able to fight.*" I watched him sigh, looking around the room we were in. "*You know, if it is a vampire or a few of them, that means those humans, or at least one of them, is helping them.*"

"*Yeah...because they're the only answer we have when it comes to who cut the fuel line on the ATV.*" I figured that much. There was no other option if there were vampires roaming the night on these mountains. "*Which one do you think it is?*"

"*You know.*"

"*Haley.*"

His big wolf head nodded.

I laid down, and he walked closer.

"*Get some sleep,*" he ordered in that Alpha way he tried on me sometimes.

"*Bite me.*"

Gentle teeth nipped my shoulder, and I growled.

"*You asked. Get some sleep, Jacky. I'll keep watch.*"

I yawned and tried to sleep, hoping we were wrong. Vampires were out of my depth, and these were smart enough to catch two, maybe three, older and stronger werecats off their guard. I almost didn't want to go to sleep. If Gaia and Titan couldn't protect themselves, if Jabari went missing, and four werewolves vanished into thin air, what chance did Heath and I have?

Too bad my own exhaustion caught up with me, and the rain starting up was like a lullaby. Sleep hit quickly.

18

CHAPTER EIGHTEEN

I woke up to the sound of a branch snap. I wasn't normally a light sleeper, but it seemed so loud, my eyes flew open, staring into the darkness I could see perfectly well in. Heath sat patiently on the couch, his head up, watching me. When he tilted his head, I knew he realized I was awake.

"Did you hear that?" I asked softly.

"No. I've only heard the rain. It's too quiet out there."

"A branch snapped," I explained, standing up to stretch out. If I were human at the time, I would have winced at the creak from the floor. It was even louder than the branch, and Heath was right. The rain was the only sound from outside, way too quiet for a world that should have felt alive. I didn't take a step, standing perfectly still as I listened to the world outside. When I heard nothing else except the soft rain, I laid back down.

"I hate this."

"I do, too, but do you really want to roam the woods at night trying to get back to a possibly broken car?"

"No. That sounds like the stupid shit a human would do in a horror movie." He huffed, which could have meant anything—exasperation, laughter, or just play annoyance. He could have been agreeing for all I knew.

"Want to sit quietly and play more questions?"

"Do you have any more questions?" The wolf practically knew my life story. I mean, not really, but there wasn't anything that came to mind he could go after that might matter to him.

"I've thought of a few while you've been asleep. Did you know that you have a somewhat naïve sense of morality?"

"I guess." I gave my best feline shrug. "I know the world isn't black and white, but...I think doing the right thing is more important than doing the proper thing. It doesn't matter if it gets me hurt or killed. I'll go down, knowing I tried, and maybe someone else out there is happier for it."

"Was that how you approached being an EMT?"

"No. As an EMT, I had strict rules I had to follow, and I did because screwing up in those situations could kill someone who needed my help. No, my attitude got me in more trouble in high school and college." I snorted as I remembered some of the downright dumb things I did with the idea I was helping other people because they needed me, and I could be there for them.

"What got you in the most trouble?"

I grumbled. "Getting kicked out of college. I caught

some mother fucker doing a procedure completely wrong on a real fucking patient. I took everything away from him, called him out, and started to do the procedure myself. We both got kicked out. He tried to shove me away to let him finish the way he wanted to do it. I punched him, and he wasn't expecting it. He hit the ground. I finished the procedure. The patient called the cops. One expulsion later..."

"And you were an EMT while your twin went on to be a heart surgeon."

"*Yup.*" I flexed my paws, looking down at my razor-sharp claws. "*Now, I'm in this world, you know? Here, doing that is everyone's first instinct. I never thought of myself as violent. I wanted to heal and help people. To save them. Looking back...I guess I was kind of violent. I was willing to get physical with anyone who stopped me doing what I needed to do for someone and...that just carried over to this life.*"

"And in this life, you aren't going to get arrested," he pointed out. "Well...never mind. You still got arrested, didn't you?" He laid his big wolf head down, staring at me with eyes that seemed to capture everything an iceberg was—cool ice-blue with a hidden depth to them like something was beneath the surface.

"*Yup!*" I probably sounded much too cheery in his head. "*Doesn't matter. I did what I went out to do that day. Now, this. I was called out for not cleaning up my shit, and it had repercussions on others I never considered, so here I am. Trying to do better. Trying to help, no matter what the hell happens.*"

"You're a good person, Jacky. Don't ever let someone make you feel guilty for that." Heath slid off the couch and trotted over to me. Plopping down in front of me, our noses nearly touched. It was the closest I had been to the man in several months. *"Without you, who knows what would have happened to the people you've helped."*

"Thanks."

We sat quietly, and I felt comfortable with his proximity. He knew what to say and when to say it. He'd said he wanted to get to know me, and I was opening up for him, just like I promised. It didn't feel as bad as I thought it would. Instead, it was nice to talk to someone who was willing to listen and understand. It was something I had been sorely lacking in my life for a very long time. The last person who tried to understand me was...Shane. I blinked as the realization came. Hasan tried his best, but he had expectations, whether he admitted them or not. My siblings were more blatant that they didn't understand me and wanted me to be more like them.

Heath was like Shane. He just wanted me to be me around him.

We were lulled into a peaceful moment, staring at each other in our animal forms, neither of us sleeping. There was no challenge in his gaze nor any in mine—just friends keeping each other company, letting words sit between us.

Then I heard another branch snap. Baring his teeth, Heath showed he heard it as well. I lifted my head and looked around the house, but there was nothing inside with us, of course.

Another branch. Then a bush getting ruffled. The particular creak of a tree branch bending.

"Could be animals," Heath said, trying to explain away the noise. I could tell he didn't believe his own words.

"Then where are the bird calls? The insects? No...all of those left long ago because something else is here." I stood up slowly, the floor creaking.

A giggle echoed outside, and my fur stood up on end.

"Another kitty comes to play," someone hissed.

There was a scratch at the front door. Heath snarled at it.

"A wolf, too," a more masculine voice growled. "Let's not forget the wolf."

"Come out and fight us like we know you want," the first voice said. I heard the thumping of something climbing over the house. "Or we can come in."

I jumped as something scratched over the glass of a window.

"They're playing with us," Heath told me, backing away from the front door blocked by the couch. I felt his hip touch mine. *"I know we haven't fought together much, but do you remember Dallas?"*

"Yup. I won't bite you, promise."

"Thanks."

I huffed. I could understand his worry. Werecats weren't exactly experts at working with others in a fight.

There was a chance I could accidentally take a chunk out of him if I was worked up and fighting for my life.

"Scaredy cat," someone taunted. "These are our woods now. You shouldn't have come."

I wished I could talk back to them, but part of me was glad I couldn't. I didn't know if that would be playing right into their hands or not. Maybe they wanted to rile us.

I heard something jiggle and snarled and turned toward the bedroom. It sounded like someone was trying to force the window open.

"They could break in if they wanted to," Heath pointed out. *"All we can do is fight when they finally do. They want us nervous."*

I didn't reply, my eyes trained on the doorway to the bedroom. The mattress didn't move.

It felt like an eternity, hearing them run over the roof and down the walls, small jests, and taunts. Laughter as if they were having fun playing this fucked up little game.

It built in me, the rage I was feeling. These were fucking monsters. They were monsters who enjoyed the smell of fear and took joy in eliciting the response they received. They were looking to have some *fun*. I understood what had made Gaia so furious now. They had played this game with her. Maybe they did it more than once. They were trying to make her fear them, and she never did. They only got the drop on her.

I'll show them fun.

I snarled louder, making Heath step away. When the laughter didn't end, I roared, making it clear I wasn't in human form, giving out mediocre snarls to intimidate. I was ready to kill too, and they needed to think better than to break in the home I had chosen for the night.

There was no response, so I roared again, making the windows shake.

What? You don't want to play anymore?

I began to pace around the living room, making Heath step away from me. Like a caged animal, I waited for one of them to be stupid enough to break the barriers keeping us separate.

"She's an angry one," one commented finally. Scurrying again up the side of the house. "Different from the wolves."

"The werewolves got cocky, then scared. They begged for mercy," the deep masculine voice whispered just loud enough for us to hear. Heath snapped at nothing, snarling hard enough drool began to fall from his jaws, making him look rabid. "The werecats all just get pissy. It's okay, though. They all died the same."

I listened for it, and once one of them scurried down the bare wall in front of me, I slammed my body into it and listened to the fucker hit the wet ground outside and seemingly roll a few feet.

"And these two put themselves in a nice little box for us," one chittered. "How kind of them."

Annoyance ran through me. They didn't care at all. They would keep on until we went out to try to kill them, or they got their rocks off and came inside.

I heard another player enter the sick dance at that

moment. The soft, so soft, fall of paws on the soil. The vampires couldn't hear. They had no idea.

But I knew. I anxiously looked at Heath.

"I think Jabari is coming," I told him. His ears popped up as he turned in my direction. *"I can hear him, I think."*

The slow prowl in the underbrush of the woods continued. One slow paw lowered to the ground and barely disturbed the underbrush. Not enough to be picked up by anyone who wasn't paying attention, but I was listening for every sound since I had no idea what was going on outside.

"I think it's time to stop playing and deal with this. We need them to stop showing up if we want to claim the mountains as our own." An older, richer feminine voice spoke with a level of boredom I couldn't believe. She wasn't having as much fun as the others or was trying not to show it.

"Maybe we should send pieces back to the wolf pack or something. We'll use these two," the younger sounding woman suggested.

"Let's drain them first and see," the man said. Now, I had heard three voices, but it sounded like four were scurrying around outside.

"Heath, how many do you think?"

"Four."

"I think the same."

"Get ready," he ordered.

I heard more scraping on the windows, making me edgy.

The front door was wrenched open in a split second, and I turned and braced myself for an attack. There stood a man, his blood-red eyes blazing in the darkness.

"Time to see who the real superior species is," he said, his white fangs visible in the darkness. "You'll regret coming out here."

Jabari forgotten, I launched myself at him and hit. I tried to get my claws into his body and was able to sink them into one of his shoulders as we flew. In a blink, though, I was suddenly staring up at the sky and hit the mud on my back. Something tore across my side, and I swiped out blindly and connected to something. It grunted with the impact and fell off me. I rolled over, growling, and snapped the next chance I had, trying to taste the dead flesh of the vampire. I didn't have time to be glad my wild guess about being alive and scents meant it could be vampires. I just needed to kill them.

The vampire was faster, pulling away before I connected. He didn't go far as another black blur of a body slammed into him. Growling and wrestling, the noise and two bodies went into the woods. Something jumped onto my back, and nails grabbed onto the sides of my neck. I bucked and tried to shake off the attacker. Screams, both animal and human could be heard all around me.

I thought vampires weren't supposed to be as strong as us, but it felt like the fingers shoving into my neck were trying to twist my head. The fucker was trying to break my neck.

I dropped to my belly and rolled over, throwing all

my nearly five hundred pounds onto the thing on my back. It screamed and let go, shoving me as hard as it could, able to push me off. A roar made me pause as the one next to me disappeared. Jabari. That had to be Jabari.

A pained yelp came from the woods, reminding me that thoughts of Jabari had to come later. First we had to live through the fight. I followed Heath's scent, knowing it was him. A werecat didn't make the same distressed, painful cry. I knocked the vampire off him and roared. I didn't move from him to chase the vampire as it scurried into the darkness.

"Are you okay?" I asked.

"Yup. He bit me, and it was a lot more painful than I thought it would be. I was surprised." He didn't sound worse for wear, so I backed off. *"I got some strong bites into him, but he was fast. Too fast."*

"Let's get back inside."

"There's another werecat here." He stood up and started walking. We stayed close to each other, our sides brushing with each step. Keeping my ears open, all I heard that could be the vampires was them running deeper into the woods, and I had no intention of chasing them right that moment. Just getting them to run off was okay with me for now.

"It's Jabari," I told him. There was no other possibility unless the world really did want to throw me another damn loop.

We made it back to the house to see a truly massive werecat standing at the front door of the house. It was hard to make out at night, but I knew the cat. He had a deep oak brown base coat with black stripes and spots similar to my own. Not quite like a tiger's stripes, but the progenitor to modern cats. His eyes were a bright amber, and his fangs were nearly eight inches. I could guess he weighed over nine hundred pounds, all of it muscle. He dwarfed me, and that made Heath look like a puppy.

He snarled at our approach.

"Down," I ordered Heath as I sank to touch my belly to the mud. Without comment or a fight, Heath also dropped down.

Jabari snarled louder, lowering his head in anger.

"Jabari, can we take this inside?" I called out mentally.

He jerked his head back and took several steps away, backing into the house. I don't think he intended to go inside. I never told my family about my fae-gifted ability to mentally talk in my werecat form. I figured they had enough to worry about, and the fewer people who knew, the better.

He pawed at the ground and turned away after a moment. I took my chance to get up and lead Heath in. With my body, I righted the couch, but there was no door anymore.

Jabari began shifting back into his human form right in front of us. I stayed a werecat, and Heath made no move to leave his wolf form, either. When Jabari was done, just about as fast as I could Change, he stood up straight and looked between us.

"Hold. I'll make the building safe." He stomped into the kitchen and grabbed a knife.

I moved out of his way as he went to the center of the living room and began to carve a symbol into the wood floors. I had never seen anything like it before, and part of that annoyed me. I knew it was a rune of power, but I didn't know werecats could do them.

"Ah. This should work...Yes. Perfect." He leaned back to examine his work. "They won't be able to enter now." His eyes fell on me. "You shouldn't be out here, little sister. Explain." After a pause, his dark eyes narrowed on me. "In human form."

19

CHAPTER NINETEEN

I began my Change and panted softly once I was human.

"Hi, Jabari."

I tried to smile a little, but he was a fearsome man. Dark skin and a face that pointed to a rich African heritage, he was intimidating and fierce. He kept his hair short, cropped close to the skull. His nostrils flared in anger.

Heath was grunting behind us as he Changed, but neither of us bothered to look at him. I was a little wary of my older brother now.

"Start talking, Jacky," he snapped. An ancient accent I couldn't place began to change his inflection. "You shouldn't be here."

"Um...you missed your reports for a week, so a family meeting was called. I was the closest and...because you had trouble talking to the local wolf pack, I asked Heath to introduce me to see if I could take them off the list of potential suspects. Hasan agreed. I'm not here without permission." I stood up slowly and tried to turn my head to check on my wolf. I hissed in pain, and suddenly, large hands were on my cheeks. One lowered to my collar bone, and Jabari growled.

"Stupid," he said shortly. "They should have sent Hisao. I don't need the local wolf pack or information from them. I need someone who can help me kill four juiced vampires."

I winced as he poked and probed the deep punctures in my neck. The bleeding was already slowing as my body worked to correct the issue.

"Please, stop. It hurts." I tried to pull away, but he snatched my jaw and held me. "Jabari."

"I'm going to look over—"

"She said stop," Heath growled as he stood up. I tried to shake my head, warning him off without pissing off Jabari more. Instead, my older brother snarled viciously.

"You. You're supposed to be a good male. That's what I've been told at least." Jabari spit on the wood floor between them. "And yet you let Jacky come out here, and she's been hurt."

"I don't need your fucking protection," I growled this time, trying to push him away. "You wouldn't do this to Zuri or Mischa."

"I would," he snarled. "Don't act like a fool. If they were hurt like this, I would kill whatever did it without considering the consequences. I also know they wouldn't get hurt like this."

I yanked my head away harder, gasping at the pain

but able to break his overbearing hold. He cursed and reached out to me, but I stepped away from him faster and leaned on the kitchen counter near Heath.

"I'm here to help," I hissed. "I'm not here to be babied. And this isn't Heath's fault. I asked him to come with me to Washington, but he came out into these woods for his own reasons."

"What could those be?" Jabari sneered in the wolf's direction. "It seems every time you're with him, you get hurt. Obviously, I heard about Dallas. Forgive me if I don't like his presence here. Or *yours*."

"I might give you that one," Heath agreed. "But I'm out here looking into the disappearance of four wolves. I was pretty sure they were connected to the missing werecats. Those vampires had some choice things to say that confirmed it."

"Ah." He shook his head. "There are no wolves for you to find. They're all dead, I believe."

"So, you...you figured it out, or did you find them?" I watched him carefully, holding a hand over the more tender side of my neck.

"You will leave at dawn and report everything I tell you to Father." He grabbed a chair from the side of the room and sat down. His nakedness didn't bother me, but I would have appreciated him having a bit more care with it. I grabbed my shirt and jeans, pulling them on. If we were safe inside, I wasn't going to sit around naked. I handed Heath his clothing, keeping my eyes up.

"I'm not leaving these mountains without you," I replied once I was clothed and feeling a little better. "Not with those vampires out there. You said they were juiced. What does that mean?"

"It means they've been feeding off supernatural blood," he answered. "They started small, taking the wolves to boost their power. It made them strong enough and fast enough to handle Gaia and Titan as a group as long as they took them down one at a time. Now, as you can see, they're strong enough to tumble with us."

"How long have they been up here?" Heath asked, finding another chair. He gestured for me to sit down, and I took it, but not before I caught the blood on his shoulder. When I reached to touch it, so I could get a better look, he pulled away. "It's the bite, and the bleeding should stop in a few more minutes."

"Okay." I sat down without bothering him anymore. I stared at Jabari, who was staring intently at Heath. I could hear him shuffling around the kitchen, drawers being opened and closed, then water running. A few moments later, he was next to me again.

"I'm going to make sure they're clean," he said gently. I tilted my head and let his gentle hands wipe down the punctures, knowing Jabari was watching and absorbing every little detail of the scene. "So, they've been feeding on supernaturals, but why out here? None of this makes much sense. The entire pack lives in Seattle. This seems like a bad place to hunt supernaturals."

"My guess? They were thrown out of their nest or left to try out something on their own."

He sat like a soldier giving a briefing, his shoulders and back straight. Did he know how to slouch? He didn't have any visible signs of injury, but he looked thinner than the last time I saw him over seven years ago. It was an unhealthy thin, though, not like he'd shed a couple of pounds because he wanted to.

"Who cares? They killed two werecats and have been drinking from supernaturals. They broke the Law in a way that gives me full right to kill them without needing to ask anyone's permission. I've been trying to track them back to their nest for days. They don't leave a trail, which has slowed my progress."

"Ah," I frowned. "So...they came up here from wherever. They captured and killed the four wolves, draining them for a power boost, then took on the werecats. Did they drain Gaia and Titan?"

"Yes, though that wasn't reported to me by the humans," Jabari answered, smiling viciously. "They'll have to answer for that. It's pretty apparent when a body has been drained. I didn't get to see the bodies, but it's the only way to account for the vampires' power."

"I can imagine," I muttered. Heath hit a particularly sore spot, and the water made something sting like a bitch. I hissed, pulling away a little. Jabari growled a warning.

"Sorry. I saw some dirt, and I didn't want to leave it," Heath whispered. "I'm listening. You two can continue."

"So, this is Heath Everson." Jabari snorted. "Hasan said he was probably harmless." I felt Heath tense slightly. "You know, sister, if you want him out of the way so you can keep the little human girl, we can arrange that."

I snarled now. "That's not funny to joke about, *brother*."

"My son won't let you take his sister," Heath said tensely.

"Then we'll kill both of you. It wouldn't be—"

"Jabari, *stop!*" I snapped. "I like Carey, Heath, and Landon. They're good. Threatening them to get a rise is not something I'm going to tolerate. I don't want to take Carey away from anyone."

Part of me knew Jabari was just trying to rile Heath as an excuse to dismiss the wolf as untrustworthy. It was a classic move of the family—goad someone into actions they can't take back. On top of that, Jabari's insane and obvious distrust of anything wolf was clear. Jabari wouldn't kill Heath unprovoked, no matter what I wanted. The family would never kill people just so I could have Carey all to myself, but Jabari would certainly use that very scenario to bother someone.

He looked over my face and leaned back, relaxing in his seat.

"I tease, little sister."

"Oh, I fucking figured, but other people probably don't realize that."

Heath was holding the back of my neck a little too tight for me to be comfortable. He had been holding me while he cleaned out the holes. Now, I had the sneaking suspicion he was trying to hold himself back.

Or he was thinking about killing me before Jabari could kill him. Then, only Landon would get Carey, or her human mother would have to be tracked down. It was the only rational response to someone talking about killing you and giving your child away, and I was stuck in the middle of my brother and a man I considered a friend.

"Heath, are you almost done?" I asked softly. His hand relaxed.

"Yes. Let me see if they have bandages around here."

"No. You know how I feel about bandages. Makes Changing harder."

He sighed and looked between me and Jabari. "Did your family teach her that?"

"My family is her family. No, we didn't teach her that. It's an interesting idea, though, the entire problem would be easily avoided if neither of you came out here." He gave Heath a cutting smile. "Forgive me. I'm protective of my siblings, and Jacky is our most vulnerable. I want to make sure you understand if anything happens, you'll be the first one here to die if I had the choice."

"I have a daughter. I understand." Heath seemed unperturbed, but I knew better. I had known this man for long enough to know when his behavior was a careful mask. His emotions were on that tight leash, and I could smell nothing on his scent.

"You also have two sons." Jabari's change in tactics annoyed me. Now, he wanted to play a nice guy? Really?

"I have one son," Heath corrected. "I had two once but no longer."

"So, you know what it means to lose a loved child," Jabari whispered. "I'm sorry—"

"Don't offer me fake condolences. He betrayed me and tried to kill his siblings. I don't regret Jacky killing him while I was fighting for the rest of my pack. No one should." His face was blank. "Yes, I know what it means to lose a loved child, but he killed what was between us before he was ever at risk of dying. Grieve for families who don't understand each other well enough to stop something terrible from happening. That's what happened to us." His eyes flicked to me before he turned his back on us.

Jabari also caught that and narrowed his eyes on Heath's back then on me. "Hasan only told me the basics of what happened last year, probably so I wouldn't come and yell at you. Would you like to clarify?"

"It's just like Heath said..." I shrugged. "I was supposed to protect Carey and get her out of the fighting over the pack. That was my Duty, you know? I killed anyone who stood in the way of that goal."

I knew Heath's look at me was about *my* family. I didn't think I had told him too much about my relationship with my werecat father, but he had obviously inferred something that hit close to home. Something Jabari realized hit close to home.

"Well. Come dawn, you two shall leave, and there won't be any more of this violence for you, Jacky."

"I'm not leaving without you, and Heath isn't leaving until he can provide proof of the fate of the wolves who disappeared here."

"Then Heath can stay, and you're going to go. I don't need your protection, little cat." He shrugged.

"I'm not going anywhere," I said, adding strength to my words. "I'm seeing this through."

He scoffed. "There's no need. Let the family—"

"I'm part of the damn family." I swallowed on a lump of fear as he bared his teeth at me. He wouldn't reject my words, but he wasn't as soft or easygoing as Hasan was. He was the battle-hardened oldest brother and was rougher around the edges than our werecat father. "As everyone constantly reminds me, I'm part of the damn family, and that means I have responsibilities. This is part of being in the family, and I'm going to see it the fuck through. I wanted to do this, Jabari. I wanted this. I wanted to make sure I didn't cause something that got two werecats killed. I...I'm not walking out of these woods a failure."

"I have a suspicion Hasan never wanted you in these woods," he growled. "Am I wrong?"

"No, but I'm here now. I tried to check something out, and we were planning on being out of here by night fall. Things didn't go as planned."

He shook his head, looking away from me. "The smell of gasoline?"

"Yeah. The ATV's fuel line was cut, and we're pretty sure our car is in the same or similar state." I rubbed my hands together. "It was a choice between staying here or trying the car and maybe having to repair it in the dark."

"And we're too far from civilization to have just run for it," Heath added.

"Yes, you are." He frowned. "I really want to be angry with you, little sister."

"You aren't?" I raised my eyebrows.

"No. I should call you careless and stupid, but I've had my own troubles this trip. They destroyed my satellite phone on my second night out there. They cut off my contact with the outside world, and since then, it's been a back-and-forth hunt. They want me because I'm a danger to them. I want them for vengeance. I don't even know how many days I've been out here doing this, but it could take weeks before they start to weaken and need to feed again. Maybe months, depending on their age."

"So, why don't we all leave?" I asked softly. "Let them have the mountain?"

"For one, that's cowardly," he answered, grunting in disapproval. "But that's not what I think you're going for. If another werecat had shoved Gaia or Titan out of their territories, they would be expected to walk away. They lost, and it's only right they move on and let the new werecat settle in. With this, it's about more than just land. These vampires are an immediate danger to anyone who comes into this area. They aren't controlled by their Maker unless one of them is the Maker. You think if we leave, they'll live peacefully out here and cause no harm? They'll prey on humans until it becomes apparent there's a problem."

"Then everyone will wonder why they weren't killed earlier if we knew about them," Heath finished. "We could let the Seattle nest know."

"No," Jabari rejected that immediately. "I won't trust the nest. They could have tossed out their troublemakers irresponsibly and might not want the blame to fall on them. I'll see them when all is said and done."

"Have you ever been in a vampire nest?" I asked, eyes going wide. "Jabari?"

"Of course. I hate it, and I wish I could burn them in their home, but I'll go if it's completely necessary. The last time was...collecting important vampires and inviting them to meet with Father to form the Tribunal and bring peace."

"That was eight hundred years ago," I reminded him. He only shrugged. "So, can I stay without being told I'm baggage you have to protect? Because I'm going to stay."

"You will follow my orders. Both of you." He glared over at Heath. "Do you understand that, Alpha wolf?"

"I do."

"Then let's start planning our next move. With three of us, we might be able to end this sooner rather than later."

For the rest of the night, I learned why the world called Jabari the General.

20

CHAPTER TWENTY

We headed out at dawn. Jabari Changed back into his werecat form while Heath and I stayed human, wearing our clothing. The plan? Well, to start, we were going to find Jabari's clothes. He'd stashed them and wanted them back, along with the rest of his things. The only problem was it left us only being able to ask him yes or no questions while we hiked.

Heath and I remained silent for most of the morning. I checked my phone, which had been safe through the night, to find that it was nearly noon when Jabari stopped at a cliffside and looked back at us.

"Is this the short uphill part you talked about?" I looked up the cliff, frowning. This wasn't uphill. This was fucking mountain climbing.

He nodded and continued walking, and I sighed at Heath as we followed. He shrugged like it didn't bother him. He'd been eerily silent all night after the initial conversation, not arguing with Jabari or questioning anything. He just fell in line, and that bothered me. Heath was an Alpha, and he was being...submissive.

"Are you okay?" I asked softly. Jabari could hear, but I didn't care. Heath's attitude worried me. "You've been very quiet."

"I don't like him," he said with a bite. "But I'm trying not to let that get in the way of surviving."

"Oh, I don't like him all that much either," I said. "Jabari is rough and always right. He's not an easy man to know."

"I'm beginning to really understand why you avoid your werecat family. I wouldn't want to be his younger sibling, either." Heath curled a lip at Jabari's back. "He completely disrespected you the first time he opened his mouth, then expected you to fall in line and do what he ordered."

I honestly expected Jabari to growl at the comment. I saw him hesitate with his next step before continuing like nothing had been said.

"You teased me when we met. I remember some choice comments," I pointed out.

"You know what I was dealing with in Dallas. I...I respected you, though. It doesn't seem like he does, and that pisses me off."

"Heath, it's not—"

"It is a problem." He was stern about it, looking down at me, his eyes hard and unforgiving. "You deserve respect. Everyone does. No one deserves to have family who makes them feel like children or like they aren't capable, but that was exactly what he was trying to say when he was telling us to leave. That you aren't capable." He growled softly. "And the way he tried to treat your injuries? If he wanted you to think you were too soft to be out here, maybe he shouldn't have manhandled you like that."

I could only listen as Heath ranted, knowing what he said was right. Jabari was an asshole. The first thing he said when I tried to explain was to call it stupid. Like sending me was the dumbest thing he'd ever heard. Then he repeatedly tried to tell me I was going to leave without listening to me.

"He's Hasan's second-in-command," I whispered. "He's in charge of the family when Hasan isn't available. If I want to be part of the family and prove my worth, I have to put up with him."

"Or he could try to be a better fucking relative," Heath snapped. "I don't like seeing you get treated that way."

"Oh, come on—"

"I treated your injuries in Dallas, but not because you were incapable, Jacky. It was my duty to make sure you were okay because you were injured for me. That's the difference I'm trying to make clear to you. Now, I see why werecats don't have real social structures that live together the way wolves do. He's an asshole, and because he's the strongest, he gets to do whatever the fuck he wants, but I bet he doesn't actually know how to lead men." Heath's words were biting and cold, the harshest accusation one could give a man like Jabari. Jabari had led scores of men and women during the werewolf and werecat war. He led real armies long before that, when werecats got away with a lot more when it came to human cultures and societies.

They were the words that finally made the werecat stop and snarl. He turned back to us, all his teeth bared, displaying just how dangerous he was.

Heath narrowed his eyes. "You know strategy, I'll give you that, but I bet your men hated taking orders from you." Bold words from a man I hadn't expected to have such a strong reaction to Jabari.

Jabari snapped the air, a warning.

"Stop it," I ordered, deciding I had to de-escalate this before it got Heath killed. I knew just how to do it. "We're not doing this. I'm sorry I fucking asked to come out here. Let's just survive the day, damn it." I kept stomping along, leaving them behind as I continued down the trail alongside the bottom of the cliff. Once I was far enough away, they both realized I wasn't kidding. I was going to leave them behind and wander off by myself if it meant not having to deal with them fighting.

Heath's words really stuck with me, though. My older brother turned and got back out in front. Finally, he showed us a narrow path up the cliffside.

"Great." I motioned for him to continue, so he knew we were following. Heath stepped up beside me and laid a hand on my back. I ignored the touch, quickly following the giant werecat up the tree-covered cliffside.

The path was so narrow, I was scared I was going to slip. How Jabari used it, I didn't understand. Looking ahead, it seemed like he had no problem keeping himself steady. Heath stayed behind me, a protective arm ready to grab me. I looked over my shoulder at it, at him, raising an eyebrow.

"So, I'm feeling a little protective right now," he murmured. "Sue me."

"I have really good fucking lawyers," I retorted. "How are you so good at this?"

"Practice. I've gone rock climbing and hiking a lot in my life."

I pursed my lips and kept moving, apparently the only one who was having trouble keeping their balance on the narrow path. Heath didn't touch me, and I refused to say thank you for his silent support, but I appreciated it.

It only took twenty minutes to get to a small cave carved out of the mountain. Jabari trotted in, and we followed. A moment later, he came back into view, holding a large hiking bag and dropped it.

"He's going to shift back now," I told Heath softly while turning my back on Jabari.

"Are you going to try to get some sleep before tonight?" he asked, directing himself the same way, his back to my sibling.

"I don't know. You should. You have one of the more active parts of this," I reminded him.

"Yeah. Bait," Heath snorted. "I never thought I would be in the sort of company where I was the weakest creature in the room."

"It can't be good for your ego," I said, smiling a little.

Then I let the smile drop. "Don't keep pissing him off. He can and will kill you if—"

"No, I won't," Jabari cut in. "He has his opinions, and I have mine, but Hasan will have my head if I killed him without cause, even though he is just a wolf."

I sighed, looking over my shoulder to see him pulling up some pants. "He's not *just a wolf*. He's Heath Everson, a friend of mine, and he's Carey's father, who is someone important to me."

"Carey...the little human girl you protected and saved on Duty." Jabari sounded like he was trying to remember as he said the name. "Eleven years old. Human."

"That's her," Heath confirmed, keeping his back turned on him. "Nearly twelve, actually."

"No, she won't let us forget that," I muttered, smiling again. "She's not very excited, though. She doesn't know what she wants."

"She asked me for a pony last year. I'm looking into getting her a horse this year."

"That's sweet of you." I patted his shoulder.

Jabari eyed us. I didn't like the look he had, but he didn't comment.

As we stood there, I tried to broach a topic he had carefully avoided all night. I tried to bring it up when he was making our plans to take out the vampires.

"Aren't you going to ask how I telepathically talk in werecat form?"

"I don't want to know why you can speak like a wolf," he snapped. "Or what you had to do to get the power."

There was an accusing note, and I let my mouth fall

open.

"You think I would offer something or sell something in exchange for—"

"Pack magic? I don't know, would you?" he asked. "I don't want you ever using it with me again. Is that clear? I don't need you or anyone in my head."

"A fae gave me the gift," I said, growling in anger. Why couldn't Jabari just fucking talk to me? "For free because he saw me injured, desperate, and running for my life, trying to protect a girl. But fuck me, I guess. I'm just a fucking traitor to my kind for finally have an edge that would make most werewolves fucking terrified of me since I can do what they can."

"Hell, I'm still uncomfortable with it sometimes," Heath muttered.

Jabari's eyes narrowed. "Doesn't matter. It's not natural. Werecats don't have that kind of magic."

"Heath, will you go out and begin laying down your scent for the vampires to find?" I asked softly. His words were ringing in my head now, and Jabari was pissing me off, giving me a whole load of hypocrisy I couldn't tolerate.

"Certainly," he said, walking away again and back down the cliffside path.

"You sent away your little protector," Jabari noted. "He enjoys speaking up for you. We won't talk about how he protects you and probably coddles you when you make a mistake."

I snarled. "He gives a damn, at least."

"Excuse me?" My brother growled in response. "You

think I don't?"

"Maybe you should try acting like you fucking do!" I yelled at him. "No, he's right. The moment you saw me last night, you started treating me like I was no better than the mud we're covered in. And this shit about the gift I was given not being natural? What the hell kind of hypocrisy is that? I saw you draw a fucking *rune of power* just last night, Jabari, and I didn't give you shit."

"Mother taught Zuri and me how, to teach it to the family," Jabari said, his tone dangerously close to rage. "Don't you dare relate what she gave the family to whatever a fae did to you. What did this fae ask for in return? Mother asked for *nothing*."

I took a deep breath. "Brin didn't ask for anything either. He had a human wife and half human children. He said he felt for my cause."

Jabari spat on the ground. "Where did you find him?"

"At some random motel. I was looking for a place to hide with Carey." His eyes told me he didn't believe me. I stepped closer, opening my arms. "Smell the truth on me, Jabari! Smell it! I'm not fucking lying to you! I have no goddamn reason to lie to you!" With a shaking breath, I went back to what else he'd said. "She taught you and Zuri for the family? To pass down?" I tried not to laugh. Neither of them ever taught me. I had no idea they even knew how to do them, not until Jabari did one. I thought it was a small trick he had, like my fae gift. "You never taught me."

"You left too young," he hissed. "You walked away from the family."

"Hasan knew where to find me. It's not like any of you really cared at the time," I said bitterly. "It's not like you gave a damn what I did or where I went. You thought I was throwing a fucking tantrum and told me so."

"You were."

"He was the love of my life. And see, that's the problem. You don't even fucking try with me. You don't *care* about *anything* to do with me." I sniffed, trying to hold back the pain. My neck hurt, but my muscles were tense as I tried to keep from crying from frustration and rejection. "Hasan spent four years telling me about how he was my family and how you and the rest of them were my fucking family now. *I ate it up.* I tried, and every time I saw any of you, you were cold to me, wary like I had done something wrong. And right when I fucking needed any of you to have a heart, you all told me to get the fuck over it." I pointed at him, stepping closer and stabbing his chest with the finger.

"Then *you* fucking called *me* and gave this big fucking talk about how you all were going to try to be in my life again. You were going to try and keep me in the loop. You also called me a fuck up. But I'm fucking here, aren't I? Being a contributing member of this godforsaken family." I sneered the best I could. "All I got from you was how *stupid* of an idea it was for the family to send me."

He didn't say anything, stepping back from my finger, his gaze on it like I had just stabbed him. When he looked up, I could see the confusion and anger in his eyes and the lines of his face.

"Now, you don't get to be an asshole to me anymore. Oh cool, you know runes of power. Everyone else in the family knows runes of power. Fun. You know what? Fuck it. I don't need them. I'll keep doing everything fucking my way."

"Stop behaving like a child," he said quietly as I went to turn away from him.

"A *child*?" I hissed, spinning back on him. "You think this is me acting like a *child*? You think the last seven years have been one giant tantrum of a child who can't take care of herself?" I snarled louder, rage building in my chest. "I run a fucking business. I keep my house clean. I pay my taxes. I do it all on my own with help from only the few people any respectable business owner would get help from, like a goddamn accountant and a lawyer. When called to Duty, I didn't go crying to anyone for help or to take the charge from me or to protect me. I did what I had to do. I asked for advice because I'd obviously never done it before, but I didn't ask *Father* to come and save me. I didn't ask him to come to the Tribunal and threaten to expose us just to save me. I took responsibility for what I did like a fucking adult should, and I was willing to die on that hill *alone*. You don't get to call me a child for telling you the truth. You're a heartless prick, Jabari. You wouldn't know love, affection, or kindness if it slapped you in the face."

"I'm not entertaining this," he declared, trying to walk past me now. "I'm going—"

"When did you teach our siblings how to protect themselves with runes of power?" I asked as he passed by.

"When they moved into their new homes," he answered. "It was the first thing we did before they moved their things in. I taught them, then walked them through it, so we all knew the home was safe."

"Think about that. You could have shown up at any point in the last seven fucking years to teach me, and you chose not to. And Hasan never forced you to come, either. He didn't even tell me about them. Does he even know you never came?"

Jabari didn't answer, walking away and out of the cave. I was left exhausted, my rage leaking out once he was out of sight. I leaned against a wall in the cavern and slid down, tears in my eyes.

I lost my human family the day I was supposed to die. For four years, I craved everything Hasan offered me— this new family. They rejected me once, based on history I had no part in. They hurt me by being callous and mean about the revelation Hasan let my fiancé die. Finally, after seven damn years, they approached me, and I opened up, just like Hasan suggested. I was again throwing myself into the effort of being one of them and Hasan's daughter. I was trying to be part of the world they loved so much.

And once again, I found myself against a brick wall I found to be insurmountable. I couldn't climb it. I couldn't change who I was to gain entry to the sanctuary beyond it. I couldn't knock it down.

All I could do was scream until someone finally heard me, and just like last time, the gatekeeper refused to listen.

21

CHAPTER TWENTY-ONE

I busied myself after drying my eyes, looking through what Jabari had brought with him into the mountains. Nothing for food, but that didn't bother me. I'm sure we were all hungry, but if everything went to plan, we would have food in our stomachs soon enough. What he did have was rope, a fire-starting kit, more than a couple of knives, an extra folded black bag, and water. I took the water and checked it. He still had some left, so I took a sip. We could all handle dirty water out of streams and lakes without getting sick, but fresh, clean water was much better.

I didn't keep track of the time they were gone. Heath came back first, which made me feel relieved. He didn't seem happy, though, or comfortable.

"Where did he go? The rule was only one of us out of the cavern at a time." Heath sniffed, his nostrils flaring. Then his eyes narrowed, obviously upset. "What happened?"

"We had an argument. Or I yelled at him until he decided he didn't want to listen to it anymore." I gave him a desperate look. "I don't want to talk about it."

"I...heard some of it," he admitted. "I walked away as the volume rose. I didn't want to intrude. I didn't think he would leave."

"I can handle being alone just fine," I said with a snap Heath probably didn't deserve from me.

"Yes, but he didn't come find me and only one person out of the cave at a time was his rule," Heath growled back.

I felt bad. "I'm sorry. He's frustrating and...I don't know how to deal with him. I should have just let Hisao come out here. I should have stayed out of all of this."

"Would you have been happy with someone else coming out here? If I remember right, you wanted to help fix this because you felt guilty. You and many others were worried this was some form of backlash over last year." He shoved his hands into his pockets, which didn't make him seem as relaxed as he probably wanted it to. He seemed tense.

"This entire trip has been about me and my problems...You're right. I wanted this and would have felt...worthless if I hadn't come out and helped when I could."

"It's fine. When we met, everything was about me and my problems," he reminded me, a small smile breaking out. "I'm just glad to get to know you."

"And I still know so little about you."

This time, he shrugged. "Maybe next time."

"Har har," I said, reaching out to slap his abdomen lightly. He dodged, quickly grabbing my wrist, and tried to pull me to him. I put my heels down and held to my spot, refusing to budge.

"Stubborn."

"Look in a mirror," I countered. He started to laugh, nodding.

"If we survive this, I'll start telling you about myself; your turn to play twenty questions."

"Like, why you feel the need for a werecat's permanent protection over Carey?"

"I've lived long enough to make enemies. I figured that one was obvious."

"Really? Nooo. I want more details than that next time." I grinned, waiting for him to either deny me or relent.

He didn't say anything for a minute. "I'm glad you're smiling again. Don't let that asshole make you feel bad. If he can't treat you right, he doesn't deserve the privilege to call you family or the ability to make you upset."

I swallowed, nodding slowly. That wasn't what I was expecting. Why did it feel like Heath was never what I expected?

"Why are you so adamant about my relationship with my family?" I asked after another moment of quiet.

"Because it pisses me off. I fucking hate seeing people treat others like that when it's supposed to be the place you find support. I told you, my sister was a Tory. Fell in love with a Red coat, and we lost contact, but I was never cruel to her. She was my sister. I...*hated* Richard that night. For one moment, I realized he was everything that pissed me off about people, and I wasn't sure how I had a son that would treat his younger siblings that way. For what? Jealousy? That's petty, and I don't tolerate petty. I don't know where I went wrong, raising him to make him behave that way."

"I don't think you did," I told him softly, taking my hand away slowly. "I think he shut you out. He was a grown ass man who decided to dwell on feelings that were unhealthy and wrong. He built up all the wrongs, instead of looking at the good things."

"You think that might be what happened between you and...them?" He moved to lean on a wall in the cavern.

"I don't know, actually. They were never welcoming. I like to think I tried, but..." I hadn't told him everything. I didn't want to rehash it all right then. "Next time."

"Next time," he agreed. "You know, my family would welcome you if you ever needed it."

"Thanks." I blinked back tears. "I mean, the holidays were uncomfortable for all of us, let's be real, but it was nice for someone to think of me." These past holidays, I had stopped in at Carey's request for Thanksgiving and Christmas dinner with the Everson family. Both times had been awkward, but the invitations mattered. They meant something.

"You're welcome to spend them with my family. For as long as you need to. Carey's right about it, and I should have thought to offer before she annoyed me into it. No one deserves to be alone during the holidays." He chuckled. "They were uncomfortable, but we were all still very new to each other."

"We were." I smiled a little. "You cook a mean turkey, though."

"Ah, thank you. Thank you." He gave a little bow. "I would hope so since I've been making Thanksgiving dinners since it was declared a national holiday."

I couldn't help but laugh. "Oh, but you need help with your sides. Your mashed potatoes are bland."

"Fine. You can make them this year and teach me better."

We both laughed at that. Then I heard the stomping of Jabari coming back.

"Fuck," I muttered. "Here he comes. We've been too happy for a split second, so he's got to come crush it and keep us on task."

"How old is he, really?"

"Born BC, at least three and a half thousand at my best guess," I said in a whisper for only him. He nodded.

Jabari walked in like a fucking storm rolling in. He looked at the pair of us standing off to the side of the cavern, then down at his bag near my feet.

"Who went through my things?"

"I did. I wanted to see what we had to work with. You'll survive. I put it all back after taking a very small sip of water, which you can deal with."

He bared his teeth but quickly pulled back his anger. "That's right, you two don't have supplies. There's a stream deeper into the cavern. I'll show you."

"Thank you." Jabari walked by us, and I gave Heath a

look, telling him everything I thought of my dear older brother. He snickered and put a hand on my lower back. With a small push, I was forced to follow Jabari, Heath right behind me.

We journeyed further into the cavern until I heard running water, and Jabari pointed out the small stream in the dark. I really should have gone deeper into the cave on my own to find it earlier, but it hadn't been on my mind.

"It's mountain runoff. Cleaner than most streams. I'm going to build a small fire," my older brother explained before stomping back to the mouth of the cave. I went to a knee, scooping water in my hands to drink. Heath did the same next to me, sighing with relief as the cool water ran down his chin. I looked back at my hands and went for a second drink as he splashed his face and ran wet hands through his hair. I did the same thing once my thirst was sated, wiping mud, grime, and blood from the night before off my face. There was nothing to be done about my hair, though. As long as it stayed in the ponytail, I wasn't going to fret over it.

We went back to the mouth of the cavern to find Jabari working to strike the fire.

"Everything is wet here," he muttered in annoyance. "We might have to go fireless if I can't get this started."

"It's fine. It's not like any of us will freeze," I said casually.

"I want us easy to find," he retorted. "They're juiced, and if they've been draining people and killing them, they're probably also high from it. They won't be smart enough to resist coming in here after us with little protection."

"You aren't going to do a little rune just for the cavern?" I frowned as I sat across from him, looking over his stack of wet firewood to catch his gaze. "We don't plan to fight them in here, right?"

"We'll fight them in here," he confirmed. "It's blocked off, and if they go deeper into the caverns, it's all dead ends. We can get them cornered and kill them if they try to escape the sun behind us. If they escape, they'll be severely injured and much easier to track."

"Are there any more in Titan's territory?" I wanted to know there wasn't going to be more of this. That there weren't half a dozen other vampires out there.

"From my investigation, they have stayed in this region for a while. When they went to Titan's territory, it was only to kill him. He lived even further from human civilization than Gaia. From here, they have the road, the small towns further down the mountains, and a lot more campers and hikers." He sighed. "They probably saw him on a visit to Gaia and realized they couldn't kill her without him coming after them. He was the older, more powerful one, so they killed him first."

"To make sure their other plans went the way they intended," Heath clarified for me.

"Yeah..." I rubbed my hands together nervously. "That means one of them is in charge and not..."

"Yes. There are two females. One of them is a little more put together, but don't let that fool you. She's just as insane as the others. I left the scent of my blood once, and she lost it. Wild eyed, feral, and hungry."

"But if they've been feeding so often off supernaturals..." I tried to put it together, the way he obviously did. I didn't have a few thousand years of experience.

"It's called a blood craze. They've grown addicted to the kill, which is why I say they're probably high beyond just being juiced up on supernatural blood. It's frowned upon. Vampires don't have to kill, and when they do, they get a rush. It's exciting, some even liken it to an orgasm." Jabari's words were professional and cold, revealing none of his personal feelings about what the vampires were doing. "From my understanding, every young vampire has a bad incident or two losing control. The nest cleans it up and continues their training to prevent further accidents. It's not against the Law for them to regularly feed on humans to the death, but it's frowned upon. No nest that wants to stay safe and hidden will allow their vampires to kill indiscriminately. Werecats, werewolves, and other species have been known to wipe out nests for being uncontrolled."

"So, these four are addicted to the rush of killing their prey and have eaten who knows how many people, four werewolves, and two werecats. Are you sure you don't want to put a rune of power on the cavern?"

He frowned at me. "Are you worried?"

"I think we need a backup plan," I said, shrugging. "We need somewhere to retreat to if we're injured. Have you not been doing that?"

"I ran until daylight, and they were forced to retreat," he explained. "But I can see the purpose of a safe zone for us." His jaw was set, taut until he stood up. "Let's go. We'll pick a back area, and you can watch me make it for us."

I raised an eyebrow at his back as he began walking off again. This time, I scrambled to keep up, Heath not nearly in so much of a rush. Jabari stopped at a dead end, nodding. It was a little thing, something one of us could lay out in and hide if needed. We would be seen, but if Jabari did that thing again, we could be safe.

"Jacky, come here," he ordered, pointing beside him.

I bared my teeth but went. He pulled out a knife and scratched a line around the mouth of the little area. I watched intently, seeing he was making a divide of sorts.

"This will keep the rune working in this area. Scratched from the same silver blade, it stops the power from affecting the entire cavern. You can do this to rooms as well by marking a door frame, for example." He knelt and scratched in the same rune as he had in the cabin. "Now, no creature of demonic origin or essence will be able to enter this space. It will burn them with pain beyond imagining if they cross it, and they will die within a few steps if they push through."

"Demonic?" Heath spoke up from behind me.

"Yes. Vampires are humans corrupted with demonic energies, thanks to an old curse on their kind. Some say it was supposed to ravage the entirety of mankind, but it never grew. So, quickly and whenever there was an overpopulation of vampires, many other supernaturals culled their numbers. We've never been able to eradicate them and finally, we let them build their own culture and societies as long as they didn't grow too big."

"You talk like you were there when they came into existence," I commented.

"I was. So were Father and Zuri."

The blood left my head. "What?"

"They originated in Mesopotamia," he informed us softly. "About three hundred years after I was born in Africa with Zuri. Father wanted to take us to see other cultures since we had spent so long living with a variety of different tribes in Africa. It had to have been..." He looked away, and I wondered what sort of mental math he was doing. "Two thousand BC? Yes, that must be it. Human civilization was still trying its hardest, and it was growing all around the world. Different tribes were appearing. Hasan once disappeared for a hundred years and explored what would later be known as North and South America. How he got here, I don't know, but he brought back many things for us to wonder at." He stopped, closing his mouth abruptly.

"Please continue," I asked softly.

"Well, we arrived in Babylon, and there were humans, of course. They looked more like Father than Zuri and I, as we take after Mother. In the hundred years we stayed there, we noticed things, bodies beginning to show up, drained of their blood. We tracked down what did it, and it was a fight, but we succeeded."

"You were there during the appearance of vampires,"

Heath whispered in awe. I looked over my shoulders to see how wide his eyes were. Mine probably matched.

"I don't know the exact circumstances, but we'd already known demons existed. From a different plane, a different world, they're monstrous, cruel, and could never be trusted. We knew the signs of them and saw those signs on the human-looking thing we had killed. It took a little testing, but we discovered our runes against demons worked for vampires as well, finalizing the connection between them."

"How do you know it's a curse?" I wrapped my arms around myself.

"It was just our theory," he explained. "But it was the best one we ever came up with. Within a century, other werecats were finding them in their own territories. Within five hundred years, they had infected the entire world. The original vampires were much more vicious and dangerous than the ones you will meet today. Ones in these modern times keep their humanity better than those who showed up in the first five to six hundred years. They quickly became feral, death addicted beasts, while today, they fight much harder and last much longer against it." He waved the conversation away. "Enough of that. I would teach you the runes of power needed for this now, but if you were to mess them up, we would lose precious time. When we're done here, I shall go to your home with you, and we will make sure you have all the protections the family can provide."

"Ah...it's not necessary, Jabari. Like I said, I can live on my—"

"Yes. You are very adamant you can do it on your own, having done it for seven years without major problems while no one knew you were a member of our family. I will teach you." He was snappy again. "That is final."

I groaned as he stomped away. "I can't win with this man, Heath. I just can't win with him."

"Seems like."

I walked past Heath, following the ancient man who was supposed to be my brother but instead, was just a pain in my ass.

"Can you believe that? He was there when vampires popped into fucking existence," I muttered as we walked after Jabari. "I didn't have any idea. I knew he was older than fucking dirt, but fuck, that's old."

"Imagine the things he's seen," Heath whispered, agreeing with me. "Too bad he's an asshole. I don't care that he's from a different time when it comes down to it, though. He needs to act better."

"You aren't going to let that go, are you?" I asked.

"No. Not when every time he talks to you, I can fucking imagine the blade cutting at you. I can see the fucking hurt flash in your eyes with every word that comes out of his mouth when he's not dismissing you completely." Heath curled a lip, mimicking a look I had seen earlier on his face. I rarely saw him disgusted and angry like this and never while in my territory—frustrated, yes, a bit pissed off with me, certainly, but nothing like the level of distaste he had for Jabari.

"Well, please, let it go for the rest of this. I just want

to get through the night alive and out of the forest without having to break you two up. I said my piece, and that's all. If he wants to follow me home to teach me something he should have taught me seven years ago, he can do that. I'm not going to fight with him anymore." I was too fucking tired to fight with him and knew it would escalate if I rejected him further. He would tell Hasan I was denying protections the rest of the family used, which would then let Hasan know I never had them to begin with, and who knew what *that* would lead to.

We made it back to the mouth of the cave, and Jabari got the fire going finally. We took places around it, watching it go, and when the quiet proved too much for me, I decided to continue asking him questions.

"How old is Hasan?"

"You need to ask him," he replied. "Every one of us has had to confront that question on our own. Consider it tradition, one he enforces."

"Damn," I sighed. "Can you tell me if he's the first of our kind?" Were all the werecats technically his in the end?

"No, he's not. They're all gone now, but we had known older. He's just the oldest left. He's from early on, I can tell you that. It took me a century to ask him. Zuri and I confronted him together about where he came from. Mischa took two hundred years. Davor asked immediately, refusing to believe he didn't know something and couldn't work it out on his own. Everyone has their own timeline about asking Hasan about himself.

He's not...an easy father to have," Jabari conceded in the end.

"No." I pulled my knees up and laid my head on them. "And this isn't an easy family to be a member of."

Jabari visibly winced that time.

22

CHAPTER TWENTY-TWO

The sky grew darker outside the cavern. Sometime during the afternoon, I napped, leaning against the rough rock wall. Heath woke me up and offered something I wasn't expecting—meat.

"Rabbit. I went out and caught a couple before it got too late," he explained. "I cooked it as best I could."

"Would have eaten it raw," I said, chuckling. "Thanks."

I took whatever the body part was he offered and bit into it. Gamey and tough, I had to pull the meat from the bone, but it was calories I was certain everyone needed. Jabari quietly sat across the cavern, ignoring us, but I could see the clean bones beside him on the ground. If he did what Hasan always trained me to do, he would bury the carcass. I was lazy about it, but this wasn't my territory where I could manage who was or wasn't on my property. Leaving evidence was a bad idea.

Heath sat next to me, leaning back on the wall as well, chewing on his own pieces.

"Did you get enough?" he asked loudly, obviously directed at Jabari.

The ancient werecat turned to us and nodded. "Thank you. It will be good to have less of an empty stomach for tonight."

"Have you been eating?" I had been a little concerned about how thin he was since I had seen him in the cabin.

"I hunted for small prey when I had time, but most days, I needed to sleep so I could continue the hunt for the vampires," he explained, eyeing me. "You haven't eaten since you've been out here until now, have you?"

"No. Like I said last night, we weren't planning on making this a camping trip. We were supposed to be back in a town by nightfall, with hot food and water," I sighed.

"Then, you need to finish that." He pointed at the piece of rabbit in my hands. I made a point to show him the bite I'd already made and then took another, chewing loudly. Heath huffed, a smile coming over his face.

His closeness made me comfortable in the strange situation we found ourselves. This was the second time my wolf and I found ourselves in a tough place and knowing he and I had survived before made me hopeful we would again.

"Do you think Carey is worried?" I asked softly. "About both of us?"

"Yes, if Landon told her. If he didn't, she'll pick up on his mood and figure out something is wrong. What about your family? You promised not to go into the woods and to call in every night."

"They're probably pissed..." I shook my head, realizing that was probably wrong. "No. Some of them are probably pissed. At least one will think I've gotten myself killed and not care, and a few might be worried, but they'll probably also say 'I told you so.' Hasan will be worried and angry, but more worried. His anger will be his focus once he knows Jabari and I are both alive and back to safety."

"Why would anyone say I told you so?" Heath's brows lowered and came together, framing his intense eyes. He obviously didn't like what I had to say.

"I'm the American daughter. The one who...does everything wrong or something. I was told not to come out into these woods, and I did, thinking I could get away with it. Here we are. Once they have me on a call, I'm going to hear about it."

"How..." Heath blew out a frustrated breath. "How do they ever expect you to be one of them if they don't give you the chance to grow?"

I shrugged. Hasan was right when I had spoken to him on the phone. I flourished when I wasn't around the family, especially my siblings—the ones who made me feel small and treated me even smaller.

He didn't continue questioning me. We sat quietly, chewing on fire roasted rabbit in dirty clothes as the sun was falling. The sky was growing darker, and it was time to put my personal issues aside. It was comforting to have one person who understood where I was coming from. Heath was insulted on my behalf, and that was a relief.

When the sun was finally completely gone, Heath dared to ask one more question.

"Why doesn't Hasan deal with them and help you?"

"I don't...really know," I admitted. "I know that in Changing me, they resented him a little too. Maybe he just hasn't found the right way to bring the family back together." Jabari snorted. I threw up my hands in defeat. "Okay, Jabari, tell me what you know. I'm only relaying what Hasan told me."

"Nothing," he said tightly.

"No, please. You obviously have a thought."

"We did resent him, but I didn't resent him because you were too soon after Liza's death. Davor probably does, but not me. I resent he made you by breaking all the rules he had placed on the family. He didn't raise you. He isn't your father in your heart the way he is for everyone else. I consider all my siblings equally, blood or not, because I know he took them in as babes and children, bringing them into this family as my siblings, and they only ever knew this family. I resent him for making you and expecting us to care for you as a sibling when we'd never even heard of you." Jabari looked back over at us. "He didn't even get your permission to join this world. You still don't know whether you want it, and because of that, you do as you please, living the life you want without considering other werecats follow rules for a reason. That's why I resent him...and you."

I didn't miss the change in his tense. His resentment

wasn't past tense. He still resented that I was in the family...could possibly always resent my existence.

"Then why did your family help her with the Tribunal if you don't want her?" Heath asked, once again growling as he spoke. "Sounds like you would be just fine with her—"

"Don't say those words, wolf," Jabari snarled. "Don't ever say those words. I might resent him for making her, and I might resent her, but I will *never* abandon a family member to *die*. None of us are that cruel."

"I could have told you that," I muttered to Heath. "Don't push his buttons, *please*."

Heath huffed, shaking his head. Jumping up, he walked away, frustration apparent in every line and angle of his posture.

"And you, Jacky, hang with wolves," Jabari muttered. "The only reason I don't consider that a betrayal to the family is because you didn't fight in the War, nor were you alive when Liza died. He's not the worst wolf, but he's certainly not one I want around. He's moral and strong, but he doesn't know when he's not the strongest male in the room or when something isn't his business."

"Not every wolf is the bad guy or the enemy," I whispered, rubbing my arms as the night grew chilly. "He's not a bad guy."

He grumbled in disagreement but didn't try to say anything against it either.

"Change. They will come soon."

I stripped and did as ordered without an argument. Tonight was important. Nothing could go wrong. If that meant he and I had to stop arguing for a night, we would. I was willing to let him ignore me for another seven years if it meant getting through the damn night.

"Remember, it will be okay if one or two get away. We're aiming to capture one, use it to find any remaining vampires and find out where they came from." Jabari continued to talk, and I could hear the old general in him. "Keep them from getting on your back. Like always, that is our biggest vulnerability except for our underbelly. I don't want them to get their hands into those wounds again, either."

I nodded as I walked up to the mouth of the cavern and stared out into the trees. Even though we had hiked up the cliffside to get into the cavern, the trees were tall enough I couldn't see the tops. While I watched the entrance, Jabari Changed. Heath was the only one staying in human form for the night. We needed someone with opposable thumbs to help restrain the captured vampire.

The plan wasn't difficult. Jabari was certain the vampires wouldn't be able to resist coming after us again, even though we chased them off the night before. We were a threat to whatever they were trying to establish, and it was either them or us dying in these mountains under the light rain that now refused to stop. If Jabari's assumption about their killing addiction was correct, they weren't in the right mind to truly consider what possible risks they were facing.

Which meant all we had to do was injure them as

best we could before they retreated, and keep one from leaving.

"I'm ready," Heath called out from near the fire. Jabari huffed and jumped out of the cavern, leaving us alone. I stepped back from the entrance, going into the darkness behind Heath to lie in wait. Our scents were around everything, which would make it hard for the vampires to tell which of us was actually in the cavern. Their noses weren't nearly as good as ours.

The night grew darker until it blanketed the world, the only light from the fire. The cloud cover and rain blocked out the moon and stars, making the world outside the cavern seem just as dark as the cavern where I was hidden. I knew everyone could see well enough, but it was still a pitch black night, and Jabari had said the vampires wouldn't be hindered by it. Their eyes were even better than ours in the dark.

It felt like an eternity. I worried they would never show. Heath moved around the cavern, tending the fire and checking Jabari's things. He toyed with a silver knife while the fire blazed. He made sure there was always wood drying nearby, ready to go into the flames when it was needed.

And we waited.

"I hate this," I said, echoing the night before. *"Do you think Jabari is okay out there?"*

He sighed and shrugged. He wouldn't speak unless it was absolutely necessary. With his indifferent posturing, I understood his answer. He thought so, but he mostly didn't care. Well, he might have cared if it meant we were going to survive, killing the vampires who took so many, but he didn't care about Jabari.

I couldn't find anything else to ask, so I went back to waiting in silence. Like the night before, the world was too quiet, aside from the rain. Maybe it was the rain that made the world seem silent, though I figured there were probably a number of creatures that were supposed to be making all their nightly noises.

Instead, it was just rain on stone and tree, our only comfort.

Until I heard the first of several branches snap and break, creaking of wood under weight, trees rustling.

"They're coming," I told him. Heath tensed but continued to pretend he was doing something important and tending the camp. The idea was for him to seem as if he was keeping everything nice while Jabari and I went out and hunted the vampires. They would come after us because they had to, but first they would take advantage of Heath being 'alone.'

Jabari was out there, hiding and waiting. He was going to block off their escape once they came inside. I was going to engage inside and protect Heath if he needed it. Jabari had made it clear, under no uncertain terms, he wouldn't purposefully get Heath killed, but then said Heath was best off being the one in human form because werewolves were weaker than werecats.

Which meant my brother had put one of my few friends and allies in the prime spot to get killed. If someone was going to be considered an easy target, it was going to be the person without their fangs and claws out.

Heath stood up and stretched, giving a fake but believable yawn. I could smell no exhaustion on him. He seemed well rested, just like I felt.

"Oh, look," someone said outside the cave. "Did they leave you to die, wolf? Were you not important enough?" The vampires were suddenly at the mouth of the cave, all four grinning, a little sick, a bit twisted, and very excited about what they saw in front of them. "Or did they think you were worthless in their hunt for us? Foolish of them. That makes them terribly outnumbered, and we've proven ourselves against two werecats already."

"You didn't fight the ones you killed in their true forms. The Moon Cursed are more powerful as beasts," he said softly. "And the cats are the most powerful of all."

"We can kill them once we have fresher blood," the younger man explained, shrugging away Heath's comment. "Our last wolf is weak. You'll be a worthy replacement."

I watched Heath's body snap to attention in a second. I could tell he wanted to jump for them and attack. My heart ached for him for a second.

They still have a wolf alive. It's probably killing him to know that.

And my heart burned for the poor wolf who must have been their captive for a month, a replenishing food source that made them more powerful than normal. He was probably starved and dying by now.

The leader, the more mature woman, stepped in further, but the others didn't. She didn't seem to have a worry in the world.

"Come on, wolf. You know you've lost. You can't beat all four of us. We're going to feast on you. Just make this easier on yourself, and the rest of your days can be comfortable." Her words were sickeningly sweet like poisoned candy. "The other wolves tried to fight, and we made them each beg for death by the end. The last one will know only misery in his final moments, but you don't have to."

"You taste so good, too," the little woman said, a mad giggle escaping her lips.

"I don't beg," Heath said with a small smile. "I'm an Alpha. Others beg me."

There was a coldness to his words that made me want to shiver. It was that Alpha power he would have for the rest of his life because he had already proven himself worthy of the role.

Never forget, he retired willingly, Jacky. He's just as much of an Alpha right now as he was the day you met him. He knows how to survive and come out on top.

"Oh? Would you like us to beg you for the privilege to kill you?" The leader laughed serenely. "You have fallen low, Alpha. There's no pack to protect you here." She waved in her companions. "Come. Let's feed. Once he's incapacitated, we can go kill the werecats, and these mountains will be ours."

Heath didn't move, letting the vampires approach him. They continued to come closer and closer, confident he was alone. I knew if they came too close, they would finally see me. My dark hideaway would only work for so long.

"I have something better than a pack," Heath finally whispered as the leader was only five feet from him. "Jabari, now!"

I jumped out, knowing the order was also for me. I landed behind Heath, snarling viciously. The leader jumped back a step, her eyes wide as I heard the thump of Jabari landing in the mouth of the cave. The younger looking woman screamed, jumping toward her leader.

"It's a trap! They tricked us!" she screamed. The younger man's mouth dropped open, and I saw he had no tongue. That was why he never spoke.

"Kill them!" the leader shrieked. "Kill them now!"

I roared in time with Jabari, causing small chunks of the ceiling and walls to crumble off from the echoing vibration.

We were done playing hide-and-seek.

23

CHAPTER TWENTY-THREE

I leapt forward as Heath jumped to the side to get out of my way. My target was the leader who reached for Heath, so she couldn't get away. I slammed into the leader, who screamed as my fangs met their mark in her upper arm. With a yank, I heard bones break and dislocated her arm. While she screamed, I shook my head viciously, trying to tear the limb off. Something slammed into my head, causing black spots to appear in my vision. I let go of her and felt someone kick me in the side, and nails ran across my hide. I swiped at the second attacker, scoring flesh and earning a scream in return.

"Jacky! Above!" Heath yelled.

I looked up as best I could and saw the leader had climbed up onto the ceiling, hissing. I jumped aside as she fell for me, trying to get on my back. She couldn't make a grab, and I spun, putting my back end to the wall, so I could see them all in front of me.

Toward the mouth of the cavern, Jabari was snapping and snarling as he tangled with the older man and the young woman. That left me with the leading female and the mute, both enraged and staring directly at me. That was good. It meant Heath could back off and stay safe while we worked on the vampires, weakening them to run or capture.

And if I killed one or two in the process, no one was going to be mad.

I snarled, my hackles rising as I lowered my head. I didn't wait for them to make the first move, pouncing forward. They both dodged, and I spun around to meet them again. The mute tried to grab for me, and I slammed my body into the wall, shaking him off. The leader slashed her wicked nails at my left flank. Since I wasn't a horse, kicking backward wasn't a very effective move. I tried to snap back at her, but she jumped away, hissing.

Before I could go after her again, arms wrapped around my neck. I snarled, shaking, and trying to get them off as they began to squeeze. I had no idea how Jabari was doing or where Heath was. The arms grew tighter, and my head began to spin. Where I had been hit began to throb painfully.

Then they relaxed as something screamed. I jerked away and found the mute with a silver knife in his back, trying to grab it. Silver wasn't special to killing vampires; sunlight and fire were best. Draining them completely only put them to sleep until someone gave them blood.

But a knife still fucking hurt, and I could see Heath reaching for it to go for another attack. The mute noticed him, but I wasn't able to intervene before the leader attacked, jumping onto my back.

I ducked my head down, trying to keep her nails from clawing out my eyes as she raged at me. I bucked wildly, hoping her grip with her legs would loosen as I made it to a wall. I jumped into the wall, letting my side slam into it with full force. It knocked the air out of me, and I heard more bone crunch as the vampire's leg was nearly crushed between me and the stone. She slid off me, screaming, but when I turned to get a bite, aiming to rip her head off, the mute was back on me. He held my jaw open, refusing to let me clamp down. And I was trying.

Then he started to push my mouth open, and I struggled, trying to pull away. When he dug his heels in, I couldn't move him. I tried pushing him next, but he moved with me, directing me with his grip on my jaw. He had one hand digging into my nose and pulling up and the other pushing my lower jaw down. I couldn't swipe him because of the angle he had, standing beside me.

For a second, I knew I was going to die if I couldn't figure out what to do. The best idea I had?

"HELP!" I screamed in my head to everyone, knowing my jaw was about to break. There was a chance the vampire was going to rip my entire snout off.

"BUCK HIM OFF, JACKY!" Heath roared over the commotion. I had no idea where he was or what he was doing, but I hoped he was fucking alive after everything because I wanted to thank him.

I reared up onto my hind legs, an unnatural stance for a werecat, bringing the little vampire up with me, his feet leaving the ground. Because he lost his ability to plant them, he couldn't hold my jaw open anymore. I snapped it closed, taking off several of his fingers from the hand holding my bottom jaw. His inhuman scream didn't bother me as I dropped back to my front feet, swinging my head to send him flying.

At the same time, a woman screamed near me. I turned my head to find the leader reeling back from Heath, who had deep punctures in his neck, openly bleeding. The leader was staring at her left hand, and it took me a full second to figure out what was wrong with it.

Heath had broken her wrist so effectively, her hand was backward on her arm and useless. He snarled, fur beginning to show on his face. He lunged for her, stabbing a silver knife into her chest. Her eyes went wide as he pulled it out. The blood loss would counteract whatever she had gotten from him.

I rushed for them, barreling into her. Something connected with my side and knocked me and her to the wall away from Heath.

"Run, Heath. Go for the shelter!" I screamed. *"Go!"*

I don't know if he listened as I rolled around with two vampires, each trying for my most vulnerable places. The mute was slower and weaker than he had been, trying to rip my head open, but his attacks on my abdomen were furious. The leader was still trying for my eyes. I pulled my back legs in and swiped out with them, mimicking a move one saw house cats do often. I tore someone open, and by the style of the scream, I figured it was the mute.

"No!" the leader screamed. "No!"

I continued to kick, shredding flesh and muscle and organs under my back claws until the vampire stopped trying to attack me, and there was only whimpering left from the body next to me.

"Retreat!" the leader screamed, jumping away from me. "Run!"

I heard screams toward the entrance and turned to follow the running woman. Jabari latched onto her, growling. The other two were already gone. He yanked hard onto the arm I already mangled, and I heard the tearing and popping of it being torn off. She screamed and slashed out at his face, scoring several lines over his snout and nose. She was already disappearing into the darkness by the time I made it to the mouth. Jabari stepped in front of me, shaking his big head, the arm still in his mouth.

I panted heavily, looking back to see what we had. The mute. Damn. He wouldn't be able to give us any information. I backed away from the mouth of the cavern, Jabari with me after he dropped the arm.

I looked around the cavern, blood everywhere. When I looked at Heath, my stomach dropped, and I began to Change back into my human form.

He had wrapped his shirt around his neck, blood trickling down his chest. There were nearly a dozen scratch marks over his chest and shallower bites on his arms. He busied himself with slowly tying up the vampire left behind by his companions, the mute with the ruined midsection.

"Heath, let me check your injuries," I said, my jaw aching more than I expected. "Jabari, are we safe for now?"

He must have Changed while I did because he was a man when he walked over to the vampire. "Yes. They won't risk attacking with the injuries they sustained. I was able to have the other two severely bleeding by the time they ran. They will lose energy and power throughout the night until they feed again.

"They have one of the wolves left alive," Heath whispered weakly. I didn't like how shallow and pale his face looked.

"Heath, please let me check your injuries," I begged softly. "Please."

"I got a few hits in. The stupid bitch got the jump on me and took a mean bite, but it's the worst of it," he informed me, keeping his eyes focused on his slow task. I reached out and took the ropes from him, and he growled pitifully at me. "I broke a few of her bones, and that hand will be useless or weak the next time we see her."

"That's good, but I think you're about to drop," I said gently. Looking down, I realized I might drop too. My abdomen was already bruising and there were long thin lacerations running across it. Blood was everywhere.

"Let her tend you," Jabari ordered. "I will handle this." He reached down and picked up the vampire who hissed before giving a pained whimper. "You have no tongue, but that's okay. I don't need you to have one."

That nearly made me sick from the implications.

"It's just some blood loss," Heath bit out. "I'll take a fucking nap and be fine."

"Yeah, but..." I felt awful. He would have never been up in these mountains if it weren't for me. He had a family to go home to—a loving one, one he should have already been back with.

"We can clean off in the stream together, but please don't coddle me," Heath said, moving to stand. When I tried to help him, swaying on my own feet, he growled softly. "They hit you in the head with a fucking big stone, Jacky. You need to be careful yourself."

I touched my head and felt the blood. I remembered being hit, but I hadn't paid attention to any bleeding.

"And your jaw," he murmured, reaching out to touch it with bloody hands. "It's going to be swollen and bruised by dawn."

"Yeah, it hurts like a bitch." Looking down, I saw scores and scores of cuts and bruises on my body again, taking them in further. "Fuck."

"Yup." Heath looked over me, wobbling as he did. "Jabari—"

"You'll both clean up and rest while I keep watch," my brother said, not unkindly. "We leave to hunt them down at dawn."

"We need to go sooner," Heath growled. "The last wolf will be dead if—"

"If they intend on draining him to heal, they will be done with it by the time we get there," Jabari growled back, baring his bloody teeth. "Let me handle this one. I didn't take as much abuse as you two did." He jerked his head, obviously annoyed, his jaw clenched. "And good job tonight. We took one out of the fight, and the others are going to be very weak and easy to track."

"So, we're still going to hit their hideout during the day?" I asked, fighting to see him clearly.

"If you two get enough rest, yes."

I grabbed Heath's elbow weakly and tried to guide him away. He pulled away, but when my hand dropped, he wrapped his arm around my waist, and we walked together to the stream at the back of the cavern. Before washing off, I drank. I wasn't worried about ingesting the blood because it would do nothing to me. It wasn't the case for humans, but Heath and I would be fine.

I was just thirsty.

Heath leaned into me as he tried to wash off. I touched his hands to stop him before taking some water into my hands and rinsing off his face. The stream was cold because it was snow melt, but that didn't bother me and didn't appear to bother Heath. I worried, though. Vampire bites had the tendency to heal slowly due to something in their saliva. Pulling the shirt back to see the bite, I watched blood push out of the punctures with each of Heath's heartbeats, which were steadily getting faster. For the first time since I had met him, something leaked into his scent he probably didn't want anyone noticing.

I ignored it and pressed the shirt back to the wound. I could ponder what it was later. It wasn't important. The lack of control was interesting from him but considering his injuries and the last two nights we'd had, I was honestly impressed he still had so much control.

"Hold it," I ordered softly. He reached out and pressed it down. "It's slow, but it hit something because it's not clotting yet. It might take time, and we might have to wrap it. Let me find my shirt—"

"Clean mine off," he said huskily, pulling it back off his neck.

"It won't dry if I dump it into the stream," I explained. "We need dry bandages for your neck. The rest will heal without a problem. Same for me."

"None of it will scar," he added to my explanation. "None of it was caused by silver, so none of it should scar."

"Yeah, I know. Are you worried about going home with battle wounds?"

"No. You." His eyes drifted down to the older gunshot scars I had. Scars I had gotten in the line of Duty protecting Carey. Scars that showed the frightening story of how I died once.

"You have some scars of your own," I pointed out softly. It was so faded, I had missed it when I first saw him shirtless. The bite mark on his shoulder and neck from the vampire was right next to the bite mark from a werewolf. "When you were human?"

"The bite that Changed me," he explained. "Fatal in most cases, a werewolf needs to bite down on and puncture the jugular or very close to the heart, so as much of our saliva gets into the wound as possible."

"Same for werecats," I said softly. "And yes, fatal in most cases, but when it's not, the bite closes up immediately as the body accepts the curse. I've just never seen it scar."

"I was unlucky, I guess," he said, chuckling softly. "Fuck, my head is spinning."

"Let's get back to the fire." Mine just ached but I could function. My injuries weren't bleeding, but everything ached. I helped him to his feet, knowing he was right about sleeping, but I still worried so much. It was funny because I had more of a chance of problems going to sleep than he did. I knew better than to try to sleep after being hit over the head, but I wanted the nap as much as he did. Blood loss, his problem, generally made someone a bit out of it, weaker, and tired.

I got us to the fire and leaned him against the wall. His eyes drifted closed immediately, and I went to steal Jabari's extra shirt, remembering he had it at the last minute. My brother looked up and saw me but made no comment when I used it to wrap Heath's neck.

I touched my own after, glad to feel scabs where I was injured the first night. They would be gone by the end of the week as long as no silver got into my system.

"Thank you," I whispered to Jabari.

He just nodded, sitting in the mouth of the cave. I caught him looking back at me for a moment and saw a frown on his face I didn't want to deal with. I sat down with my back to the same wall as Heath, letting my body's need to heal take over.

"You..."

My eyes were closed, and I was fast asleep before he finished.

24

CHAPTER TWENTY-FOUR

I woke up to something being dropped on my lap and jumped.

"Good morning. You forgot to get dressed," Jabari said as I looked up at him with a glare.

He was clothed, thank god, because the angle was terrible. I looked down at myself and noticed what he was talking about. In my haste to pass out and let my injuries begin healing, I had forgotten to get dressed, naked as the day I was born. Behind Jabari, Heath was squatting next to the fire, poking it with a stick. There were no fresh logs on it, and I realized that meant we were about to leave. I was also too embarrassed to say anything or look too long at Heath, who was not looking at me at all.

I grabbed my underwear and slid them on first without standing up, trying not to think about how I had been sleeping fucking naked in a cave with two grown ass men—one I was kind of related to and one who I found much too attractive for my own good. My bra and shirt went on next because I didn't have to stand up to get those on either. My jeans were more of a struggle, forcing me to stand up and lean on the stone wall.

When I was finally decent, I looked around to see that it was dawn out, and there was a vampire, wide-eyed and terrified at the mouth of the cave, just out of the sun's rays, stripped bare. I looked back at the fire, hoping either man there would acknowledge my question.

"Um. Why is he still alive?" I asked softly, pointing at the mute vampire.

"I wanted you to be awake. This is educational for you." Jabari gestured to him. "I'm going to show you what we do when we have to kill a vampire who might have belonged to someone, and we must report the death."

"Wolves do it too," Heath commented softly. "Good morning, Jacky." His gaze was guarded. I felt like he was shutting me out, and I had just woken up. "When this is over, I want—"

"No. You shall report to the werewolves in Seattle," Jabari snapped, cutting off Heath. "I shall handle the nest. Divide and conquer. Don't worry, I shall make sure reparations are paid to all appropriate parties, including the local pack." Heath settled, accepting that from what I could tell.

"What are we about to do?" I had no idea what they were even talking about.

"Come." He waved me to follow him. Other some slight dizziness and a minor ache around my injuries, I was fine. The dizziness was the more worrisome problem.

We stopped in front of the vampire, and Jabari grabbed him by the ankle. His head began to shake violently, and he screamed. I wondered if he was trying to beg for mercy. By his face and Jabari's slow walk, dragging him along, toward the sun, that's exactly what I thought he was doing.

"Jabari, what are you—"

He let go of the vampire once most of it was in the sun. I couldn't breathe as blisters formed, and the vampire screamed.

And screamed.

And screamed.

He was struggling to survive, trying to lift his arms to drag himself back into the shade.

I was horrified. The blisters burst, and the skin began to...melt.

The screaming didn't stop. I could only stand there, shell-shocked by the horror unfolding before my eyes.

Chunks began to solidify again and crack like drying mud, crumbles of dust falling from the vampire. When I jerkily stepped forward, Heath grabbed me. Jabari looked up from the vampire dying below him.

"This is the exact same execution vampires would have given him."

I wanted to be sick.

The body began to crumble except for the piece Jabari left in the shade—his head. When the vampire was dead, and the screaming stopped, his face was frozen in a look of sheer terror and pain, the likes of which I never wanted to see again.

Jabari picked the head up. Heath left me, carrying a black bag. The head was dropped in, and the bag was closed.

Then I was sick. I staggered to the wall after the first ejection of everything in my stomach. The second had about as much as the first—chunks of rabbit and water.

"It's hard seeing it for the first time," Heath whispered, understanding dripping off him like sweet honey. I was overwhelmed by the urge to punch both of them in the face for making me see that. "We could have beheaded him, but...Jabari felt you needed to see."

"Did my family come up with that?" I demanded, looking past Heath, gagging again just from the memory burned into my mind. Fuck both of them: Jabari for thinking I ever needed to see that, and Heath for letting him get away with showing me.

"No. Other vampires did. Certain crimes must always be punished in certain ways. They broke the two most important rules of their kind, and to show respect to other vampires, I will execute them in the manner dictated by their section of the Laws." He didn't seem bothered. "This is just one way we keep peace among the different species, honoring the customs of others when necessary."

"They wouldn't have known," I mumbled.

"Yes, they would have. If I had cut his head off and sun-burned the body, they would have known."

The screams echoed in my head. "Not...that was *wrong.*"

"Do you think the execution wasn't justified?" Jabari sounded deeply confused now.

"No, I just..." Of course, I thought the execution was justified. He had helped kill so many supernaturals without cause, and there had to be a punishment that was final in the end. I took a deep breath, hoping my stomach didn't try to leave my body again. "That was gruesome. I wasn't ready for it."

"You still have a human constitution. You'll grow out of it." His voice sounded weird and awkward. He stepped closer to me and patted my shoulder, obviously uncomfortable with his own actions. "You fight well. Now, you just need more experience with the harsher parts of our world, so they can't catch you off guard anymore."

Is he trying to comfort me and talk me up?

I wasn't sure what my expression was saying to him, but he pulled away quickly. Heath was left next to me, holding the black bag with a head in it. I stepped away from the bag, looking down at it, my stomach doing a couple of flips.

The screaming was all I could hear.

"We have to get moving soon. The vampires were bleeding last night, which should make visually tracking them easy. We need to get to their nest and kill them before another night comes around. I burned the arm, so don't worry about there being any evidence of a fight left behind." Jabari was back to a stony General, ready for his army to pack up and fall in. I found my socks and shoes, slipping them on. Jabari kicked out the fire and buried it under dirt and sand in the cavern. Heath repacked Jabari's bag and handed it off to him, throwing the black bag on his own back. Heath's lack of disgust at the execution surprised me, but he had said werewolves did it too. When we started walking out of the cavern, I let Jabari take the lead. I didn't ask as we walked down the steep, thin path on the cliff face, but the moment my feet were on solid ground, I turned on him.

"Have you seen that before?" I asked quietly as we walked.

"Yes. A few," Heath answered. "I was in the Boston pack for a very long time, probably a hundred and twenty years. We had a vampire nest, and every couple of decades, someone in the pack caught a vampire doing something illegal. I was part of the inner circle to another Alpha, so I attended with him when he and the local Master executed the vampire."

"Did you..."

"Puke? Yes, the first time I saw it. Everyone does." He gave me a small reassuring smile. "You aren't the first, and you won't be the last."

"Davor still retches at the thought," Jabari said loudly from the front. "I won't tell anyone you threw up if you don't want me to. You might have lost your stomach at the end, but you held out for the entire thing. Better than most. The only person I never saw get sick was Niko, but he was exposed to it growing up."

I sighed, not wanting to continue this line of conversation. I couldn't even hate on Davor for his physical reaction because it was completely understandable. The part about Niko didn't surprise me, for some reason.

"How far do you think they are?" I asked, hoping he had some sort of answer. Jabari only shrugged. *Great.*

"Look at the blood, little sister. This is what we're following," he said, pointing to a bush. I stepped up to see what he was talking about. Blood was splattered on the leaves, and the dirt was stained with it. "One stopped here, exhausted from the loss of blood, and because of that, we have a trail to follow. Consider this your introduction to tracking lesson." He gave me a pondering look. "You can also look for fibers caught on branches. I would pay attention to footprints as well, but vampires generally walk softly and don't leave many traces of their activities."

"I know how to track," I told him softly. "I do it all the time."

"With your nose. It's our best resource to track, much like the wolves, but you need to learn to track with your eyes. Do you ever hunt in your human form?" He continued to stare at me, waiting impatiently for an answer I knew was going to upset him or annoy him.

"No," I said, crossing my arms.

"We'll go hunting together. We'll start with easy game like your deer in this country. When you get better, you will visit Zuri and me in Africa, and we'll teach you the thrill of hunting real game." He awkwardly patted my shoulder and started walking again.

I gave Heath the most confused look I could muster.

When Jabari was once again some distance ahead of us, I dared to speak again.

"What changed? Did you talk to him again?" I asked softly.

"I woke up to him mumbling about how he didn't understand you. I didn't say anything but heard a lot of grumbles about what his father would do."

"Oh, dear god," I muttered. "He's trying to be Hasan and turn everything into a lesson. All my favorite times with Hasan were when we pored over a book, and I was learning something new. He was the keeper of knowledge into my new life, and I soaked it in." I sheepishly shrugged. "I soaked it in as best I could. You know, applying knowledge helps one remember the lesson, but until recently, I didn't have to apply a lot of it."

"The way you talk about him sometimes is so... different from the relationship you seem to have with him," Heath pointed out. "You have fond memories and get a relaxed look on your face when you think of him as if he really is your doting father. But you don't treat him like that now."

"Her fiancé was alive when Hasan found the accident. Hasan only Changed Jacky," Jabari said loudly ahead of us. "She hasn't told you?"

My stomach dropped, and the snarl that ripped out of me, uncontrolled and vicious, made Heath take a step away, his eyes flying between Jabari and me, waiting for another bomb to go off.

"Why?" he asked softly after a moment. "Why would Hasan do that to you?"

"I don't know," I snapped. "And it's been the... problem. He lied to me for four years, saying my fiancé was dead upon his arrival. Then his story changed to my fiancé was too far gone to survive the Change, and even that was a lie. In the end, he let Shane die and kept me in this world. Do you know the answer, Jabari?"

"I always have," her brother said. "But you aren't ready for it."

I growled at him before turning back to Heath.

"See? So, four years after trying to be part of the family with siblings who resented me for things I had no control over, I found out that the man I had come to love as a father in my new life was...a liar. It took me a while to catch it because I was still learning what different scents meant, but when I did, he didn't...tell me the truth."

"I'm so sorry." Heath reached out to touch my arm, but I pulled away before he could. "Jacky, that's..." He looked back at Jabari. "And none of you thought about how painful that would be to learn?"

"What do you know about it?" Jabari snapped.

"I watched my human wife die of old age," Heath said softly. "And if there's one moment in my life where I didn't want to continue, that was it. The pack around me forced me to eat for a year. They didn't let me run off and waste away. So, I would think I know a lot about losing a loved one and finding the future ahead of me very painful, one I can't fucking imagine."

Jabari's eyes went wide as he looked back at us. Then he started walking again, away from us, following the blood trail. Heath growled, about to rush after him, but I grabbed the wolf.

"It was a long time ago," I said softly. "Just leave it. That's why Hasan and I are complicated. That's why I spent seven years pretending none of them were my family."

"If my pack hurt me like that, I would have disappeared too," he said. "That's hard. I'm sorry, Jacky. Let's get through this and get home, away from this jackass. The fact that you're even here helping him and that family of yours is...amazing." He shook his head in disgust.

"Yeah, well...I thought I had started a war," I reminded him. Now that wasn't the case. It was clear the vampires were a seemingly random occurrence, but I wanted to see it through. "I wanted to clean up my mess and prove I could. Turned out, it wasn't my mess."

"Or mine or anyone else's," he said, nodding slowly. "But really, let's get this over with and get back to Texas. I hate this rain, and I hate your family."

We kept trudging through the evergreen forest, the rain falling on us. Heath didn't seem any worse for wear from the night before, and other than my aching pieces, I was feeling fine. Jabari looked like he wasn't injured at all. Every so often, Jabari called me up and pointed out something and made me find the next piece of the trail to follow.

A few hours in, I checked my phone and sighed. It was dead, so I couldn't check the actual time. Looking up,

I had to guess it wasn't noon yet, maybe ten or eleven in the morning still.

"I think we've found them," Jabari announced.

Heath and I stepped around him to see what he saw. There was a cave, but not one in the side of a mountain. It went kind of down into the ground, 'under' the mountain. What lay inside, no one could see. We walked closer together, Jabari setting the pace, which was cautious.

"If this is their hiding place, no wonder they were able to come after us both nights. We've been in the same...ten- to fifteen-mile area since we left the cabin," Heath pointed out. "Meaning they aren't completely out in the middle of nowhere."

"It's good hunting," Jabari commented. "They are close enough to the campgrounds and hiking trails to attack humans."

"And if someone goes missing out here..." I looked around. "Well, they would just be one of many who have gotten lost out here."

"Yes, Jacky. That's exactly the conclusion I was coming to. They're using the forests and mountains in the area for a hunting zone where no one has to know they killed anyone."

"Then they ran into two werecats when they got here," Heath continued, crossing his arms. "Two werecats who took it personally when humans were in trouble and helped them. Guardians of the area. They were in the way of freedom to vampires, who had no way to defeat them."

"Then a group of werewolves decided to take a camping trip," I said, helping put the story together. "Easier prey, something to power them up to take out bigger problems."

"And once all was said and done, they thought they would get away with it. Until we showed up with Jabari," Heath sighed.

"Unless they cut our fuel line in broad daylight, they have help from a local human, though I'm still trying to figure that one out. I don't see any of those three having a real motive."

"They'll talk once we deal with the more dangerous group." Jabari nodded down at the cave.

We were close enough now, I could see it was part of some sort of cave system. How big it was, I didn't know, but it was terrifying to think I was about to go in it after vampires.

"Then, let's go kill these vampires," I said, hoping the courage I portrayed covered up the waver in my voice.

CHAPTER TWENTY-FIVE

W e planned to Change together, shoving our clothing into Jabari's bag. He tucked it away in a bush, covering it with foliage to stop curious hikers and animals.

"There's no food in it, so it should be fine," he said. "Remember the plan. We're going down there together, and even if it takes all day, we're going after them one at a time. Incapacitate them, drag them out here, then burn them. If one of them offers information, I will go into my human form and get it." He eyed us both. I rubbed my hands together, nervous. "Then I can communicate with both of you, and Jacky, you can tell me what Heath has to say."

I nodded quickly. "Can do."

Heath nodded beside me, remaining silent. I knew he just wanted to get this over with. He looked like he was doing fine, but he was a little pale in the light. He would follow orders if it meant never seeing these vampires or Jabari ever again.

"Good. Let's Change and get through this. We'll be out of this forest by nightfall."

I fucking hoped so because I was done with stomping around the woods in the rain.

We Changed, bones cracking, growls, and grunts accentuating the pain and transformation our bodies were going through. Jabari was done before me, and we waited the few minutes it took for Heath to finish. He was fast for a wolf, just like I was fast for a werecat my age. I wondered if there was some similarity between us that caused it, or maybe we were just both lucky.

Jabari walked into the caves first with Heath and me able to walk beside each other behind him.

"He's a big motherfucker," Heath pointed out. *"Every time I see him, I wonder if he can crush my damn head with those paws."*

"Probably. He would wipe the floor with me, that's for sure." There were reasons I never got physical over the insults my siblings threw at me. Mischa and Zuri were more my size, maybe a little bigger, but they were older, more powerful, and more resilient, so size essentially didn't matter. Davor was the smallest of the guys in the family, still bigger than me, while Jabari and Hasan were the biggest werecats on the planet. I didn't think anyone would ever match them in size.

We entered the cave, going down. It smelled of dirt and water, along with some other choice things like decay. They had left bodies down in the mud, apparent to anyone with a nose. Even humans could have walked down here and known there were dead bodies of some sort—it reeked.

Heath growled softly. There was one problem with the reek of dead for our noses. We knew they were dead wolves.

"Do you think they're asleep?" I asked Jabari and Heath, wondering what they thought about the welcome we weren't getting. Jabari's big head nodded, and Heath provided more information.

"Most vampires feel an undeniable urge to sleep once the sun comes up. From what I know, as they get older, they can resist it but not well. It's just safer to hide and sleep." Heath sniffed the air. *"There's a small draft, and I can smell...a wolf on it. I think the last one is still alive."*

"Then we'll find him," I promised. My nose, not being as sensitive, couldn't discern that. All I could smell was earth, death, and wolf. Unless I was missing some key way death changed scents, I had no idea how he came to the conclusion the last wolf was still alive. Maybe it was just hope.

Jabari continued in the lead, deeper into the caverns. We walked silently, placing our paws carefully to keep from causing too much of a disturbance. If we hadn't woken them up already, there was no reason to wake them up now. Sleeping vampires had to be easier to kill.

We cut into a small passageway, a thin, narrow walk into what seemed like a back chamber. Jabari crouched, which allowed Heath ahead of me to see over his head. And I could see over Heath's head.

Inside the chamber, there were mattresses and furniture. Couches with throw blankets and pillows. A power generator, probably using gasoline to run electrical items like the TV I saw. The vampires had set up a nice home in their cavern.

The only reason it wouldn't be a cool little clubhouse was the werewolf in human form on a small blanket in the corner. Even from where I was, I could see how gaunt he was. Heath pawed at the ground, anxious. I sniffed and realized he was right. This werewolf was alive. How I didn't know, but he was still fucking alive.

Jabari began to walk again, low to the ground. Once he was out of the small passage, Heath moved out faster, though still very silent, and went toward the werewolf.

"Don't. He could wake up and wake them up," I said.

"He's going to die if we don't get him out of here now," Heath snapped.

I shook my head. *"Let Jabari and I get into position, then you can run him out. We can handle the vampires, but you have to wait for the right moment."*

Heath looked from me to the sleeping, half-dead werewolf, then nodded. I moved toward Jabari and saw what he was focused on. In the corner of the cavern I couldn't see from the narrow passage, the vampires had set up an impressive bed and were sleeping together on it in a tangled amalgamation of bodies and limbs. They looked peaceful and clean, nearly harmless. They must have washed the blood and mud off themselves when they had run from the trap we had set. Now, injured and sleeping, they were easy prey.

Jabari and I stalked to the bed. We didn't touch any of the pieces hanging off, not yet. The leader was in the center, the hole where her arm used to be closed up. The younger woman looked perfectly fine if a lot paler than she had been the night before. I couldn't see most of her, which annoyed me. The man had vicious claw marks all over his chest, where Jabari had nearly cut him in half.

Jabari sat on the other side of the bed, and it looked like he smiled for a moment, his teeth bared and his eyes on me. He nodded his big head, letting me know he was ready for me to make the call.

"Heath, are you by the wolf?" I asked.

"Yes. I'll wake him up the moment you get started on them. Hopefully, I can get him on my back and run him out to daylight before any of them divert their attention from you."

I took a deep breath, flexing my claws into the dirt, feeling it between my paw pads.

"Now!" I ordered. Jabari and I jumped onto the bed, attacking the first bodies we could sink fangs and claws into. The werewolf screamed across the room, but I didn't hear Heath's response. Underneath me, the vampires screamed and struggled. One of them punched me in the head. One was able to scramble away and ran somewhere I couldn't see. Jabari pulled one off the bed, dragging it by a leg.

I focused on the one beneath me, the leader. With her remaining arm, she clawed at my face as I shook her by the shoulder, not connected to an arm. My five-inch fangs were buried into her, through bone and muscle.

Tired of her clawing at me, I jumped back, yanking her along with me off the bed. Once I was on solid ground, I pinned her to the ground with a paw and tore, taking a giant piece out of her. Her screaming wouldn't stop, so I flexed my claws, letting them dig into her chest and tore down, tearing bones and muscle open.

Some part of me knew I should be sick from the carnage. Vampires had a human face, and it was disturbing when you could tear off pieces and cut them open, and they kept screaming, still 'alive.' Their animated corpses continued to fight as you pulled their intestines out.

"I'm dragging this one out," I told Jabari as I grabbed her good arm and yanked, listening to her scream further. She tried to stand, so I swiped at her legs, listening to the bone crunch, probably one of her femurs. She fell to her knees, yet she still tried to pull her remaining arm from my mouth.

I yanked her and was able to get us to the narrow passage. Instead of fighting to drag her alongside me, I walked backward down the little hall of stone. Once we were in the main area of the cave, her screaming picked back up, probably realizing how we intended to kill her. A howl came from behind me. Heath probably letting me know he was there, out and free with his saved werewolf.

The stupid bitch of a vampire pulled her arm hard, and I felt muscle and tendons tearing apart. I released for a second, let her gain an inch, then slammed my jaw closed again, snapping the bone in her upper arm in half and making the hand fall limp. With a snarl, I yanked her harder, making her fall to the ground. As I approached the mouth of the cave, Heath appeared before me, his ice blue wolf eyes watching me carefully. He ran in and grabbed one of the vampire's legs and turned her to go into the sun, feet first. We were big enough, we lifted her off the ground and slowly marched outside. I halted before her head was exposed to the sun. The light felt good to me.

It did *not* feel good to her. In Heath's mouth and broken on the ground, her legs went first. Beyond him, I could see the freed wolf, eyes wide with terror and awe, watching as the bitch that had tortured him melted, crusted, cracked, then crumbled as dust into the wind and rain. I didn't feel sick this time, forcing a vampire to suffer this. She had helped torture the poor werewolf for a month. The poor thing who had to watch his friends die and was probably would've died soon if they hadn't rescued him.

I dropped her arm once I knew there was no hope for her. The screams echoed around in my skull, though. She never stopped screaming until her lungs were dust. Heath nudged the arm and shoulder into the light, which quickly went to dust.

We were left with just her head, which I carefully pawed back deeper into the cave.

"There's one more left. Jabari is bringing the man. I'm going back in for the other woman. Keep an eye on him." I pointed with my nose at his saved werewolf, who shook weakly. The poor young man looked to only be skin and

bones, but at least he was out in the sun and not down there being torn apart any longer.

"Be safe," Heath said, bumping his head to mine. I nervously danced back from him and went into the cave once more. As I traveled back down to the narrow passage, Jabari passed me with the man, who was missing both his arms and one leg. I didn't let it faze me; Jabari had done what he needed to.

"I'm off to find the last one. Heath will help you position that one to burn," I told my brother as he went closer to the sun. Jabari, holding the man's remaining leg, nodded.

I went through the narrow pass, hoping there would be another one inside the caverns that could show me where the little bitch fled. They had brought this on themselves. I understood now what it meant for Jabari and my siblings when it was said they were Hasan's judges, juries, and executioners. There was no oversight. We knew the Law, and we fought to avenge those werecats whose lives were lost unnecessarily. While the execution was gruesome, seeing that poor werewolf made it worth it. We were all monsters, but that didn't mean we had to be monstrous. We could live wonderful lives, have fucked-up families, and still be monsters.

There was no reason to do what they had done to that werewolf. They should be thankful. Their deaths were quicker than the one they had wanted to give him, wasting away as leftovers for them to snack on.

I snarled as I prowled around the little mansion they had set up for themselves. I sniffed the air, realizing the dead werewolves' bodies weren't being kept in this area, which meant there had to be another. They weren't buried because the scent was too strong, too pervasive.

No, they had stashed the dead werewolves somewhere, and that was probably where the little bitch had gone to hide.

I found a small opening and growled into it. A whimper came out the other side. I listened harder, tilting my head to hear everything.

"I don't want to die. I don't want to die. I don't want to die," the younger vampire whispered to herself.

I pawed at the stones and realized she had half-buried herself in while we were handling her friends. I went on my hind legs and shoved my paws against the loose rubble, knocking some over on the other side and digging to clear out the side I was on. Her breathing grew heavier inside as I dug out stones, some nearly as big as my head.

Finally, I could see her and swiped a paw inside. She screamed, backing away and curling into a ball.

I roared, trying to dig her out and get my body inside. I was nearly in a frenzy with it, desperate to take my prey to meet its end. I snapped and snarled, wanting a piece of her.

"Jacky, back away," Jabari ordered behind me. I hissed, turning to see him in human form. "I need to ask this one some questions."

"I'll tell you anything!" she screamed inside. "Please don't kill me! I don't want to die!"

"I won't let you die," he promised, smiling. The little

vampire relaxed immediately. "How long have you been a vampire?" he asked, grabbing the scruff of my neck. I resisted, but amazingly, he was able to pull me back from the hole. I pulled and tugged, trying to get free from his grip, fury pumping through my veins. I wanted this bitch's blood. I wanted her head to roll. I wanted her *dead*.

"Jacqueline, daughter of Hasan, you will let me question her," Jabari snarled down at me before pulling me further away and swinging us, so his body was between me and the vampire. I roared in his face, but he seemed unfazed. "You can't beat me, little sister."

I could. If I wanted to kill him right then, in his human form versus my werecat, I could kill him. I snarled until he released me and backed away.

I didn't want to, and he nodded slowly as he recognized that as well.

"Now, vampire, how long have you existed?" He turned back to the little bitch in the hole. I paced behind him, waiting, frustrated something stood between me and it.

Soon. He'll let me have her soon. He better.

"Twenty...twenty-two years," she answered softly.

"Then you know the Laws," he said professionally. "And you know how you've broken them."

"It was just so good, you see?" She dared to lean out a little. "And who cares about the Laws anymore? They can be changed. I heard it. But it doesn't matter. My Master thought he could teach me better, and I said no."

"Why?" he asked gently. "Why did you tell your Master no?"

"Because I'm a fucking vampire. I can do whatever I want. I didn't think..." She looked at me, her eyes going wide. "I didn't think this would happen. It started, and I just wanted to try it out. They said it was so good, you see?"

"See what?" Jabari asked, kneeling. I didn't like him so close to her, so vulnerable.

"Killing! The blood tastes so much better as they get closer to dying, then they die, and you get all of that...*good shit* from it. It was just going to be some humans. No one had to make such a fuss about it."

"Ah. Did someone make a fuss?"

Jabari sounded like a caring uncle or an older brother who just wanted to know why his little sister got into so much trouble.

It tore at my heart because he had never spoken like that to me.

"Yes, my Master, but Essie, she said we weren't killing anyone important, and it was so good, and he was just jealous. Then he threw us out! He made all of us, and he tossed us out!"

"So, your Master knew before you left. Why did you come out here? There are much nicer places."

"He suggested it! He said no one would miss some campers. He couldn't bring himself to hurt his precious children. Seattle wasn't safe for us anymore, he said. We didn't know there would be werewolves or werecats. We didn't think they would care about us, but the werecats did. We had to kill them because we had to stay here."

"You didn't think to stop what you were doing?"

"Why? They're just humans, and I'm a vampire. They're food. Who gives a fuck—"

Jabari reached out and grabbed her neck so fast, I barely saw it happen. With a single twist of his wrist, he broke her neck.

"She was Changed young," he said as her wide eyes stared up at the ceiling, her body unmoving. "And she's not...right. They indulged her and never taught her better. She couldn't have been more than fourteen," he whispered, running a finger over her face. "A waste. At least she told me everything we needed to know. Come. She can heal that. We must burn her before she gets back mobility."

I grabbed onto her arm and dragged her after Jabari, who didn't spare her another glance as he walked away.

When we reached the mouth of the cave, he took her from me. Heath had already Changed back into his human form as well and held my clothing as I Changed, turning away while I dressed. The starved werewolf was asleep in the dirt now.

The last vampire, her neck broken, didn't scream as her body went to dust, and only her head remained.

26

CHAPTER TWENTY-SIX

I put the heads in the bag. Together, there was
barely enough space to close the damn thing. Jabari
went back inside with a torch, and we all knew
what he was doing—burning the remains of the dead
werewolves. That was gruesome work I didn't want to be
a part of.

Which was why I put the heads in the bag.

Much better, Jacky.

Heath walked in behind Jabari, holding every piece
of timber he could get his hands on, leaving me with the
sleeping werewolf. I ignored the poor man, deciding he
didn't need me scaring the hell out of him by trying to
wake him up to perform an exam. I would do it later once
I knew we were going to get out of the woods. The EMT
in me wanted to do it right that instant, but I knew there
was nothing I could do for him, anyway.

There was still a lot we had to do before leaving. I
wondered if they were going to burn all the evidence the

vampires had been down there, or leave it for someone to think squatters had moved into the park.

When they both came jogging out, I didn't get the chance to ask.

"Don't go in there. You'll get some serious lung damage," Heath said to me as he passed by me to the werewolf on the ground. "We're burning it all."

"Ah. I was just wondering," I commented. "So, now we need to get out of here."

"Yes. I have a vehicle..." Jabari frowned. "I parked it along the main road, but I don't know where it is in relation to where we are now."

"Can you get us back to the cabin where you found us?" I asked, throwing the bag with the heads on my back.

"Yes. That's easy."

"Then we can get to our car, probably do a quick repair, then pick up your car," I said, taking a deep, steady breath. I was so ready to get out of the woods. Hasan had been right, I shouldn't have come out here, but now, it was finally over. Except for some shit we still needed to work out, that was. "We need to get ahold of those three fucking humans and find out which of them sabotaged us."

"We do," my brother agreed. He was preoccupied, and I turned to see what he was looking at.

Heath was trying to wake the werewolf who was sleeping so deeply, but nothing was stirring him. I felt the pain of anger flare up in my chest again. I had really wanted to tear that last little bitch to pieces. A hand touched my shoulder, and Jabari moved around me.

"Let me carry him," he suggested, kneeling next to Heath. "I am the strongest."

"He's a werewolf," Heath growled softly. "You think I would trust you with him?"

"He's a warrior who has survived an ordeal. I'll suffer with the fact that he's a werewolf and carry him." Jabari was serious.

"Heath...let him," I whispered from behind them. My wolf turned, showing me his eyes were still his werewolf ice-blue, not his normal grey-blue. He wanted to protect the other werewolf, but there wasn't a threat anymore. I didn't like Jabari much, but I wouldn't question his honor when it came to another warrior.

Heath backed away slowly. My brother picked up the sleeping wolf so gently it nearly broke my heart, leaving Heath to grab the bag of gear.

We walked in silence, Jabari holding the wolf carefully. It took hours, but we reached the cabin. As we passed it, I sniffed the ATV once more, just testing to see if there might be a scent that would help us. Heath did the same. We had to find out who left us out here to die and told the vampires our location. It was the last thing we had to do before we could return to the city.

"Anything?" I asked him as we both walked away.

"No. I can smell all three of them, but I don't know who was touching what. They all used it regularly."

With a sigh, we continued down the trail that would finally reach the service shack where we left our car. Dusk was fast approaching as we found it, and Heath did a quick check on the car.

"Busted," he confirmed. "But I can fix it with some jerry-rigging. Shouldn't take more than an hour. Jabari, can you put him in the back seat?"

"Of course." He shifted the young man's body around, but I rushed over to help, not wanting to see him struggle. I opened the door and helped Jabari lower the sleeping wolf inside. I wondered if this was the first safe sleep he'd had since he was captured, and it was par for the course he only slept during the day, thanks to the vampires' schedules. We closed him in to keep him safe if he woke up and freaked out.

"What's wrong?" Jabari asked, walking back to the front and looking down at what Heath was doing. "I was never very good at these things."

"It's...just leave it to me," Heath finally said, shaking his head. "Do we have any tape?"

"No." I groaned. "He cut the electrics, didn't he?"

"Yeah..." Heath frowned. "We can drive, but we might not have lights or anything. It would have been hell trying to get out with this at night. Sure, we can all see, but the tree and cloud cover blocks all the natural light, and we would have wanted to rush because someone messing with our way out would have meant we were being hunted. It could have been dangerous."

"And we would have been an easy target," I pointed out. "Driving slowly, they could have easily caught up to us."

"Exactly. Or we would have driven off the road. As it is, we can get to the main road before night falls. Let's go." He slammed the hood shut and pointed for me to get in.

I opted for the back seat with the werewolf, keeping an eye on his breathing and pulse. He would survive as long as we didn't seriously injure him before getting him to a hospital. He was dehydrated, malnourished, and probably low on blood he couldn't replenish due to the other issues. My worry was organ failure.

"Why didn't they drain him?" I asked softly, reaching out to move matted hair off the werewolf's face.

"They probably wanted to feed come nightfall to fight us again," Jabari answered. "I was also a little surprised, but they were healing well by the time we got there. They might have not wanted to kill an easy resource before they had to."

I didn't say anything to his explanation. All of it made sense.

The car got moving, and Heath was right. Much of the dash didn't work at all, and I couldn't turn on any of the lights in the car, so as night came, it grew very dark.

We reached the main road, and I jumped out to open the very gate I had seen John, one of the humans, open on our way in. Jabari was pointing to the right when I got back in.

"My vehicle will be that way. I took it to one of the stops where a hiking trail begins. It had some parking spots that didn't require the local permit."

Heath nodded. "That's toward home. Let's go."

It wasn't long before Jabari pointed us at the right turn, and we saw a nice SUV waiting.

"There it is. We must decide how to handle things further. Jacky and I can talk to the humans while you take the wolf back to the city. Does that work for everyone?" He looked between us.

"Be safe, Heath," I whispered to my wolf before jumping out of the car. I grabbed the bag of heads out of the trunk and followed Jabari.

"I'm going to get pulled over!" Heath called out as we walked away.

"Good! That means a cop can help you get that wolf to safety!" I waved at him. He would figure it out. I didn't want him waiting around for us to track down and deal with the humans. That wolf needed attention as soon as possible. "Or you can get to a station or something and call for help! Like a medical evac!"

I saw him nod, then he drove away. I jumped into the passenger's seat of Jabari's ride, amazed it hadn't been broken into while he was running in the woods.

"Do you have a charger?" I asked, holding up my cell. He went into his glove box and pulled out his and turned it on.

"Use this one," he said, holding it out to me.

"It has no service. We'll have to get to the closest town...did you pass through Darrington?"

He smiled, and I could see his white teeth in the darkness.

"I did. Do you think we'll find them there?"

"I think we might," I said, smiling back. I let him drive and waited for even a single bar to show up on the cell phone. Once it did, I dialed the number I knew by heart for Haley. It was etched into my memory, it seemed. In a few weeks, I would forget it, but not now... definitely not now.

"Hello?" she answered. "This is Haley."

"Haley! This Jacky. I'm calling from my brother's phone. I wanted to let you know we handled everything, and we need to see you, Gina, and John as soon as possible."

"Oh my god, you're alive!" She sounded genuinely excited. "Oh, this is amazing! I was so worried when you never came down. John said he would wait for you when Gina and I were called to help some hikers. He said you never showed up, and we got so worried!"

I glanced at Jabari. John was left alone with our things.

"The first night, we ended up staying in the cabin you had shown us where Gaia and Titan met up. Jabari met us there, and we went further out to...fix what was going on. I'll explain soon. Can you meet us in Darrington? Somewhere private?"

She quickly gave me an address I committed to memory.

"I'm so happy all of you are safe. Who will be there?"

"Just my brother and I. Heath is taking a werewolf in our car to find medical care, so I'm in a big ass black SUV."

"Oh, shit. He must be the med evac I just heard over the comms. All right, well, I'll meet you there. I'll tell John and Gina to come too."

"Thanks," I said, smiling to myself. She hung up, and

I dropped the phone into a cup holder, sighing. The smile died quickly. "What kind of impression did you get from them when you met them?"

"They were upset over Gaia and Titan. Haley thought she knew everything about our kind. I didn't bother dealing with her because I didn't care to or have the time to properly educate her. John has cancer."

"What?" I sat up straight again, frowning at him. "How do you know that?"

"I got close enough to smell the illness on him. No, not the illness. I could smell the medications and had run into the scents before. My human lawyer in Botswana passed away about five years ago, and I knew everything about his care, from his disease to his medications. I know the smell of a man who is battling for his life against his own body."

The explanation stunned me into silence for a long moment until he turned his dark eyes on me.

"I'm sorry," I whispered.

"It happened. He rests in peace now on my property. Back to the problem at hand, please." He looked back to the road, and I was left trying to process how to go back to the conversation.

"So, yeah...I got the same vibe from Haley. She was a bit bitchy when I explained some things to her because they weren't what she expected. I didn't know John is sick. He didn't mention it or act like it. Um..."

"Gina was just a crying woman. I don't think it's her. John or Haley," Jabari declared.

"Yeah..." I wasn't sure how to react to that statement,

either. "John or Haley. What do each of them get out of it?"

"Depends on what they were offered. We'll find out when we see them."

I had the odds of flipping a coin, but I already decided which one I thought did it. I had a feeling Jabari was on the same page.

CHAPTER TWENTY-SEVEN

W e arrived in the pitch blackness of the night. Jabari turned our lights off but kept the SUV running. Quietly, we waited for the humans to roll up and meet us in the park they had picked out. There was no one around, which made it perfect.

I tapped him and pointed to the two trucks that came in at the same time. They must have lived nearby and driven at the same time on their way to meet us, because it was the same thing they did when meeting Heath and me.

We got out of our vehicle first and let them approach. I sniffed the air, paying attention this time to John's scent. My brother had been right. There was a smell of chemicals to him I hadn't noticed before. I was focusing too intently on what I had to deal with and didn't catch what had been right in front of my nose.

"So..." Haley stepped up closest. "It's really good to

see you both alive..." She looked between us and frowned. "Are you really related, or is that just something you tell people? Because I'm not seeing it."

"My father Changed her into a werecat," Jabari explained. "That makes us siblings, though it doesn't have to. We choose to have that relationship."

"It's not a biological relationship at all," I made sure to point out when Gina raised an eyebrow. "It's complicated." It was funny because the relationship between werecat siblings was an odd one. Like Hasan had mentioned on the phone, talking about Davor and Liza, it was perfectly acceptable for it to become romantic as long as the werecats weren't actually related. I glanced at him, frowning. Jabari and Zuri were from a different time, though...

No. Stop. Don't need those images.

My mind was going interesting places now that I was safe from immediate death.

"Ah." Gina nodded slowly. "So, will you tell us what happened?"

"Certainly." I took the lead, letting Jabari just stand there and be intimidating. "We discovered that you had a small infestation of vampires who had gone rogue and were looking to take over this area for easy feeding. You know how Gaia and Titan regularly helped save humans? Yeah, that was about to be flipped on its head. They were setting up so they could take any random hiker or camper, feed on them, then kill them without being noticed. There's a lot of space out there to hide a body." I waved a hand at the surrounding mountains. "And no one would have found them, but your missing person reports would have skyrocketed."

"Oh my god..." Gina covered her mouth. Haley just let hers drop open.

John was uncomfortable. He was the only one who hadn't yet spoken and seemed fidgety.

Yeah, motherfucker. I knew it.

"So, we killed them. They won't be a problem. You're looking at a long time without any supernaturals in those mountains." I smiled blithely. "Heath and I hadn't planned on staying out there. We wanted to get back out before dark. We're lucky Jabari got to us. He had already been actively hunting the vampires when they attacked us."

"Why were you still out there?" Haley asked softly.

"That's the part we're here to deal with. Someone cut the fuel line on the ATV you left us. We didn't want to risk walking back to the car and getting there after dark because if someone was smart enough to sabotage the ATV, they would have also sabotaged the car. Turns out, we were right. When we got to the car earlier today, the electrics had been cut. We got it running, but some things weren't working." I stopped, deciding to change the subject for a moment. "If Heath got our saved werewolf to a medevac, that means he didn't wreck the car. He had to drive at night without headlights."

"Yeah, I checked in on that. It was definitely two werewolves being flown out. The Seattle pack asked for them to be taken there, then information after that is classified. You know how the werewolves are." Haley was rubbing her hands together. "Could the vampires have cut the fuel line?"

"No. We made it back to the cabin in broad daylight. They wouldn't have been able to." I sighed. "Which makes me need to ask a question. John, did they offer to turn you?"

John took a step back as the human women gasped in their shock.

"What kind of offer would you-"

"You have cancer," Jabari commented blandly. "What kind?"

"Lung," he answered, bitterness tainting his words and features. "Never smoked a day in my life and got fucking lung cancer."

"Life isn't fair, is it?" I said gently. I felt for him, I did, but I didn't let that change the cold rage that the sympathy couldn't bury. "So, you what? Did you approach Gaia and Titan to Change you, and they said no? Then you were approached by the vampires because you had information they wanted about the locals?"

"Pretty much," he snapped. "What are you going to do about it? Are you going to kill me? Humans are protected, right? You can't."

"Not today," Jabari hissed. "We have more pressing things to do than cover up the death of a human." He glanced at me, and I knew what to say. Deep in my bones, I knew what needed to be said, and I wondered where I heard it before.

"But one day, you'll get a knock on your door," I explained to him. "One day, a werecat will come to have you pay your debt, and you'll be left wishing you'd let the cancer take you. I would recommend running. Run as far as you can and as fast as you can. You might earn yourself more time if you do it well enough." I grinned viciously. "I make no promises that the werewolves won't come for you immediately."

John paled. Ignoring the betrayed women, he turned and ran back for his truck, jumping in and screaming off.

Haley looked back at me, terrified.

"You can..."

"By supernatural Law, if a human is introduced to our world, they are beholden to our Law. They face the same punishments as the rest of us, based on our species. Gaia and Titan were open to him about what they were, and he betrayed them. Not only that, he helped a pack of vampires break the Law, several times over." Jabari's explanation was one I couldn't have put better myself. "Humans are generally considered innocent in our world. Werecats particularly like to protect you, but he lost that right and place in our eyes. He's no more than another animal who will eventually have to be put down for the crimes he committed against our kind. Because he's human, we'll give him a chance to run." Now my brother smiled. "He won't make it very far."

I wondered who he would call to fly out here and deal with it if he wasn't going to do it himself. While I was capable of giving the threat, I wasn't sure I was ready to kill a human.

"I asked them to Change me once..." Haley whispered. "Would either of you come back one day—"

"No," we both answered. I looked up at Jabari, who gestured for me to continue first. "Changing someone into a werecat is adding them to your family. The werecat becomes your parent and must spend years making sure you can survive in this world. Neither of us is looking for that sort of responsibility, and you don't want to invite either of us or our family into your life. You have a good life here. Live it. Leave the monsters to the monsters."

"Is that why they said no?"

"Probably. Gaia seemed like she didn't want much company, not even from her mate." I shrugged.

"She...how do modern people put it? She strung him along for years and was constantly changing her mind like the turn of the seasons," Jabari said softly. "Their romance was one for the ages, always back-and-forth, hot-and-cold. It was why their territories didn't overlap. One decade, they would be the perfect mates, the next, she wouldn't want to see him." He chuckled sadly. "She never wanted children. Neither did Titan. They spent their centuries entertaining themselves with each other."

"I'll miss them," Gina murmured, wrapping her arms around herself. "And John...how could he?"

"The possibility of death drives many to do things that seem out of character," I said gently. "You two will be able to move on. It just takes time. Now, we have to go. It's a drive back to Seattle, and we have things to take care of."

"Of course. Thank you for...everything." Haley reached out to shake my hand, and I accepted. I waved at Gina, who seemed utterly heart broken.

As we drove away, I watched the women console each other over the loss of not just two friends, but the betrayal of a third.

"What's next?" I asked Jabari.

"We get to Seattle and contact the family. After that, shower, sleep, and spend a day taking care of ourselves. We haven't eaten properly in days. Hasan will notice and chastise us both for not taking better care of ourselves."

"After that?"

"We need to visit the Seattle nest and have a discussion with the Master. He threw out his vampires knowingly and left them to be someone else's problem when he should have executed them himself."

"All of that sounds fun. Care if I sleep on the drive?"

"No. Go ahead."

I let the lull of the engine take me under. I was tired, but we weren't done yet. A small nap wouldn't kill anyone now.

28

CHAPTER TWENTY-EIGHT

J abari woke me to ask what hotel I was staying at. I yawned as I told him, then stretched out.

"Why? Where are you staying?"

"I never got a hotel room since I wasn't planning on staying in the city."

"Of course," I muttered, shaking my head. "My room has one bed, but there's a couch that might pull out into a bed. I didn't pay attention when I booked."

"Thank you. Do you have any way to contact our family?"

"Yup. A laptop. Did you forget one of those, too?"

"I brought a cellphone and a satellite phone. I didn't need a laptop. I was only going to report in nightly with Hasan."

"Then the cellphone was out of service, and the satellite phone was broken. This is why you have backups," I told him, crossing my arms.

"Says the one who walked into the woods and her

ways out were sabotaged," he retorted. "We'll tell Father all of it, and he'll judge us accordingly."

"Joy, but since it's my room with my money, I call the shower first."

He sighed heavily. "But I was out there longer."

"I don't care." Well, I did because he probably looked and smelled the worst. I was pretty sure we both reeked, but, in the end, I was getting my shower first.

He silently shook with laughter, something I wasn't expecting. When we pulled up to the hotel, it all stopped as we saw several obvious werewolves hanging out at the front. I stepped out first, frowning.

"Can we help you?" I asked loudly. It probably seemed out of place, but I wasn't walking closer or letting Jabari get near them. Not because I was worried about his safety—I was worried about theirs.

"We were just in a shift change...You're Jacky Leon?" When I nodded, the wolf who spoke stepped closer to me, straightening up to seem more professional. "Alpha Lewis asked us to wait here and report when you arrived, so Alpha Everson knew you were okay. He should be here soon. He's debriefing Alpha Lewis on what happened."

"Thank you for the report. You can clear out now. I've got an edgy, pre-War werecat who probably wants to come inside without having to deal with you." I tried to sound like I was joking, and I kind of was, but the wolves also knew that no matter how casually or teasingly I said it, the threat of a very old, cranky werecat wasn't to be taken lightly.

"We'll head out, then. Thank you for everything. I know you guys only brought back one of our boys, but it's good hearing at least one came back."

"It was my..." I almost said pleasure, but nothing about the last few days was a pleasure. "It was my honor to help," I decided on, smiling at them kindly.

Once they were gone, Jabari went to find a parking place while I waited at the front door. He was carrying both bags as he approached and gave me the one without the heads. Together, we walked into the hotel and got up to my room while I explained where Heath was. I had booked it for a month, so I knew it was still mine.

Upon getting in, I threw Jabari's gear bag on the table and went to the bathroom, jumping in without giving anything else any thought. I needed that shower, and I was going to have it.

I could hear him moving around in the room, and it died off while I was shampooing my hair. Finally, something surprised me.

"JABARI!" Hasan's voice came through my laptop speakers, loud and crackling. And he was both relieved and angry. "You're alive! Where's Jacky? Why are you on her laptop? Answer me while I tell your siblings—"

"Here, Father!" Zuri said quickly. I heard the jumbled mess of the rest of my siblings all jumping on. Had they been waiting around for us to contact them? Most were excited to see Jabari on, but after Hasan asked about me, I only heard Zuri and Niko wonder where I was.

"Quiet! I can't tell you anything while you're all

yelling," Jabari snapped. It went silent. I began to rinse the shampoo from my hair, and once it was out, I leaned on the wall of the shower to listen better.

"So, continue," Hasan ordered. "Where's Jacqueline?"

I wanted to snicker as he went back to calling me Jacqueline. Jacky was apparently only for the rare slip.

"We're back in Jacky's hotel room, and she's in the shower. I decided to get this call moving so she could talk to you when she gets out. Now, I'll get the report done for both of us. I know the majority of what went on with them, so I'll relay that."

"So, them. The wolf was out there too and survived?" Niko asked quietly. I almost didn't hear him.

"He was." Jabari was getting annoyed at being interrupted. "It was four vampires thrown out of the local nest, pointed toward the mountains to cover up their killings. Has happened before and will happen again. These nest Masters and Mistresses always have a hard time killing their creations. They were riding death highs and juiced on supernatural blood. You know how it goes. Stronger and faster than usual." Jabari snorted. "We're going to need another night here to handle the politics with the nest. I'm going to take Jacky, so she can experience it—"

"Inside a vampire nest after you accuse the Master of a crime is not safe. I don't want Jacky going," Hasan snapped. He must have been insanely worried about me, which made me feel a little better.

"She handled herself well out in the park. All her

injuries are minor, and she stomached some traditional executions. I even saw her go into a frenzy for one of them. Had to haul her away and force her to back off to get the information I needed. She'll be fine in the nest, and I want the back up."

"You want Jacky as back up?" Davor snorted. "What the hell happened out there?"

"I met our sister," Jabari answered softly. "And I saw the loyalty she commanded from the werewolf, Heath Everson. He's a werewolf, and I hate him, but he's one of the best I've ever met."

"You hate him, but he's the best of them?" Zuri sounded incredulous. "Please explain."

"Don't worry about it, sister," Jabari said in a calming tone. "It's not important. What is important is, I think she's completely capable of handling a trip to the Seattle vampire nest with me. Maybe Heath can join us to represent the wolves. I'll inquire with him on his return. I told him I would handle it but I hadn't known everything then."

"Where is he?"

I closed my eyes. He respected me as backup now? It hadn't felt that way the entire time out there. Looking back, I remembered how he had started to teach me things, started to listen to me, and stopped making rude comments.

Jabari quickly gave them the same explanation I had given him. Then he backtracked and began his tale about what happened in the woods.

I purposefully took the slowest shower of my life,

listening in. I wonder if he knew what I was doing, or if he wasn't paying attention to the time. There was one part I was most interested in hearing, and when he finally got to it, I finally had to move on to rising off the soap all over me to get out of the shower.

"I had to make a rune of power to protect the cabin. They didn't have one and had been completely vulnerable when I arrived and helped them against the vampires."

"Why didn't she make one?" Hasan demanded. "All of you..." The snarl that came from those speakers made me want to sink to the bottom of the tub and hide.

"I never went to teach them to her," Jabari answered softly.

"Neither did I," Zuri admitted as well.

"Damn you both. Your mother gave you one job. She gave you one of her most valuable skills to help protect our family and..." The restraint it took Hasan to stop was more than I could have ever mustered. "We'll talk about this. You'll both fly to me, and we're going to discuss this."

"Can she even do them?" Davor asked, derision in his voice. "Talentless—"

"You'll show up too, so I can put you in your place," Hasan snapped. "Actually, all of you will be coming home in the next three days for a long talking to. She is my daughter, just like all of you are my children. You might not care about her as your sister, and that's fine, but I am done with this level of disrespect and lack of care for her safety."

"Father, we have lives—" Mischa tried to say, but Hasan wasn't having it. My heart was racing.

"You will put them on hold. That's an order."

"I was going to stay on her territory for a couple of weeks to make sure it's safe and teach her. She had some choice words for me when we last talked about the runes of power." Jabari sounded like he was completely willing to take the beating. "I've failed her as an older brother enough already, and that was made very clear to me. I'm not going to continue to do so."

I had to close my eyes. Tears unexpectedly threatened me, and I couldn't figure out why those words meant so fucking much. I hadn't come on the mission expecting I would get that much.

Damn you, Jabari. You heard every word we said about you out there and never told me.

"I'm proud of you," Hasan said, much gentler than he had just been. "I won't accept more neglect from any of you when it comes to her safety or inclusion in this family."

Jabari launched back into the talk, how we planned the next couple of days, what our game plan was. I finished cleaning off and stepped out of the shower, grabbing a towel. I dried off slowly and didn't use the hair dryer, wanting to keep the ability to hear. I was able to check my injuries in the mirror, wincing at the nasty bruising on my jaw and face. It would wear off quickly, but it looked pretty bad. They would know when they saw it that something had nearly happened. The rest of the cuts were scabbed over, and since nothing was deep or fatal, I didn't worry.

Slowly, Jabari got to where we were now, in my hotel room and how the next few days would go. My clothes were in the room, so I finally left the bathroom, and his head jerked, his dark eyes landing on me.

"Good shower?" he asked.

"Hi, Jacky!" Zuri called. "Glad you're alive!"

"Yup, good job out there!" Mischa said next.

"Thanks," I tried to say as the rest of the brood tried to talk at once. Davor was the only one who didn't say anything...not yet. "Good shower. Let me put some clothes on, then you can go, and I'll talk to them, so they can see I'm alive."

Jabari only nodded before looking back at the screen to continue talking to the family. I honestly didn't want to talk to any of them, but once I was dressed, I switched places with Jabari.

"Hi, everyone," I said, aiming for cheerful.

"Jacqueline," Hasan whispered in a sad and concerned tone. "What happened during those fights that led to that?"

"One of them got a good grab on me and tried to tear my head in half, using my snout as the starting point," I answered, swallowing. One of them gasped at my explanation, but I didn't catch who. "So, Jabari left something out."

"What?"

"I have a fae gift," I said softly. "And before any one of you freak out like he did, I didn't ask for it, nor did I trade for it. It was a gift. Ran into this fae that decided I needed some help last year when I was protecting Carey."

"Fae are known to meddle if they feel it might benefit them down the road. They walk roads we can't understand, and some of them are known to see the future," Hasan explained carefully. "What was the gift?"

"Pack magic," I whispered. "I can communicate like a werewolf while in my werecat form."

"Oh." His eyes went wide. Others in the family weren't much different. "And you've had this for...several months now."

"Yeah. Only a few trustworthy people knew before Jabari, and that was because I used it while we were rescuing Carey. They've kept it quiet, and I don't have much reason to use it. I figured...if it got out, it would be bad. They all agreed with me." I could name those people on one hand. The only people alive who knew about the gift were Heath, Landon, Carey, and Tywin, the current alpha in Dallas.

"If a wolf pack you didn't trust learned that, they would hunt you down," Niko said plainly. "We'll keep it a secret, but that's really useful. Really useful. Hasan, the ways we could—"

"We'll discuss it another time. Did it help you deal with the vampires?" He was leaning on a hand now, much like The Thinker.

"Yeah. It just made communication easier. It's not like I am suddenly a superhero or anything. Being able to talk in werecat form is useful." I shrugged. "Should have told you sooner, Hasan. Sorry."

"You live and learn," he said, dismissing my apology and forgiving me at the same time. "Who was the fae?"

"Nope. Not telling you that. Don't need or want anyone tracking him down. He might remember he gave it to me, and I might suddenly owe him something."

That made half of them laugh, including Hasan.

Before I could continue, Jabari was out of the bathroom and clean. I narrowed my eyes on him.

"Really? You were in there like...five minutes."

"I don't need an hour to get clean," he retorted. "Move over so they can also see me."

"Put some fucking clothes on!" I yelled, pushing him away before he could sit down. "And actually dry off! Don't get my shit wet, asshole!"

Jabari backed away, his hands up. He went to get a towel, dried off as I asked, and put on some clothes. When he came back, I moved my chair over and let him bring the second chair around to sit next to me. The entire time this was happening, our siblings either sat with horror on their faces or snickered, nearly an even split between the two. Hasan just had an indulgent smile on his face.

Right as Jabari sat down, there was a knock on the door, and I sighed.

"Let me get that. It's probably Heath."

I jumped up before any of them could say otherwise and went to the door. I was right. When I opened it, there was Heath, still dirty from the forest, the rain, and mud.

"Hey," I said softly, leaning on the door frame. I had missed him a little, realizing it as I saw his tired grey-blue eyes. He felt sane compared to the ones I left on the video call.

"Hey. I just wanted to let you know I got in safely. I'm going to shower and order some room service. Want to join me? Some real peace and quiet while I give you an update on what Geoffrey wants?"

I glanced back at Jabari, watching over the top of the laptop, listening to our siblings talk about the last couple of weeks. When I turned back to Heath, his eyes had narrowed, and he was looking over me at Jabari.

"Yeah, I'll come over. Just knock on the dividing door when you're ready."

"Thank you."

I closed the door as he walked to his own. I didn't sit next to Jabari on the call, lying out on my bed instead, trying to stretch tired muscles.

Jabari and the family talked about what they thought was the best course of action to reprimand the Master of the Seattle nest. There was a chance that could go sideways, but I only half listened. He would probably drill me on it repeatedly before we went.

When Heath knocked on the dividing door, I jumped up and ran out of the room.

29

CHAPTER TWENTY-NINE

I felt at home sitting at his table, watching him sigh in exhaustion as we waited on food to arrive. On his way back to the hotel, he'd bought a case of cheap beer, which made me laugh, but I totally took one.

Jabari better not give me shit when I go back over there. I fucking earned getting a little tipsy before passing out.

"Have you called Carey and Landon yet?" I asked as I cracked it open.

"No. I had Geoffrey send them a message I was safe as I flew in with Carter, but I haven't slowed down enough to call them yet. I don't want to be yelled at."

I looked over my shoulder and sighed. "Yeah, I took a long shower, so Jabari had to deal with the brunt of Hasan's anger. I'm sure he'll remember that he hasn't yelled at me soon and demand my presence, but I'm safe for now as they discuss the last couple of things we have to do before we go home."

"Like?" Heath frowned.

"We're going to talk to the Seattle vampire nest."

"Ah, fuck, Geoffrey was mentioning that. He doesn't want to send his wolves because he doesn't trust them at all. He wasn't sure what to do about them."

"Would you like to represent him and come with us?" I asked, sipping on the beer.

He shrugged. "Let me text him and see if that works for him." He pulled out his phone and sent a quick message to the Seattle Alpha. His phone dinged immediately with a reply. "That's an affirmative. He would love an outside wolf to go represent him."

"Doesn't it make him look weak?" I leaned back in my seat, kicking my feet out.

"Sure, but his wolves are all wary now. After I debriefed him, his inner circle passed the news. He's going to keep it from going to violence by imposing a ban on seeing vampires until tempers cool. If one of his pack went, there would be a fight, and that makes him look stupid. I'm a safer bet since none of my wolves died," he growled softly.

"Carter. That's our living wolf's name?"

"Yeah. He should survive. They put a feeding tube in him and half a dozen IVs. He didn't have any major organ failure, but his body was eating away at his muscles. He'll be in rehabilitation for months. I've never seen a werewolf that starved, and it was only a month."

"A month where a naturally high metabolism body was also being depleted of his blood at a rate that would have killed most things," I reminded him. "As an EMT, I would have rushed him to a hospital, but where we were made that impossible, and we had things to finish. Once we were in the car, I kept an eye on his vitals, but it was all I could do."

"I figured that's why you sat in the back with an unknown werewolf," he said, smiling a little. "Thank you."

"Of course," I murmured, pulling my beer to my chest, a little uncomfortable. "Right now, the plan is we take a day to eat, rest, and heal. Tomorrow night, we'll go to the nest and handle it, then leave in the morning."

"Good. Only two more nights until we get to go home."

We get to go home. We. I smiled at him.

"I miss Carey. Call her before the food arrives. I'll answer the door." I slapped the table a couple of times to rush him. He chuckled and started dialing while I waited impatiently. It only had to ring once.

"DAD!" she screamed. "Dad, you're okay! We were so worried!"

"Hey, baby girl!" he said happily. "I'm fine. I'm safe. A little bruised and cut, but nothing I can't handle."

"You promised everything would be fine! That you would be back before the end of the weekend and..." I heard her sniff, and my heart broke a little. "You promised." Another sniff and I knew she was crying.

"I know. I did promise," he consoled her gently. "This is life sometimes, baby girl. It's going to be okay. We're only going to be here for two more nights, then we can come home, and everything will go back to normal."

I hadn't told him Jabari was planning on following us home for a short time, so I let him keep that delusion for the moment. I would break it to him after we finished our business in Seattle. No reason to piss him off unnecessarily when we had shit to do.

"And where's Jacky?" she demanded. "She promised not to get hurt too! Landon couldn't tell me anything!"

"Where is your brother?" he asked softly. "And Jacky is fine, she's right next to me. We're waiting on dinner."

"I'm behind her. She grabbed the phone before I could." I snickered at Landon's annoyed voice. "Are you really well?"

"I am and should remain so." He eye-balled me hard as he said that. "But I would like to talk to you about business when you send Carey *to bed*."

"Dad! Let me talk to Jacky, at least! I've been so worried!"

He held the phone out to me, sighing heavily and dramatically—the man who was jealous of his daughter's best friend. I took the phone with a smile.

"Hey, Carey," I greeted happily, not the fake cheerfulness I had used on my werecat family. The joy was genuine for her—always.

"Are you really okay?" she asked softly, the worry in her voice making me feel loved.

"I am, kiddo. It was messy, but we did it. No, we're not going to give you the details."

"Was it bad?" She was so quiet.

"It was pretty bad," I answered. "But we're all okay."

"Good. I guess I should let Dad and Landon talk now that I know you're both okay, huh?"

"That might be good. Don't worry, we'll catch up when we get back. You might be interested in something when I get home." I eyed Heath, who gave me a narrowed-eyed stare.

Oh, that makes you curious, wolf? Wait until you find out I'm talking about introducing her to Jabari.

"Good night, Jacky."

"Good night, Carey."

I handed the phone back to Heath, and he told her good night as well, then launched into an explanation of the last few days to his son and what we were planning next. When room service knocked, I got it and separated our food out, the same order we had last time. I heard another knock right after, and Jabari received his own food.

I started eating and tuned out Landon and Heath, focusing on Jabari alone in my room. Oddly, I heard my siblings still, meaning the family meeting wasn't actually done yet.

"Where is she? Why are you eating alone?" Zuri asked, her voice a little tight.

"She's having dinner with Heath and talking to his family. He'll be going with us to the nest tomorrow night, it seems."

The walls were so thin. I didn't think Heath could hear as well as I could, but I figured it was common knowledge among the group now that nothing said was secret. Maybe Jabari thought I was too preoccupied to listen to him because he continued.

"Heath is protective of her. She's very protective of his daughter. It's not normal. I've never seen a friendship quite like it before, but they trust each other beyond measure."

"Interesting. I figured it would be a phase, and they would go their separate ways, eventually." Hasan sighed. "She's treading ground none of us have before, allying with a werewolf so closely."

"She is. After I was Changed, none of them would accept me, and I tried." Niko that time.

"Is it appropriate? She's a member of this family. It's funny to tease her about it, but she's eating with him and not Jabari."

"He understands her better than I do," Jabari admitted. "Much better than me. She's probably spent more time with him than I ever did with her. It's really our fault. We neglected her, and now, we must suffer the consequences."

"Everyone calls Niko the traitor," Davor mumbled. "I wouldn't even protect a wolf's kid—"

"Davor, I swear on everything I am, if you do not stop, I will come, claim your territory, drag you home, and reeducate you," Hasan snapped. "She isn't Liza. She doesn't try to be Liza. You must stop hating Jacky for something out of her control."

"No, she has more backbone than Liza," Jabari said. "She's tough when she needs to be and righteously angry when it's called for. Not what I was expecting. Not the naïve girl I thought she was, just still learning."

"Now you're on her side," Hisao pointed out with a bit of bitterness I didn't expect. "I should have been out there with you."

"It would have gone smoother, yes, but she was effective and followed orders. No reason to be angry at how it went." Jabari paused, and no one cut in. "She said I was heartless."

"Excuse me?" Zuri sounded offended, the precursor to a rant.

"She was angry," he said before his twin could continue. "And she was correct, in a way. We were all callous about the death of her human fiancé. We've all lost people and learned the hardships of this world over the centuries. We never gave her the chance to grow and learn. We expected her to be like us immediately, and she wasn't, so we thought she was a failure."

I finished my food and walked to the dividing door. Heath frowned at me as I sat down, my ear angled at it to hear better.

I didn't want him to see the tears in my eyes.

The silence stretched out before one of them sighed. Another coughed for a moment.

"And there's one last thing I wanted to discuss before letting you go for the evening."

"Please, Jabari, then yes, you need to rest." Hasan was back in concerned father mode.

"Have you ever encountered someone who can block the emotional currents of their scent? Heath Everson's scent tells one nothing about his emotional state. You can smell the powerful Alpha, his age and sex, but if his face is angry, his scent won't be. When he shows you nothing, there is nothing to get."

My heart thudded. This was about Heath. I wasn't the only person who noticed the intense control my werewolf had over his emotions and scent.

"No, but considering how the body works, those scents should be uncontrollable," Hasan said, thoughtfully. I heard a weird tapping sound, realizing that must have been him tapping his desk. "Some werewolf lines have Talents much like werecats. It could be possible that's his, and he doesn't announce it like I don't announce mine, and Zuri doesn't announce her own. I wonder if any of his children picked up the ability."

"None of us have picked up your Talent, so I wouldn't put much hope on the werewolves passing along theirs any more successfully. I'll do some research," Zuri told everyone professionally. "If that's all, I'm heading off. Jabari, stay safe dealing with the vampires tomorrow. I'll wait at Father's for you after you're done helping Jacky with the runes of power."

"Thank you, sister."

There were goodbyes, and I was left listening to Jabari pull out the mattress in the couch. Heath was watching me, his conversation with Landon finished.

"It's time to get some sleep," I said, yawning to punctuate the point.

"Do you want to stay over here?" he asked softly. "You can have my bed."

I almost said yes. He was more comfortable than Jabari and the family. We fought and nearly died together more than once now.

"No. I'm going back to my own bed," I said with a yawn. "Good night, Heath."

"Good night, Jacky," he replied, his eyes never leaving me as I left the room. I felt that gaze burning into my skin long after I closed the doors between our rooms.

Jabari said nothing from his bed, and I slid into mine without bothering him.

Finally, we were all asleep in relative safety with one last thing to finish up before leaving for home.

30
_____

CHAPTER THIRTY

The day was spent making sure we all had something decent to wear to the nest. For Heath and me, that was easy. We had both brought extra clean clothing and had nice enough outfits for a small political affair. I didn't have a dress or anything, but I wouldn't wear one of those into a vampire nest, anyway. Clean black slacks and a professional blouse worked and allowed for movement in case something happened. Heath went with a black suit I couldn't help but admit looked dashing on him. Jabari had to run out and find something, unprepared for a political affair, but he was ready by the time we had to go.

We loaded up into Jabari's SUV, and he drove the winding roads of Seattle. I wasn't sure where we were going, but we left downtown and stopped at a mansion that had an amazing view of the Puget Sound on one side and a beautiful forest on the other. I had no idea where we were, but it was a place I wouldn't mind living if it weren't for the vampires I knew were inside.

"This is it," he announced. "They're expecting us. Jacky, what did I tell you?"

"Don't make eye contact with anyone except the Master for long periods of time. Don't allow any of them close enough to bite me. Growling, snarling, and hissing are frowned upon but not offenses they can call me out for. None of these vampires will be juiced or riding death highs, so we can easily defeat them if it comes to it. If they threaten our lives, we threaten them with our family and complete annihilation."

"Good." He nodded once, satisfied with that. "Heath, all of that also goes for you as well."

"The North America Werewolf Council briefed me earlier today. I'm allowed to push the Council coming down on the nest if it's needed. They are also already talking to the vampires of the Tribunal about possible charges being pressed." Heath yawned, seemingly unworried.

"Hasan is also already beginning discussions with them," Jabari said. "Good. That means we're a united front. A first for our kinds."

Yay! Look, the big boys in the sand box can *play together!*

I snorted at my thoughts, and we all left the vehicle. Night had fallen a few short hours before, and together, we went to the front door and knocked.

I was kept in the middle of the two men, holding a black bag containing the heads. We had gone over this as well. While I might be stronger than Heath because I was a werecat, neither of the men wanted me in the vulnerable position of flanking another. It also put me in the talking position, something Jabari wanted to 'test my political skills,' promising to help if needed.

I couldn't argue with both of them, so I didn't bother trying. I stood in the middle, and that was that. I held the bag because it was less likely to get stolen from me than it was from them.

The door creaked open, and a beautiful man smiled at us.

"Jabari and Jacqueline, children of Hasan and Heath Everson, Alpha?" he asked politely.

"That's us," I said brightly. "I'm Jacqueline, and this is Jabari." I gestured to the very tall werecat on my left. Then I moved my hand to the very tall werewolf on my right. "This is Alpha Everson. You are?"

"You may call me Kevin. I will be escorting you to the Master of the Nest. He's been waiting for you."

"Thank you."

Kevin ushered us in, and I went to follow first until Heath stepped in front of me, looking around. Jabari held me back for a moment until the werewolf seemed pleased and nodded. I was allowed to enter, then my brother.

We followed, ignoring the large double staircase that looked like it belonged in a palace in front of us and went for the doors underneath them. Everything was dark wood with dark fabrics and low light. It would have been sensual if it wasn't the home of vampires. That fact only made it reminiscent of several horror movies I had seen in my lifetime.

Kevin pushed the doors open and paused in the center of the doorway.

"Presenting Jabari, son of Hasan. Presenting Jacqueline, daughter of Hasan. Presenting Heath Everson, Alpha." Like any good movie, he spoke so loudly he echoed back, and everyone in the room was very aware of who was waiting behind him to enter. Around the room, I could see vampires feeding on humans, licking their necks as blood dripped down.

There was a smell that couldn't be ignored. Some of the humans were close to death. Many were much too pale. The vampires fed hard and well, taking their meals to the very edge. I didn't know if it was allowed, but I had a suspicion it was the reason four death-addicted vampires had come out of the nest. It seemed like it was all too easy to kill one of the humans and begin a terrible addiction.

"Thank you, Kevin," someone said in a whispered voice, seemingly weak, but I found the one who spoke and knew he was anything but. He exuded power and was definitely in charge of the room.

The Master sat at the center of a long table in the back of the room, directed at the door we walked through. Vampires parted in front of us, and Kevin led us to him. As we drew closer, I could see he had the same blood-red eyes as every vampire in the room. His skin was too pale, and his fingers were too long as he steepled them in front of his chest and waited on us. His dark hair was past his shoulders.

I realized what I didn't like about him.

He was a clichéd motherfucker.

"What important task has brought you to my home this evening?" he asked, not bothering to stand on our arrival. Jabari had told me he would stand due to our positions in the werecat world. Was this an offense I should be paying attention to?

Neither of the men with me spoke, so I went for it, quickly throwing together an idea based on Jabari's suggestions.

"We've come to discuss with you a problem we recently encountered in the Cascades and possible reparations between your nest, the Seattle pack, and the family of Hasan." I swung the bag off my shoulder and unzipped it as I began to walk up to his table.

"Why would I owe the werewolves or werecats reparations?" he demanded.

I didn't stop walking forward. We weren't offered seats to speak to him as equals, and he didn't stand, putting us in a position of lesser power. I pulled out one of the heads at random and put it on the table. Several vampires hissed.

"Do any of these belong to you?" I asked, reaching in for the second head. When it was placed on the table, I noticed the Master's still face twitched. With the third head, he couldn't stop his lip from curling up ever so slightly. With the last head, he was glaring at me. "They killed two werecats, three werewolves, and tortured a fourth werewolf for a month."

"No. None of them belong to me," he answered, a noticeable tension in his words.

"Are you sure?" I asked, pretending to be confused.

"They don't belong to me because they left of their own free will. What they did with their time after leaving here isn't my concern." He didn't move, didn't lean forward, didn't do anything. His gaze was blazing hot, though. I could tell he was pissed.

"One of them claimed her Master in Seattle didn't want to kill her, so he threw her and the rest of the gang out, along with the ringleader." I gestured to all the heads then pointed at the one that died with a serene face, the one Jabari had questioned. "This one said it." I frowned at him.

"What else did that one say?" he asked softly, his eyes narrowing. "She was always unstable."

I pondered, not taking him or his anger seriously. "That her Master told her no one would miss some campers, but that Seattle wasn't safe for her anymore."

"And you say they killed five supernaturals and kept another hostage to torture?"

"Well, they were using him as a feeding source after all the other wolves were dead. You know the penalty for these things, of course. Decapitation by sun burning and brought back to their nest of origin. Reparations are to be paid if the Master is found to be negligent in his duties." I leaned in close. "And you were."

"You have no right to say that to me!" he snapped.

Still, he didn't bother standing up for me. "You have the word of a dead vampire who was known to be—"

"Master, I know someone who can perform the ritual to reanimate those heads and make them talk in front of the Tribunal," Jabari called out from his place behind me. "Do not push me to it. Reparations for the wolves lost and injured will be paid to the Seattle pack. Reparations for the two werecats, Gaia and Titan, will be paid to Hasan directly, and he will make sure it is delivered to any family they might have."

"Why should I? You don't have a case." He reached out to grab the head I pointed out. Before he could reach it, I snatched his wrist and snarled viciously.

"That belongs to me," I warned him. "Heath, Jabari, come put these away."

Both men rushed up and quickly stored the heads again.

"If they used to belong to me, they belong to me in death to make proper arrangements for their disposal," the Master hissed. "Unhand me."

"No." I yanked him, forcing him from his seat onto his feet. "And while I have your attention, when guests of equal rank walk into your home, you fucking stand up and greet them. Now, I might be a rough American, but I am a daughter of Hasan, a member of the Tribunal and leader of the werecats. Jabari is his oldest son and heir. We aren't equal to your rank, we're *above it*. Alpha Heath Everson is an Alpha who once served on the werewolf Council in North America. He *is* equal to your rank if not *higher*."

Words I never thought would come out of my mouth. Social ranking was something I had avoided and run from for years. Now it served me. If it meant getting what was due for the deaths of several innocents minding their own business, I was going to wield it like a sword.

"You're an upstart who hasn't earned her place," the Master retorted. "Everyone knows you should be without your head and would be if not for your father."

"She might not have earned her place yet, but I have," Jabari growled, leaning over me. "You will pay reparations. These heads shall be sent to the fae Tribunal members, an uninterested and unbiased party, for their interrogations."

"The fae aren't unbiased!" He tried to yank his hand from me, but I squeezed, my grip growing tighter and tighter.

"Maybe you shouldn't have been so callous with your creations," I hissed. "You might have still had an ally at the end of this. As it stands, your Master and Mistress of the Tribunal are going to have to smooth over your mess. Pay the reparations."

"Screw you," he growled.

I shoved him away. "Jabari?"

"That's his only chance of smoothing things over before they get worse. If he doesn't want to, the Tribunal will make him. Let's go. We're done here." He turned and held out an arm for me. I rolled my eyes and walked past him. When I reached Heath, who had backed off a few steps, I gestured for him to keep moving with me.

We walked out of the ballroom and the mansion together.

As we loaded the bag into the back, all staying together, I heard rustling in the woods. I wasn't the only one. All three of us snapped to attention and stared at the woods to find several vampires with sickening red eyes. One hissed as I made eye contact with it.

They drew closer, some skittering across the ground on all fours, some walking slowly.

"Halt," Jabari snarled.

I went for something a bit more intimidating.

"If you start this fight, we're going to kill as many of you as we can before we fall. You won't win in the end, though. Kill two of Hasan's children and their ally, and he will bring the entire weight of our family down on your head and every werecat that respects and follows him. You will be dust. Your Master will be dust. Everything to do with you, including your home, will be dust. Then our family will build a mansion in its place and eat holiday meals together, knowing they earned the spoils of war, not ever giving you a second thought."

Heath and Jabari turned to me, both surprised by my words. Maybe I was being a little too dramatic...it was possible.

The vampires didn't continue their approach, several hissing viciously at my threat. We hurried into our SUV, and Jabari hit the gas, screaming down the driveway like it was a racetrack.

After the mansion disappeared behind us, I breathed

again. Once we made it out of the gates, officially off the driveway, I relaxed completely.

"They outnumbered us bad enough, we could have gotten killed," I said softly.

"The Master was considering his options. If he killed us and destroyed the heads, there would be nothing for the Tribunal to use against him, even our deaths. We would be unfortunate accidents, or he could say we threatened him unduly, and no one could say otherwise. He plays a dangerous game inside his nest and doesn't want anyone to know it." Jabari's voice was tight.

"You noticed that?"

"I noticed it," Heath said softly, looking out his window with a frown. "He lets them nearly kill humans. I bet many die after those sorts of parties, and he just disposes of the bodies. I'm going to call Geoffrey and fill him in as we head back."

"I'm thinking the same thing. I'll report it to Hasan, then we shall go home," Jabari said. "We're done here. The rest is up to the Tribunal."

"That it is," I whispered, looking at the trees as we drove. I could hear Heath already on the phone, rattling off the meeting as I considered Jabari's words.

Home sounded good.

Then our ride flipped as something slammed into the side of it.

31

CHAPTER THIRTY-ONE

I couldn't think. This was my second time in a flipping vehicle, and even as a werecat, it wasn't a pleasant sensation, fear pumping through my veins. My head hit the ceiling, the door, and other parts of the car, rattling painfully as it still remembered being hit with a rock only a couple of nights prior. I heard the crunch of metal and the groans and yells of pain from the men in the car with me.

I couldn't think. I barely registered that I needed to protect my head, finally trying to wrap my arms around it, hoping I broke an arm before I cracked my skull.

It was all too similar, all too much.

It settled after three rolls, rocking as it rested upside down, skidding a little further.

I couldn't think.

Outside the car, other sounds could be heard— rustling in the bushes and trees, a wind blowing hard.

A small part of me wasn't in rainy Washington anymore.

Part of me was on that little tropical island with the rain coming down, hoping I would be able to get out of the car.

"Shane?" I whispered. "Shane, are you okay?" He had to be okay.

A groan was all I heard in response.

Not again. No. This can't happen again. Not this. Anything but this.

I fought to free my legs from between the seat and the dashboard. The airbag had gone off, and I fought against it as well. I snarled as I finally freed my first leg.

"Shane?" I called again, my voice not as loud as I wanted it to be. Then my brain started to function again, thanks to my nose. Werewolf and werecat, both male and bleeding. Not Shane. This wasn't Shane. He was dead already. Dread made my throat grow tight. Not Shane, but two other very important people. "Heath? Jabari?"

A louder groan.

More rustling outside the car. Something or someone trying to pry one of the doors open. Talking, but my ears were ringing, and I couldn't make out any words. Something about that made me desperate to get moving. The impact had been on the driver's side, where Jabari and Heath were, which meant I had more space. I didn't take the brunt of the accident, which meant I had to get moving. They could be dying for all I knew. Desperation made me fumble with the seat belt, finally getting it to release as the door behind me flew open.

I fell to the ceiling and growled, trying to turn to see what was in the back.

I could barely think, but I could feel. I could feel the pain of the accident, the need to defend the others, and the need to figure out what had just happened.

A blur was all I saw in the backseat, and I tried to grab for it, fumbling as my vision spun, and my coordination made me fall onto my belly. Something dripped down on me, and I looked up slowly to see Heath's grey-blue eyes. He was conscious, and I was in the way. Blood was dripping off his left arm, but I didn't see any other injuries.

"Who's Shane?" someone asked. I turned to the open door and saw red eyes in a pale face.

"My dead fiancé," I answered, not sure why I even wanted to answer. "He died in an accident like this one. Almost killed me too."

"You should have died with him. Divine retribution, then." The vampire smiled. "No one threatens our nest and Master."

I grinned back, knowing there was blood in my mouth because I could taste the rusty thickness of it. I probably bit my inner cheek or tongue during the accident.

"I'm not going to die tonight," I promised. Reaching up, I tore out Heath's buckle, then dodged as he fell to the ceiling. I didn't look back at him as I scrambled out of the open door and tackled the vampire who hadn't thought to get away. I snarled as I got my hands on its head and twisted as hard as I could, listening to the clear and perfect snap of its neck breaking.

"Don't stop," Heath growled as he climbed out after me. "Tear its fucking head off and finish it."

I obliged, using my weight to hold the limp vampire down and continued to twist. Muscles tore, blood poured, and slowly, I broke all the connecting tissue and threw the head aside. Heath stood over me, looking out into the darkness. I followed his gaze and saw red eyes growing larger.

"Fuck. He was supposed to report us dead, wasn't he?" I asked softly.

"Yes, and this is probably the clean-up if we weren't," Heath muttered back. "Jabari?"

"Alive when I got a whiff of him, but I don't know what sort of state he's in. Can we do this?" I swallowed, hearing the running vampires speeding toward us. They wouldn't be as strong as the ones in the park, but they were healthy. We weren't.

"We're going to try," he growled. "Jacky—"

I didn't get to hear what he said as a vampire landed on the SUV behind us. I turned and met it as it jumped for me. I landed squarely on my back and tried to roll backward, kicking up at the same time, sending the vampire flying. I went all the way over and tried to stand. One barreled into me, and I felt ribs crack. I roared and grabbed its arms and slowly pulled them off my waist, my muscles straining. I didn't stop once I was free, breaking one of the arms at the elbow, listening to the resounding scream of pain in response.

I didn't really have time to think. Going on instinct, I tossed that vampire to the ground and swung around, lifting an elbow to slam another in the jaw. When I saw one trying to crawl into the car, I reached out and grabbed it by the ankles as another jumped onto my back. I pulled with all my might, letting it drag over the broken glass and threw it away from the SUV.

I screamed as teeth hit my shoulder, and I reached up, grabbing a handful of hair. I ripped the locked jaw off my body, tearing open my shoulder, flipped the vampire over my shoulder with a roar of rage, and stomped down on its face twice.

It felt like a street fight, something I had never been a part of but had seen enough in the movies to get the gist. They wanted to dogpile me, and I kept having to toss them off, trying to keep them off me. I took a punch to the face, making my head throb, and stumbled for a second. Two tackled me together, and again, a set of fangs sank into me, this time on my arm. The second went for my neck, and I grabbed its neck before it could land the strike. I put my medical knowledge to use and squeezed tightly, putting all my werecat power into it. Everything beneath my hand crushed, and when I pulled, it all came with me. The vampire wasn't dead, but it was completely incapacitated by the action. I threw aside the pieces of vampire in my hand, grabbed its bottom jaw, dropped open from the pain, and pulled it down further, breaking bones and causing more blood to rush out of the vampire's mouth. It covered my face, neck, and chest now, putrid and stale, pumping out of veins it didn't originate from.

Once that one was dead, I shoved the body away

and grabbed the hair of the one chewing on my arm, taking long swallows of my blood. Pulling it off with a scream, I wrestled it to its back in the mud. Before it could attack me, I tore out a clump of its hair. While it screamed in pain, I grabbed its neck and tore it open like the previous one. I reached into its mouth and ripped out its fangs.

I was feeling particularly vicious. I could barely think, but I could feel.

Rage. Pain. Insult.

Sorrow.

"Jacky! We've got them retreating!" Heath called. My head snapped up, and I snarled angrily.

I didn't want them retreating. I wanted them to fight me and meet their fucking maker. I wanted them to pay. The callousness of their Master got innocent people killed. Their need to hide their crimes nearly got me killed...nearly got Heath and Jabari killed.

They didn't get to run away.

I stood up slowly, kicking away the vampire's body.

"Where?" I demanded in a growl.

"We need to check on Jabari," he reminded me quickly, reaching for me as I went to find a blood trail. I shook him off hard, but he latched back on. "*Jacky. We need to check on your brother.*"

I stopped, letting the words sink in. Jabari. Yes. He was in the SUV. I protected him. I needed to see if he was alive.

If he wasn't, there was going to be a purge the likes of which the world had never seen. I would personally ask

Hasan to have every vampire nest in the country raided and exterminated.

I could only nod at Heath, though. He relaxed just a little and stepped away from me, not going into the SUV, leaving the space for me to try.

I crawled in and found my older brother breathing slowly.

"Jabari?" I asked softly, finally finding my voice. The entire left side of his face was cut open from the glass, and bruises were already beginning to form. There was no smell of silver in the air, a blessing.

"Sister," he murmured, a raspy attempt at speaking. "Vampires?"

"Yes. Heath and I protected you from the clean-up crew. We need to get help. More could always come."

"They will," he said, gasping. "My chest."

I cursed and put my hand up to his chest, gently feeling. Sure enough, every rib on the left side was broken. I couldn't tell if one punctured a lung or not, but I was guessing none had because he wasn't coughing up blood while upside down.

"I need to get you down. Does your back hurt? Can you feel your legs?"

"Hurts...not broken," he answered, groaning. I reached up and braced myself for him to fall on me. When the seatbelt released, the fall wasn't pretty, but my body kept his head from taking the brunt of the impact. He fired off something in a language I had no hope of ever learning and moved so I could get out from underneath him. "Help coming?"

"No idea. Let's get out of the death trap first." I crawled out of the SUV, then helped him out. He staggered as he tried to stand up. "Heath, do you think someone is going to come to help?"

"I was on the phone with Geoffrey when we were shoved off the road," he said, stepping closer. "There's a chance he's coming. There's a chance he just thinks the call dropped."

"Let me find your phone. You protect Jabari. He's got several broken ribs and probably more problems I can't see. Right, Jabari?"

Her brother only groaned and sank down to the earth. My gut twisted. This was the great General, and a car accident nearly did him in.

I crawled back into the car, searching around for any of our cellphones. I found Jabari's in the center console and nearly cried in relief when I saw it wasn't in pieces. Where mine and Heath's had gone, I had no idea, but one phone was better than none.

I crawled back out, showing off the phone.

"Do you remember Geoffrey's number?"

"Not by heart," Heath answered softly, frowning. "Who could we call..."

"Hasan," I answered, already looking for the contact. If I couldn't get someone close by to save us, I was going to call the biggest, baddest mother fucker to avenge us.

"Jabari, how did—"

"Hi, Hasan. We were run off the road and attacked by the nest. I'm certain more are on the way. I'm calling to tell you everything, so I need you to not interrupt me at all. I don't know how much time we have."

"Talk fast."

I gave him the rundown about the Seattle vampire nest, listening to him hum and scratch notes down. I explained the crash and the attack. Jabari's injuries. Mine. Hell, I even gave him the injuries I could see on Heath, whether or not he cared about those.

"What do you need?" he asked when I paused.

"I need you to find some way to contact the local wolf pack. Go through the Tribunal or whatever, I don't know or care. They might be the only ones who can keep us alive tonight, but we can't reach them. If...if we don't make it, I promised this motherfucker that the family would destroy him. We would raze his home to the ground and claim his land as spoils of war. I want you to make sure they don't get away with this."

"They won't," Hasan promised softly. "Stay on the line. Please."

"You might have to listen to me die," I whispered.

"I know. I have other phones to make calls."

I looked at the two men with me and saw they were staring back at me.

"I want to kill them," I growled softly. "I want to kill all of them for this."

"I've got one of the werewolf Tribunal members on video conference," Hasan said quickly. "Hold on, my children. We're going to get you help. Jacky, put the phone down and Change. Be ready."

"Yes, sir." I handed the phone to Jabari and nodded at

Heath. I wanted him at my back. Needed it. I wanted to know we were both in our most powerful forms to defend ourselves.

We Changed at the same time with me finishing first.

"Father...she Changes so fast," Jabari mumbled into the phone. "You told me, but every time I see it, I'm proud."

"I know," Hasan whispered. "Hold on, Jabari. We're getting help."

"She's good..." Jabari said softly, groaning. Then he coughed, and I looked over, whining as I saw blood begin to go down his chin. He was deteriorating faster than he could heal, and his lung must have been punctured. I had missed it. He shook his head at me. "Stay focused. Tend to the wounded...after...the fight."

"Fine. You're going to heal at my place, though. You're not leaving until I know you're fully healed." I was just beginning to find common ground with my brother. I wasn't going to lose him now.

Heath growled deeply, staring off into the woods. I followed his line of sight and saw the problem.

The vampires were coming. We had Changed just in time.

32
———

CHAPTER THIRTY-TWO

I snarled as the Master of the Seattle nest stepped to the front of the pack of vampires coming toward us through the trees.

"Since you seem to have so much fight in you, I guess I have to soil myself to finish this," he said with a dramatic sigh. "You should have just given me the heads and let it go. I won't let my paradise be taken away from me and destroyed."

"Warned you..." Jabari said as loud as he could. My heart ached. I wondered if the accident targeted him, being the strongest in the group. "Dead anyway for this."

"Yes, I heard your warning. My nest and I will be long gone before your family comes to get their vengeance. I'm not scared of a grieving old man and his children."

If I could have laughed, I would have. Idiot didn't really understand who Hasan was, did he?

"*Are you ready, Jacky?*" Heath asked me softly. "*We're being surrounded.*"

"*I know.*" I could hear them moving through the brush of the small forest around us. Smell didn't matter for this fight. Even if there wasn't a hulking piece of hot metal and fuel behind me, I wouldn't have been able to smell them. I could only listen, and I was paying the utmost attention.

The Master of the nest waved a hand, and suddenly, they were coming at us. I jumped in front of Jabari, who was leaning against the SUV. It was only a couple of seconds later when one jumped on my back, and another came at my front. I snapped at it, only to feel the slice of something I wasn't expecting to deal with.

"*They have silver!*" I screamed at Heath. I hoped Jabari heard. I hoped we weren't going to die.

But fangs sunk into my feline back as I dodged the thrust of a silver sword, and I had a very bad feeling.

Until howls filled the air—lots of them.

I had heard a song like it once before when Heath and I fought off the traitors of the Dallas-Fort Worth werewolf pack.

The vampire biting on me pulled away, and I took my chance to snap at her, making contact with her thigh. I didn't get the grab I wanted, but one would be limping a little now.

"*Jacky! Look!*" Heath ordered. A nose prodded my hip, and I turned, realizing everyone was standing still.

Through the trees, upwind of us, a pack of werewolves headed our way. One in the front lifted its head and howled as it ran, and the rest answered. I couldn't take my eyes off it as the vampires faced their new adversaries.

The wave of wolves rolled into the battleground and began helping to tear the nest to pieces.

"*Geoffrey?*" Heath called out. I backed up to Jabari again, wanting to stay close to him. He needed my protection. I didn't hear anything from the pack, but Heath stood close to me and watched the carnage unfold while keeping me up to date. "*He heard the accident over the phone and started calling in everyone. They already had a small force prepared just in case, a typical procedure if a meeting goes sour.*"

"*Are they going to take out the entire nest?*" I asked.

"*Yes. This is considered an act of war against the North American Werewolf Council now. He already called it in...*" Heath growled, but it seemed satisfied. "*We've been given free rein to obliterate the nest by the Tribunal Master and Mistress. Our retribution.*"

Politics. I was never one for them. All of it happened so fast. I looked down at Jabari, whose eyes were drifting closed.

"*Brother. I'm going to get the one responsible for this.*"

"Go," he coughed. He was holding his chest carefully. "I'll be fine. Take Heath. Ask some wolves to come over here? Fuck, got to ask wolves for help."

"*They're all we got right now. Don't complain,*" I reminded him. I didn't think the Seattle pack was going to be stupid enough to kill Jabari the General right now. And I owed it to him, Gaia and Titan, and four innocent wolves to take the fucker down. I was going to do it.

"Go, Jacky," he ordered. "Kill him and bring us honor and victory."

I nodded my head once and took off, looking for the Master of the nest. I didn't even know the man's name, as sad as that was. I never needed it for anything that was supposed to happen tonight. Maybe Heath knew it, but I didn't care to ask.

In the end, I'd probably never know any of these vampires' names.

And it didn't matter.

Heath followed behind me, but we couldn't find the Master of the nest anywhere in the fighting. I took a shot and began running back toward the mansion, remembering how he said they would be gone before our family ever showed up. Heath followed me without question. Neither of us was at top speed, running on pure adrenaline at this point. I knew Heath was just as banged up as me, and there was nothing either of us could do about it until the mission was over.

We were able to find the road and make it up the driveway to the mansion again. The vampires must have known the area well because I'd needed those to find my way back.

"There," I growled. A growl in my chest and throat matched as I bared my teeth at the Master of the nest, who was busy throwing things into a car.

"Time to die," Heath snarled in agreement.

Together, we stalked up to the vampire, hidden in the

night while he was busy trying to run for his life. He left all his people to die to save himself.

Disgusting coward.

I ran for him first, going for the jump at his back. He blurred and was out of the way by the time I landed. A whoosh and silver cut through my flank. Heath howled and jumped in next.

"He's a Master for a reason," Heath snapped. *"He's older and better than the rest! They gain power with age like we do!"*

I didn't really care. I lunged for him again, keeping his attention off Heath, who snapped at his legs behind him. The vampire was fast, dodging out of the way in time to strike at each of us. We needed to wear him out before we dropped, but I wasn't sure how. Then I had a damned bad idea. We were going for his legs—I wanted his neck.

I lunged higher, causing him to bring up his sword. It slid over my ribs, and I roared in pain and fury. My attack missed.

But Heath's didn't. He jumped onto the vampire's back and pushed him to the ground. I turned and grabbed the vampire's leg and shook hard, holding him down as Heath placed his jaws over the vampire's head and bit down. *Hard.*

More than a bit morbidly, I thought it sounded like cracking a watermelon.

And like that, the reason for everyone's troubles was dead. I looked up at Heath, who looked back at me, blood and gore falling from his mouth. He lifted a paw and tried to wipe it out. Mentally, I smiled a little as dizziness washed over me.

Then I passed out.

I woke up in the back of a vehicle. Someone was rubbing my hair, but it wasn't a scent I recognized.

"Where am I?" I demanded, groaning as everything began to catch up, and my body ached. My head throbbed.

"I'm Emmy. An old friend of Heath's. We had to get him into treatment as well, so I decided to stay with you." She kept rubbing my hair. "Do you remember your name?"

"Jacqueline Leon, daughter of Hasan," I answered. "Jacky. We came up here to investigate the deaths of two werecats and help my brother, Jabari, son of Hasan. We learned there were also four missing werewolves. We saved one...then we killed the vampires who killed the others, and the nest wanted to cover it all up by killing us. Did I miss anything?"

"No, it seems your memory is just fine," she said with a chuckle. "We're getting you to the hospital where Jabari was flown. We have a few werewolf doctors in the pack who are willing to help him reset the broken bones before they heal wrong. You have a few cracked ribs yourself, you know. Also, a not so minor concussion."

"You a doctor?" I asked. Where had I heard the name

Emmy before? That was where I was blanking. An old friend of Heath's didn't sound right.

"No. I married one, and he trained me to be a field assistant."

Married.

"You used to fuck Heath," I remembered, though I probably shouldn't have said it out loud.

She sputtered for a minute, and I finally opened my eyes to see her. Cascading red hair matched the blush on her face. Maybe I could have been less crude.

"Sorry. Not thinking straight..." I felt a little bad. "Good for you, marryin' a doctor. Heath's got bad history with ladies, I think."

"Oh yeah. Twice a widower before I met him, and a baby momma since I left. I know his history with women." Emmy laughed. "And now you."

"Oh, it's not like that," I said quickly. "No. He's a nice guy, but he's a werewolf and an Alpha with it. Not my type." *Without the werewolf problem, he would totally be my type.*

"Of course. He wouldn't be your type, would he? A werewolf would love him, but then, you aren't one of us, and that's okay." Her gentle hand ran over my hair again. I could see why a doctor married her. She had an amazing bedside manner. "Why don't you rest? We're almost at the hospital."

I nodded, closing my eyes. When the vehicle pulled to a stop, my eyes opened again as the back was opened. Emmy climbed out first as I let them lift me out on the stretcher I was on.

It took some time, but I was cleared to get up and move once I was in the hospital. Only a few hours, but too long to me, for some reason. We were somewhere in Seattle, but I didn't know the name of the hospital. If I had my way, I was never coming back to this state for as long as I lived, even if that was an eternity.

"Where's my brother? His name is Jabari," I asked a nurse who passed through my room. I had been left alone when I was cleared to move around, and while that was fine, I had people to look out for. Heath would be fine. He was with other wolves. Jabari was an old werecat who could prove to be a problem for a lot of people if he suddenly decided he didn't feel safe.

"Come with me. I'll show you." She smiled at me kindly, and I trotted out of the room after her. My head hurt with each step, but that was fine. Everything was settled in my mind. I just needed to get my brother and my werewolf and go home.

She led me into a quiet, lonely room at the end of the hall.

"We put him in here under heavy sedatives when the doctors were done with him. His age and species means he'll burn through them soon." She waved me in, and I left her at the door, going to the large man in the bed in an unnatural sleep.

Bedside vigil wasn't something I was good at, but there was no one else there. If Zuri had been in the States, she wouldn't leave his side. None of them would. I couldn't.

It felt like hours, but he began to stir. The first thing I

saw that showed he was waking up, though, was the deep inhale and flaring his nostrils, letting me know he was sniffing for enemies or allies.

"Little sister," he greeted softly. "I'll be fine. Tell me you saw a doctor."

"I've been done. Waiting on you to wake up so we can go home. You wanted to come to my territory for a little while, and I don't want Hasan yelling at you when you're not one-hundred percent."

"Ah, now you grow protective. I'll be sure to tell Zuri there's a sister here in the States willing to baby her brother when she feels he needs to be babied."

"It's nice to turn it around on you after everything you did," I retorted.

"I bet." He groaned and pushed himself to sit up. "A couple of weeks and I'll be fine. There was silver in the fight. How are you, really?"

"I'll have a scar on my ribs from a silver blade. Nothing else permanent. My concussion will give me a problem for a few days, but it shouldn't be bad."

"And your wolf?"

"I don't know. I was more worried about you in a hospital full of them than I was him. I knew they would treat him like royalty."

"Good wolf. Don't like him, but good wolf. What happened? Do we know anything new?"

I sighed. "I'm hoping Heath will know more. In the end, it doesn't matter, but it would be nice to know the whole story."

"We'll wait together. I don't think I'm ready to get out

of bed. Modern technology strikes again with a car accident. I told Father when cars were beginning to get made, they were death traps. They just keep getting faster, though. Every year, faster and faster."

"Stop complaining, old man. You don't get to. I've been in two of them now that should have killed me. I get to complain. Not you."

"Fine," he huffed and smiled at me. "Hopefully, there won't be a third. I heard you. You called out for him." I looked away this time, but he reached out and grabbed my hand. "I'm sorry. I should have never been so cold. I never understood, but I see how deeply losing him hurt you."

"It was a long time ago. You know what? After all of this, let's call it even, shall we?" I tried to smile back at him, but it scratched my weary emotions raw to realize someone had heard me calling out for a dead man. On top of that, Jabari's words were too much.

"We'll call it even, as you modern ones say," he agreed.

We waited in silence after that, just enjoying each other's company. It felt like hours later when Heath stumbled in, his arm bandaged to the shoulder and a crutch to help him walk.

"Two broken ribs," he said. "You?"

"Six," Jabari replied. "Punctured lung. Some other minor fractures"

"Three and a concussion," I added. *What a weird dick measuring contest to be a part of.* "Any news?"

"No. They used a group to shove our car off the road

and sent it flying. A couple died in the effort to kill us before we could report back. I have a feeling the Master of the nest was desperate to stop us, even if it meant his own downfall. There's nothing left for us to do, though. Geoffrey wants me to get out of his territory. The Tribunal wants to come in and clean it up and offered their sympathies to us for this mess."

"Then let's get home," I declared, trying to stand up. When I wobbled, he moved as fast as he could to my side. When he tried to help me with his good arm, I narrowed my eyes at him, making him laugh.

"Fine. Let's get home. Jabari, where's home for you?"

"Botswana this decade, but I'll be staying with Jacky for a couple of weeks," he answered. Heath froze, then slowly looked down at me. I gave him my most innocent smile.

"Carey will love him," I promised, hoping it wouldn't be a lie.

CHAPTER THIRTY-THREE

THREE WEEKS LATER

"Have a safe drive, Jabari," I said, smiling at my older brother as he finished loading his things into his car. "And have a nice flight."

"I shall. You stay out of trouble." He smiled back up at me. "Are you confident with the runes? Do you want me to run through them one more time?"

"I'm fine. We're good. I think I've got a handle on them." I knew why he was worried. He ended up staying longer than he planned when I had a hard time getting the hang of the runes. No matter what I did for the first two weeks of his visit, I couldn't make them work. It wasn't until the third week I finally made one that worked. Even then, he made all of them for my home and bar. I was now protected from demonic things, vampires, fae, and all manner of things I didn't really know.

"If you have any questions, Zuri and I—"

"I know," I confirmed, gently pushing him toward the

open driver's side door. "Go home, Jabari. I'm ready to get back to normal."

"I'm worried. Most of our siblings do them much easier. You are the worst at them yet." He was frowning now, and I kept pushing.

"My self-esteem doesn't need the reminder. You left me that little book in case I forget any, and I'll keep practicing. Promise." Honestly, I had been serious when I said I didn't care if I knew them or not. The pain had come from never being told about them, never being offered them. Now that I had them, I was grateful, but I wasn't going to practice them for hours on end, the way Jabari wanted me to. I had a business to run.

Speaking of which... "Jabari, really. I have to get the bar up and running for today."

"You need to hire help," he mumbled petulantly. "As your older brother, I should tell you it's unhealthy to work alone like this without assistance."

"And I will take your concern into consideration." *Not.* "But it's time for you to leave." *I want my own space back, damn it.*

"Fine. See you later in the year for the holidays at Father's." He turned around and wrapped his arms around me. It was the first time he'd ever hugged me, and I accepted it with an open heart, hugging him back. The events in Washington and the last three weeks had helped Jabari and me find the very thing we had both wanted—understanding of each other. With that, we became the siblings Hasan always wanted us to be. I still had work to do on the others, but Zuri was backing me up more and more.

"Did Hasan tell you what he was planning?" I asked softly.

"Yes. Do you want to know?" He pulled away when I nodded. "He wanted to give you temporary free rein to be his contact with North and South American werecats much like Zuri and I handle Africa, Mischa handles Russia..." He trailed off, staring at me with concern. "Jacky?"

"Are you serious?" I sounded like a dumfounded fool.

"You aren't to do anything dangerous in the beginning. We'll all be ready to step in if you need help, but you wanted to help this time, and...I recommended to Father you might need a job with the family. You need a place equal to ours, something you can be proud of. Did you like helping me in Washington?"

"I did," I answered, kicking a rock as I absorbed what he said. "What if I fail?"

"If you ask for help when you need it, you won't fail. He's planning on approaching you with it in a few weeks, so act surprised when he tells you. He likes surprising his children, and I just ruined that for him."

"I'm not ready," I said, my voice stronger that time. "Damn it."

Jabari laughed. "No, you're not ready to do what Mischa does or what Hisao and I do, but no one is when they start out. If you don't want it, you don't have to accept."

I shouldn't want it, but my newfound feeling of

responsibility demanded a different answer. "This is what our family does. As long as I can continue to run my bar and live my life, I'll help the werecats of North and South America as best I'm able, and if I can't, I'll find the werecat who can."

"Good. He also wants you to be our direct liaison with werewolves for any political problems that don't require his presence with the Tribunal. The North American Werewolf Council is the strongest of their councils right now, but he wants to introduce you to the Tribunal werewolves, or you can ask Heath to..."

He was still talking, but I'd checked out. I turned away from him and started walking for my bar, letting those words ring in my head.

Hasan was giving me a whole lot of responsibility.

"Sister, wait! One more thing!" he called out. I turned slowly and saw him looking through a briefcase. Yeah, even ancient African warlords had briefcases now. He pulled out a piece of paper, sighing. "Father told me to give this to you at the right time. Since I've healed, and you've learned the runes, you've decided to throw me out. That makes it time for you have this."

I walked back and took the paper. It was a deed.

"Oh, fuck."

"You said we would take their lands as spoils of war... so we did. Father has decided since North America is yours, and it was your idea, it belongs to you. He'll have someone burn the home down later this week if you want to go watch."

I started walking away again.

Jabari didn't follow me, laughing as he got into his car. I went into my bar, only turning to wave at him as he pulled out.

I hustled to get the bar ready for opening, and once I was done, I had to turn on the Open sign and wait.

It only took thirty minutes for Heath, Carey, and Landon to walk in.

"Wait!" I ordered them at the door. "This is a reputable establishment, and we do not allow minors!"

"Jacky!" Carey whined. I grinned at her.

"But you can sit nicely at the bar before others show up, and no one has to know." I winked at her, and her replying laugh made my heart easy. I could worry about whatever responsibilities Hasan wanted to throw at me tomorrow. Or when he finally told me. There was no reason for them to ruin my day.

"So, he's gone?" Heath asked, looking around. "He's not going to pop out and ruin my drink?"

"No, he's not going to pop out. He drove off about an hour and a half ago. I'm sorry your Saturday nights were ruined the last few weeks."

"He hovers, and it's odd. It was like he thought I was trying something." Heath sighed. "Landon, do you want anything?"

"Yes, please." Landon stepped closer but didn't sit down. He watched me carefully, and I waited for him to come to his judgment about me today. "He has something to tell you." He gestured to his father. I raised an eyebrow at Heath for a second, who growled softly. "And I would like a brandy if you have it," Landon continued.

"Coming right up. Heath, what's this thing you need to tell me?" I grabbed glasses down and began to get everyone what they wanted. Carey would only ever drink juice in my bar because I refused to serve her anything else except water. Heath wanted a beer. Landon was the one who always switched it up. Brandy, mixed drink, beer, water—he was the most inconsistent customer I'd ever had.

"We'll talk about it after these two leave," he answered, gesturing at his children.

"All right, then." That meant it was important and not for Carey's ears.

"Dad!"

"No," we said to her at the same time. She frowned but didn't fight us. I sighed.

"Your birthday is in a week, right?" I asked, leaning over to talk to her as I slid her drink to her. She grabbed it like a pro before it went over the edge of the bar.

"Yup."

"Have you figured out what you want me to get you?" I waited, and she shrugged. "Carey..."

"I mean..." She made a face. "Surprise me."

I groaned, letting my head hit the bar. Impossible. Heath and Landon were no help, laughing in delight at my situation.

And so, it went. Another day with some of my favorite people. Carey refused to give up an answer to me for two hours, and when a human customer walked in, Landon ushered her out to take her home. I was able to snag a hug before she was whisked away.

"I'll give you a list of things we need to grab before the horse gets here," Heath offered. "You can grab some of the items off it, and we'll make it a gift from all three of us."

"Really?" That touched me. It was lazy, but...I was being included in the family gift to her. Somehow, that privilege felt more like a gift to me from Heath than it did a gift for Carey.

"Really. We'll let you sign the card and everything." He smiled at me. "So, that important thing..."

"Get on with it," I ordered, waving my rag at him.

"The North American Werewolf Council asked me to take a special role. Ambassador to werecats. I was offered this role thanks to my friendship with a particular werecat who happens to be part of a very important family, and that means we can—"

"Stop." I held up a hand. "I don't need to hear any more. I'm about to be offered a few family positions too. How about we pretend none of that is going on while we're in this bar and try to have a normal night?"

He chuckled, and something curled in me. I hated his chuckle, but it sounded so good.

"Yeah, we can do that," he said, leaning on the bar with that small smile.

I caught something in his scent. I had before, but the circumstances had prevented me from putting too much thought into it.

Now I had the time, and what I caught made my eyes go wide. I met his grey-blue gaze, confused what the man could possibly be attracted to.

"I figured if we're going to be friends, you should know the feelings are mutual," he explained softly.

Heath Everson was attracted to *me*.

"No." I pointed at him. "No. We're not doing this. Nothing weird tonight. Drink your beer. I'm going to tend my bar."

He only laughed.

Keep reading for more information about the next release, special news, and more.

DEAR READER,

Thank you for reading!

I adore writing this woman. Jacky is honestly more of a story about family than anything else. She's part of several and each one of them have a definite impact on who she is and the decisions she makes. They will probably always play a very important role in her stories, and there's so many family members to explore, I honestly can't wait.

Just so you know, here at the end of book 2... this is going to be a 15 book series.

If I still have you, head over to my website to get the latest updates on the next book in the series. Head over to my website and sign up for my mailing list! There are exclusive teasers for those who are signed up: Knbanet. com/newsletter

Also, I have a Patreon, where I write a monthly short story or novella. You can check that out here: Patreon. com/knbanet

And remember,

Reviews are always welcome, whether you loved or hated the book. Please consider taking a few moments to leave one and know I appreciate every second of your time and I'm thankful.

THE TRIBUNAL ARCHIVES

The Jacky Leon series is set in the world of The Tribunal. Every series and standalone novel is written so it can be read alone.

For more information about The Tribunal Archives and the different series in it, you can go here:

tribunalarchives.com

ACKNOWLEDGMENTS

I'm very bad at giving really public praise. I shower people in praise in private. But that's not everyone's love language and that's okay.

So this little page shall now be dedicated to everyone who helps me get these books from the concept to the release and beyond. From my PA, to my editor and my proofreader, to my wonderful friends helping me through the hardest moments. To my husband, who doesn't read my books, but loves that I write them and is willing to listen to me talk about them for hours.

And to you, the reader, for without you, I wouldn't have anyone to share these stories with. I'm a storyteller at heart and you have given me the greatest gift of listening.

I love all of you. Thank you for continuing to go on this journey with me.

ABOUT THE AUTHOR

KNBanet.com

Living in Arizona with her husband and 5 pets (2 dogs and 3 cats), K.N. Banet is a voracious... video game player. Actually, she spends most of her time writing, and when she's not writing she's either gaming or reading.

She enjoys writing about the complexities of relationships, no matter the type. Familial, romantic, or even political. The connections between characters is what draws her into writing all of her work. The ideas of responsibility, passion, and forging one's own path all make appearances.

facebook.com/KNBanet

instagram.com/Knbanetauthor

bookbub.com/authors/k-n-banet

amazon.com/K.N.-Banet/e/B08412L9VV

patreon.com/knbanet

ALSO BY K.N. BANET

Servant of the Blood

Blood of the Wicked

Tribunal Archives Stories

Ancient and Immortal (Call of Magic Anthology)

Hearts at War

Full Moon Magic (Rituals and Runes Anthology)

Made in the USA
Middletown, DE
04 October 2023

40159514R00239